Riders and Hunters
The Magic of Dragons
Book 1

Laura Burton

Burton and Burchell LLC

Copyright

The characters and storylines are fictitious, and any resemblance to real-life people and events are purely coincidental. No part of this book may be distributed or shared without the written consent of the rights holder.

© 2025 Laura Burton

To discuss rights: laura@burtonburchell.co.uk

First Edition

ISBN: 978-1-962068-30-7

Edited by Vanda O'Neill
Cover Design by Lara Wynter
Chapter Heading Artwork by Katryn Designs
Published by Burton & Burchell LLC

This book is written in U.S. English

Dedication

To Ryan, Alex and Nicholas - For giving me the courage to write a book about dragons

To Ross - For making my dreams come true.

To Susan Burchell - For believing in me

Finally, to my readers, without whom, I would have no business writing these books. I hope you love Kayla's story

In Memory of

Brian Burchell
1950-2017
He would have loved this book the most. I'm sorry it took me so long to finally write it.
Miss you dad.

Chapter 1
The Valley Gazette

"Horror in the Skies: Arizona Plane Crash Kills Three Family Members, Only One Survives"

San Tan Valley, AZ – A devastating plane crash in the mountains of San Tan Valley has left a young woman fighting for her life while her parents and younger sister perished in the fiery wreckage.

The single-engine aircraft went down just after 3:30 PM on Monday, crashing into the rugged mountainside and igniting upon impact. Frances and Connor Whitman, along with 14-year-old, Shelby, were tragically killed before emergency responders could reach them. 16-year-old Kayla miraculously survived but remains in critical condition.

Eyewitnesses say the plane appeared to be in distress moments before the crash. "The plane made a strange puffing sound, as it wobbled over my ranch. I'd say the engine was failing," one local resident reported. "When it reached the mountain, it fell out of the sky like a rock—then there was a ball of smoke."

The Whitmans were well-known in their community, with Frances working as a beloved elementary school teacher and Connor operating a small aviation business. Shelby, a high school freshman, was an aspiring artist with a passion for music.

A GoFundMe campaign has been set up to cover funeral costs and support Kayla's medical expenses as she fights to recover. Meanwhile, federal investigators from the FAA and NTSB are working to determine the cause of the crash.

As the tight-knit community mourns this heartbreaking tragedy, friends and neighbors are rallying around Kayla, the sole survivor of a nightmare that changed her life forever.

More updates will follow as the investigation continues.

Chapter 2
The Invitation

"Kayla Whitman."

My name echoes around the gym like a distant roar.

I step forward, my feet sluggish, heavy, like I'm wading through water.

The applause reaches me in waves, distorted, too slow to be normal. My sights flicker over the sea of faces watching me.

I sense their lips moving at a rapid speed behind cupped hands as heads turn to their neighbor.

Even though it's impossible to hear the whispers, I can guess what they're saying.

"That's the girl from the plane crash."

I swallow, curling my fingers into my sweaty palms, and try to ignore the attention.

High School Graduation is supposed to be a moment of celebration. The end of one chapter and the beginning of a fresh one. It's a day of relief, a day of hope.

I'm a survivor.

This is my moment to revel in that.

I suck in a determined breath and hold out my hand as I approach the front of the line.

Mr. Sterling, the school Principal, hands me my scroll.

"Well done, Kayla." His voice is warm as he clasps my hand, but I feel cold.

No.

Not cold.

Numb.

My school counsellor told me grief does that.

My fingers curl around the scroll, but it feels wrong. Weightless. Like it belongs to someone else.

The room is too bright. The crowd too loud. Or maybe too quiet? It's hard to tell.

I force a smile and jerk my head in an awkward way to resemble a nod.

When Professor Sterling's hand releases mine, I catch a flash of emotion behind his eyes. His lips part and for a second, I think he's going to say something.

I wait, hoping for him to bestow some wisdom upon me. Something to give me direction as I head into the unknown.

About what happens next.

But then–

"Jackson Harper."

And just like that, the eye contact is broken, and I'm staggering off the stage to a happy ruckus.

This time, several people wolf-whistle. Someone shouts, "That's my boy!"

I cast my sights over the crowd of people propped up in chairs that have been set out just for the graduation.

The gym still smells like rubber and sweaty socks. But it's filled with loved ones beaming at the line of new graduates.

Chloe, the valedictorian, gives a speech about taking on whatever new challenges life throws at us with a can-do attitude and a good sense of humor.

Her words echo in my brain like church bells.

I'm hoping that my future is not full of new challenges. To me, challenges just equal more trauma.

I prefer... boring.

Uneventful.

That sounds nice. Peaceful, even.

The graduates in front of me whisper excitedly, sharing dreams of getting into a sorority at college or traveling the world on a gap year.

All I want is a steady, monotonous routine to fill my days and enough money to keep a roof over my head and warm food in my belly. I don't even need a partner. If I get lonely, I'll rescue a cat.

When the ceremony is over, everyone files out of the double doors to the school grounds. Graduates are dotted about, surrounded by their loved ones as they take photos.

Teachers weave in and out of the bubbles of families, shaking hands and exchanging compliments to the parents for their shared work in getting the students to this point.

Then there's me.

Alone.

I clutch my scroll, rolling on my heels and wondering when it will be socially appropriate to leave.

My eye catches Hollie, my...friend?

I lift my hand with a faint smile and for a splinter of a second, I think she's going to smile back. But her eyes dull, and her gaze drops away from me.

She returns her attention to her father who is speaking to Mr. Clark, our science teacher. Probably discussing her plans to study microbiology at Princeton and how proud they both are of her achievements.

"Kayla."

I whip around under the weight of a hand pressing on my right shoulder. A strong waft of familiar perfume floods my nose, and my stomach tightens.

"Mrs. Murphy." I try, and fail, to smile. Instead, the left corner of my mouth twitches.

I'm not sure what's worse; being alone for graduation. Or being seen in public with the school guidance counselor.

"Here." She hands me a gold box wrapped with a black ribbon. She pushes her glasses up the bridge of her nose, then clasps her wrinkled hands in front of her pinstripe skirt. "I thought you'd appreciate the colors."

I blink up at her. "You got me a present?"

Mrs. Murphy waves a hand in the air like it's nothing. "Of course. I happen to know that it's not only your graduation..." She leans in close to murmur in my ear, "Happy Birthday."

I clutch the box like my life depends on it, and my eyes prickle. "You didn't need to get me a present."

Mrs. Murphy's wide nostrils flare, then her thin lips disappear as she gives me an odd smile. "You've been through a lot this year. Most students would have dropped out of school long before now. But you stuck it out, and I'm proud of you. I wanted to give you a little something."

Swallowing the emotion bubbling in my chest, I look at the gift in my hands.

The silky black ribbon is a stark contrast to the golden box, perfectly reflecting my hair. Honey blonde, with a layer of black underneath.

Curiosity piqued, I unwrap the ribbon and lift the box lid.

A flash of light blinds me for a second.

I squint, then angle the box so the contents do not reflect the sunshine.

When my eyes adjust, I lift my brows at what's inside.

"A dragon?" I inspect the pendant.

A tiny red dragon with its tail curved to form an outer ring hangs delicately from a gold chain.

"The necklace is made of titanium metal, and the dragon is hand painted with a metallic red glaze, designed to catch the light just right."

I run my thumb over the tiny creature's curved tail, tracing the smooth metal before it dips into intricate scales.

The craftsmanship is flawless, almost too perfect for something trivial.

Mrs. Murphy watches me closely, her gaze unreadable behind thin, silver-framed glasses. "I noticed you'd doodle dragons in your notebook during our sessions. I thought you'd like it."

A swirl of guilt makes my stomach churn.

I never paid much attention during our sessions, but I hadn't realized I made it that obvious.

"I do like it. It's just—" Odd. Unexpected. The only gift I'm getting this year.

A lot of things.

But why is Mrs. Murphy still being nice when I'm always aloof and moody around her?

A lump forms in my throat.

I want to apologize for acting like an ungrateful jerk. For refusing to open up about my feelings and wasting so much of her time during our compulsory sessions.

But I can't. It's impossible.

I settle for, "Thank you," because anything else might break me right now.

Mrs. Murphy inclines her head like she understands, then shifts her weight as though debating whether to say something else.

I watch as she nips her bottom lip and blinks rapidly. I can't figure out if she's trying to make a decision or just keeping her emotions at bay.

Maybe both.

In the end, she pats my arm with a nod. "Take care of yourself, Kayla."

And with that, she's gone, disappearing into the crowd of graduates and their waiting families.

The sunny scene grows misty as my eyes flood with tears. But I refuse to let a single one fall. Not today. Not now.

I focus on my breathing, letting the world move around me oblivious to my internal torture.

My family should be here.

My imagination opens up, letting me fall into an alternate timeline where my parents are standing side by side.

My dad has his oversized camera raised to his eyes, while my mom is beaming at me. "Shelby, stand next to your sister."

The air shifts, and my red-haired, rosy-cheeked sister joins me.

My breath hitches at the weight of her arm on across my shoulders.

"Cheese!"

The scene slowly fades like wisps of smoke, and the harsh sunlight casts a glow over my new reality. The school grounds are almost empty, and the warm evening breeze ruffles my gown.

I shudder and hug myself.

Alone again.

Just like always.

Later that night, the smell of grilled cheese and grease clings to my uniform as I wipe down the counter at the diner. The clock on the wall reads 10:42 PM.

My shift is almost over.

The door opens, and I glance up, my stomach tightening when I recognize a few familiar faces.

Graduates. People I sat next to in class, who I once considered friends.

Of course, they're out celebrating. I'm probably the only one who didn't take the night off to let my hair down.

The bell jingles as they step inside, laughter bouncing off the walls. But the second they see me, it cuts off. Not just awkwardness—something sharper. Like they forgot I existed until this moment and now don't know what to do with the knowledge.

But the moment passes when one of the boys coughs and makes a joke. Shoulders relax and no one looks in my direction as they slide into a booth, talking and laughing, again.

Serving them is the last thing I want to do, but I'm the only one left on shift while Rob works in the kitchen.

Sucking in a breath, I approach them, and their conversation dies. Their gazes flick to me and then away, as if pretending I'm not there.

I clear my throat. "What can I get you?"

Silence stretches for a beat too long. Then, finally, Hollie—Hollie of all people—mutters, "Just a few root beers."

I jot it down, forcing my hands not to shake.

I knew people acted weird around me since the crash, but this? It feels like something else. Like I'm a ghost haunting my own life.

I hesitate before stepping away, glancing at them. "So... any big plans after graduation?"

They exchange glances, awkward smiles flickering before disappearing.

"Uh, yeah. Chloe's heading to UCLA," one of the guys says, rubbing the back of his neck. "And a bunch of us are doing a road trip before college starts."

"That sounds fun." I offer a small smile, though my throat tightens. "Where to?"

"Just, uh... around," Hollie says quickly, fiddling with a napkin. "To the East Coast, maybe."

I nod, though the tightness in my chest expands.

She used to tell me everything. But now? She can't even meet my eyes.

"Sounds great. Hope you guys have an amazing time." My voice comes out too light, too fake, but none of them call me out on it.

They just nod, offering half-hearted smiles, as if that somehow makes up for the gaping space between us.

I turn on my heel, heading for the soda fountain, pretending I don't feel their stares burning into my back.

How does a group of friends turn into strangers? Was it me? Did I freeze them out in the haze of grief and shock after the crash? Or were they just cowards, afraid to be near me in case grief was contagious and they got infected?

Either way, the distance between us feels deliberate, like a chasm neither side is willing to bridge.

* * *

My muscles ache as I lay on my bed.

The laundromat below hums with the steady churn of washing machines, filling my tiny attic room with a familiar white noise. The ceiling slopes just above my head, the walls are bare except for a single shelf of secondhand books, and my unpacked suitcase sits in the corner waiting for a plan I don't have.

This is my life now.

High school is over.

No more classes, no more structure. Just a job and bills and the terrifying uncertainty of what comes next.

I exhale and roll onto my side. Then I flop back on my back with a frustrated huff.

Despite my aches and pains, sleep does not come.

Mrs. Murphy's gift sits on my bedside table.

I reach for the box and open the lid once more.

The dragon's tiny eyes glint under the lamplight, daring me.

Mrs. Murphy was right. I do like dragons. And I did doodle pictures of them during our sessions, but I never thought she was that observant, after all, I thought I'd been subtle about it.

Ever since I was a kid, I've always been fascinated by stories of mythological beasts. Dragons were both feared and revered in cultures around the world. But I always associated them with wisdom and protection.

People have often said that dragons are not real. But I have to question, how could there be so many ancient writings and drawings of such beasts, even when it was not common for people to travel all around the world?

The hairs on my arms stand on end as a memory flashes before me.

One that haunts my dreams and lingers in the back of my mind during the day.

The day my life turned upside down, and I went from grumpy teenage daughter and sister, to depressed orphan.

I'm trapped with my seatbelt stuck, pinning me to my seat in my dad's plane. Fire blazes all around me, dancing in front of my eyes and licking my body in a way that feels... freezing.

My lungs scream under the choking stench of smoke and burning flesh.

Then, a shadow in the shape of a huge dinosaur with wings.

I hesitate, staring at the dragon pendant once more, admiring the way it catches the lamplight in an almost ethereal way. As my heart makes an all-too-common throbbing sensation in my chest, I yank on the pendant, then loop the chain around my neck.

The metal is cool at first. But the moment the pendant touches my skin, heat lances through my chest.

Heat.

Not warm.

Holy crap, it's HOT.

Too hot.

Scalding.

A breath seizes in my lungs as a sharp, searing pain claws through my chest.

My fingers fly to the necklace.

But it won't budge.

I choke, clawing at the chain, but it's fused to me—no, sinking into me.

A sound rises in my ears, something between a whisper and a roar.

My vision swims, the room warping. And then—

Blackness.

When I wake, I'm on the floor. My skin is slick with sweat, my breath ragged, my heart thudding against my ribs almost as if wanting to escape.

I push myself up on shaking arms, wincing at the dull ache in my chest.

My body is tingling, and there's a pressure rising to my head, making my temples throb.

The heat is still unbearable.

I stagger to the small basin in the corner of my room and splash cold water over my face. The drops leave an icy trail down my neck and when I swipe them away, the absence of metal has me pause.

I pat around my collarbone, feeling for the necklace. But my fingers only collide with flesh and bone.

I squint in the dim light at my reflection.

Then I see it.

The necklace is gone.

Instead, something dark and metallic gleams on my skin.

I scramble to yank on the light cord and take a closer look.

A black and red tattoo-like mark is etched into my skin.

I lift trembling fingers to my collarbone, tracing the raised, ink-black outline of a dragon, its tail curled into a perfect circle—just like the pendant.

I swallow hard. My pulse pounding in my ears.

What the heck?

My gaze snaps to the bedside table, where the box still sits.

With unsteady hands, I reach for it, flipping open the lid.

Nestled inside the velvet lining, a single slip of paper awaits folded neatly in half.

I unfold it.

My breath catches as I read the words scrawled in sharp, precise ink:

Theridon Academy of Dragon Riders
Official Summons

To Miss Kayla Prue Whitman,

It is with great honor that we extend to you an invitation to Theridon, the esteemed Academy of Dragon Riders. You have been selected for enrollment based on extraordinary potential.

Your escort will arrive no later than 3:00 AM to ensure your safe passage to the Academy. You are required to gather your belongings and be prepared for immediate departure.

Classes commence on Monday.

A new chapter awaits you—one of strength, courage, and fire.

Welcome to Theridon.

May your wings carry you beyond the stars.
King Siberious
Headmaster at Theridon Academy of Dragon Riders

A shiver races down my spine as I mouth the words several times, trying to make them imprint in my brain. But they slip through my mind like grains of sand between my fingers.

Dragon Rider Academy... Is this a joke?

I run a hand down my face, still trembling.

This has to be a prank. Or a mistake. Or maybe, just maybe, I finally lost my mind.

But the words won't change no matter how many times I blink at them.

Theridon Academy of Dragon Riders.

At this point, I don't know whether to laugh or cry.

I've either truly turned insane, or someone is playing a cruel trick on me.

A tap on the door jolts me out of my daze, and I glance at the clock.

2:57 AM.

A floorboard creaks somewhere in the hall, and my heart stops.

Someone is already here.

Chapter 3
The Visitor

A shadow moves in the hall, erasing the thin strip of light under the door, and my breath stills in my throat.

I clutch the thin sheets tangled around my legs, the weight of the letter still heavy in my lap.

This can't really be happening, right?

The clock on my nightstand flicks to 3:00 AM, and I hold my breath.

A sharp rap echoes against the door.

My analytical brain is too slow to consider what the heck is going on or reason anything. Instead, I'm frozen on the fantastical idea that I'm going to a *freaking* dragon school.

I swallow hard, heart thundering.

I guess this is it.

My *"you're a wizard"* moment.

The moment that changes everything.

Another knock, more insistent this time. More like a thump from a fist.

I rise cautiously, stepping over the creaky floorboard as I inch toward the door.

My throat constricts, and every hair on the back of my neck is on its end. My fingers tremble as I twist the knob and pull.

I half-expect to find a giant with dark, shaggy hair and a pink umbrella to be on the other side.

But instead, I'm met with an ominous hooded stranger.

"Yes?" The word comes out dry and weak. I clear my throat and try again. "What do you want?"

The stranger flinches, then slowly rises a hand to their hood.

After a moment of hesitation that has my nerves on end, the person yanks the hood back and I'm met with a pair of beady eyes boring into mine.

The stranger is a man.

He leans in close, bearing several gold teeth.

My imagination is running on overtime.

Could this be a pirate about to steal me away and take me on a sea waring adventure?

An overwhelming stench of alcohol washes over me.

The man stumbles forward, barely catching himself on the doorframe. His brown eyes, bloodshot and unfocused, squint at me.

"Oh," he slurs, dragging a hand down his unshaven face. "Wrong room."

My heart sinks.

He swivels in a full circle and gives me a lop-sided smile when his sights land on me again. "Got any quarters?" He jerks his head. "You know, for the machines."

I blink, reality slamming back into place. This isn't my escort from a mystical academy. Or a morally gray pirate captain here to take me away.

Nope.

He's just some drunk who wandered too far from the laundromat below.

I shut my eyes, annoyed by my foolishness.

"No. Sorry." I shut the door before he can stumble inside my apartment.

Exhaling, I press my forehead against the wood. My pulse is still racing, adrenaline buzzing under my skin.

As I wait for my body to calm down, I listen.

The floor outside creaks, and the man's grumblings grow faint.

I peel away from the door, rubbing my collarbone.

The skin is still raw, the tattoo-like mark tender to the touch.

The necklace must have been old, tarnished metal, causing an allergic reaction. That has to be why it burned. Why the dragon pendant left its imprint on my skin.

As for the necklace? It must have fallen off somewhere. I'm sure I'll find it in the morning.

How could I be so easily led into the fantasy of being whisked away to some magical school?

Have I secretly been waiting for my Hogwarts letter since my eleventh birthday?

Yes, totally.

But have I ever truly believed in magic?

No way.

I curl up, wrapping myself in the thin sheets, and exhale long and slow.

It's all in my head.

My subconscious is concocting weird illusions to make my life less dull and depressing. Even though I tell myself I want a simple, boring life, there's a part of me that craves something more exciting and full of purpose.

"You're an idiot, Kayla," I mutter under my breath.

I let my imagination get the best of me. Again.

My body relaxes, and I sink into the lumpy mattress, allowing sleep to take hold.

But my dreams are haunted by the ghosts of my past.

I toss and turn, lost in the visions playing in my mind's eye.

Flashes of light.

Clouds of smoke, burning the back of my throat.

"Where's Dad?"

There's a distant scream. Or maybe it's me.

"Kayla!"

I wrestle with the belt that has me pinned to the seat.

A crackling roar of flames.

More screams.

I thrash in my sheets, sweat slicking my skin as the nightmare swallows me whole.

My mother's cries, my father's shouts, "Mayday, Mayday, Mayday. We're going down."

Shelby's desperate sobs. "Daddy."

"Close your eyes, my darlings, be brave." Mom's voice is like hot milk at the end of a stressful day.

But then an almighty bang roars in my ears, bursting both eardrums.

And a deafening silence follows.

I swallow ash, tasting something bitter and sharp.

Flames lick at the side of the plane, and my vision grows hazy.

I can't see anyone in the cockpit.

I clamp my eyes shut and chant to myself.

"Not real. Not real. Not real."

My body jerks awake, gasping. My pulse pounds, my breath ragged.

Sweat clings to my face, sticking my hair to my temples.

I swipe it away with a shaking hand and reach for my phone. But my hand falls through the air where my bedside table should be.

I jolt up, my pulse hammering.

My stomach lurches as my body rocks to the side.

The ground isn't solid beneath me—it's moving.

Velvet cushions press against my palms. A low hum vibrates through the air.

My brain struggles to catch up as I blink at the dim golden lamps above.

Polished wood paneling, strange wallpapered walls, and flickering reflections in a dark window.

I'm not in my bed.

I'm on a train.

Great. Somehow, someone has taken me from my

bed without my consent and put me here. Love that for me. Not terrifying at all.

My vision is still hazy, while my brain is sluggish with sleep.

I blink hard, trying to focus on my surroundings, and that's when I notice *him*.

The man sitting across from me is dressed impeccably—a thin pinstripe suit, tailored to fit his lean frame. His hands rest neatly folded over a small black book in his lap, the leather cover worn smooth.

He's staring out the window, his profile strikingly sharp yet ageless, like a marble statue carved with a perfection that doesn't quite belong to any era. His skin is smooth—too smooth—untouched by the lines of time, but his eyes...

His eyes are ancient.

There's wisdom in their depths, the kind that comes from years, centuries, maybe, of seeing more than any human should. They flicker slightly in the reflection of the window, as if catching light in an unnatural way.

But it's not his eyes that make my stomach drop.

It's his ears.

Just barely peeking out from the strands of silken blond hair, the tips are unmistakably pointed.

Chapter 4
The Train

I don't move. I don't even breathe.

Because if I so much as blink, it might shatter whatever fragile illusion this is, and the real world, the world of cheap sheets and fluorescent laundromat lights, will crash back down on me.

Except... I *know* that's not going to happen.

Because as the train hums beneath me, the steady vibration thrumming through my bones, and the air remains thick with the scent of polished wood and something faintly metallic, I know this is real. *Too* real.

I glance down and try to ground myself.

My hands are trembling, my fingers curled into the plush velvet of my seat.

Across from me, the man in the pinstripe suit hasn't moved. His hands are still folded neatly over his small black book, his posture straight, elegant.

Slowly, his head turns, and his regal gaze lands on me.

My heart flutters.

Finally, he speaks. "You're awake."

His voice is controlled and void of emotion. I half-wonder if this person is even human or an advanced AI robot.

I swallow hard, my throat still raw from the nightmare.

"Yeah, well..." I rub the back of my neck. "Not sure if that's a good thing or a bad thing."

I pause and stare at the man with pointed ears as a horrifying thought crosses my mind.

"Am I dead?"

The man doesn't answer right away. Instead, he turns a page in his book, his movements slow and deliberate, as if he has all the time in the world.

As if he isn't sitting across from a girl who is staring at him like he's sprouted two more heads.

"If you are dead, I suppose that would make me an angel. Do I look like an angel to you?" The corner of his mouth tilts up into an amused smirk.

I pinch myself, and the sting grounds me.

Okay. I'm not dead.

A dazzling blur of colors flashes across the window as the train moves at an unimaginable speed. Yet, despite our velocity, the carriage rocks lazily.

If this were any other situation, it might be enough to soothe me.

But not today.

I lick my lips. My mind is screaming at me to do something—ask questions, demand answers, freak out completely—but I can't seem to make my body cooperate.

So, I settle for the default questions.

"Who *are* you, then? And where am I?"

The man sighs, almost like he's disappointed that I started with questions so... predictable.

"You may call me Eliyah. And we are... in transit," he says, as if that answers everything.

I clench my jaw. "Right. Super helpful. Thanks, Eliyah. So... where is our destination?"

He finally looks at me, his piercing ancient eyes locking onto mine. There's no warmth there, no amusement. Just cool, assessing calculation.

"Theridon Academy."

My brain burns with recognition as a chill trickles down my spine.

Theridon.

The name from the letter. The one that invited me to a Dragon Rider school. The one I had rationalized away as some trick of my overactive imagination.

I shake my head, my pulse thrumming faster. "No, see... that's not a thing. This isn't a thing. Schools for dragon riders don't exist. *Magic* doesn't exist."

Eliyah doesn't react. He doesn't even blink for several long moments.

"And yet..." He tilts his head finally. "Here we are."

I open my mouth. Then shut it again.

Fair point.

Then I narrow my eyes on Eliyah, trying to ignore how surreal this is. "And *how* did I get here? Did you kidnap me?"

Eliyah's brows twitch, and he looks at the open book on his lap. Then he hums to himself, following a sentence with his index finger dragging along the page.

I shift in my seat, the realization settling in. I guess that is exactly what happened. After all, the letter said someone would come for me.

The fact that they came while I was unconscious isn't creepy at all.

"Okay," I say slowly, my voice only slightly shaky now.

I'm still in my bed. And this is just a fever dream.

I cross my legs and strum my fingers on my knees as my brain works on a new theory.

"Let's say, *hypothetically*, I believe you. Let's say this place, *Theridon,* exists, and I was... summoned."

Eliyah looks up and inclines his head, waiting for me to connect the dots.

But I shake my head. "You've got the wrong girl. Magic? Dragon riders? No way. I failed AP biology. I can't even parallel park without panicking. You want someone special? You're looking at the wrong freaking person."

Something flickers across his face—so fast I almost miss it.

Almost.

But the emotion is too strong to evade me.

Amusement.

"The dragon mark suggests otherwise." He gives me a pointed look.

I freeze.

My hand flies to my collarbone, fingers pressing against the skin.

The mark is still there, raised and warm to the touch, like it's alive. An energy burns through me, and my heart squeezes.

But then my stomach drops.

"How do you know about that?" I whisper.

Eliyah shakes his soft hair out of his eyes and leans forward just slightly, his sharp gaze never wavering.

"Because it means you were chosen," he murmurs. "A dragon has already claimed you."

A breath punches out of me in the sound of a laugh, but nothing about this is funny.

My brain immediately rejects the information.

This has to be the fakest news I've ever been told.

"Nope." I shake my head. "No, see, I don't know if you've noticed, but there's no dragon here. No one 'claimed' me. I put on a stupid cheap necklace, it burned me, and now I have a weird tattoo. That's it. That's all."

I fold my arms and jut out my chin like a stubborn child, while Eliyah sighs and pinches the bridge of his nose for a moment. "I was warned you might be hard-headed, but this is—"

I scoff. "Are you kidding me right now? You expect me to just go along with everything you say? What next? I'm guessing you're going to tell me you're a... a...an elf?"

Eliyah's ears burn red, and his jaw bulges.

The man is clearly offended, and guilt nips at my insides.

Have I stepped over a line? I didn't mean to insult the guy, but my brain is scrambling to make sense of anything that is happening right now.

Instead of correcting me, he purses his lips tight and closes his book. "You truly don't remember, do you?"

I narrow my eyes. "Remember *what*?"

For a long moment, he just studies me. I get the distinct impression he's deciding something—whether to tell me or not.

Then, just as I open my mouth to press him further, the train shudders.

I glance at the window and hitch a breath.

For a fraction of a second, my own reflection isn't staring back at me. An ominous shadow stands there instead.

The lights flicker.

When they stabilize, the shadow is gone, and my reflection is back. But my blood has already gone cold.

"Oh, no," Eliyah whispers.

Then there's a deafening bang.

Smoke creeps under the door to the next carriage and fills the space in slow motion.

Eliyah launches into action, his eyes piercing and intense as he raises a hand.

Another bang has the train screeching to a stop.

I scramble to my feet and clamp my hands over

my ears against the jarring sound of metal scraping metal.

"Get down," Eliyah barks, swirling his wrist in an unnatural way.

His iris turn gold, and an ethereal light pours out from his palm.

My mouth falls open as I watch him, too transfixed to care about my safety.

The light chases the smoke away and floods the cabin in a glow that is warm and oddly peaceful.

My cells tingle and shudder all at once. As if I'm vibrating at a new speed.

Then a shadow crosses the window, and the glass shatters into a million tiny shards of glass that sparkle like glitter.

The shards hang in the air for a few moments, while Eliyah focuses on them.

"I said, get down and cover your head," he barks.

The authority in his voice has me doing as I'm told, but another shadow appears—and something whistles past my ear.

I yelp and duck, heart hammering. "What the heck?"

Suddenly, the entire train tilts and groans.

Has something just landed on top of it?

"What... what is that?" I whisper.

Can dragons be real after all, and one has come to get itself a little snack?

Eliyah's expression hardens instantly as he waves his hands and forces more swirls of light and power to flood the space around us. "They've found us."

My heart slams into my ribs. "Who's 'they'?"

Before he can answer, the train rocks again, the lights flicker, and an ear-piercing roar tears through the air.

And then the roof explodes inward.

I throw my arms up as shards of metal rain down, the wind howling through the shattered ceiling.

But Eliyah's palms create a veil between us and the chaos. The splintered pieces of debris fall away, leaving us both unscathed.

I barely have time to process the chaos before something massive drops through the wreckage. And lands directly in front of me.

I gulp, frozen under the hard gaze of two glowing yellow eyes.

But it's not a dragon.

It's more like...a dog. A big one.

My jaw drops as I blink up at a wolf the size of a bear.

It's looking right at me.

Chapter 5
The Wolf

Chestnut brown fur ruffles in the air like fields of corn, and I'm so mesmerized by it I can't move.

A deep growl emits from its open mouth and rolls through the wreckage.

My breath catches in my chest.

Run, Kayla. Get up and run.

But telling myself to move is no good, my body is totally immobile.

Everybody talks about fight or flight, but nobody talks about freeze.

And that's exactly what I do.

I'm like a statue, at the mercy of whatever happens next.

The wolf—the massive, bear-sized creature—locks its glowing eyes onto me. Its breath comes in slow, measured huffs, misting in the cold air.

We're trapped in the oddest staring competition of my life. And I'm so stunned, I forget *how* to blink.

The logical part of my brain is screaming at me to

hide, to do anything but stand here like an idiot. But my body is still pinned by the weight of its stare.

Then, it speaks.

No, not speaks. At least, its mouth doesn't move, but a voice enters my head and intuitively, I just know it's not my own.

"You don't belong here, Kayla Whitman."

The voice is low, ancient, and laced with something sharp—like it's peeling back the layers of my mind just by speaking. It's somewhat pleasing and yet...intrusive.

Also, how does a giant talking wolf know my name?

I flinch.

My stomach knots.

That—that's not normal.

The wolf spoke to me.

I whip my head toward Eliyah, expecting him to react.

He doesn't.

Instead, he steps between me and the wolf, one hand raised, fingers pulsing with golden light. His wings—he has wings now?—flare slightly, glowing like molten metal in the dim air.

"Stay behind me," he murmurs.

I barely register his words. My heart is slamming against my ribs, and my ears are ringing.

I grab his sleeve. "Did you hear that?"

His gaze flicks to me as he cranes his neck to look at me over his shoulder, puzzled. "Hear what?"

"The wolf," I whisper back. "It talked to me."

Eliyah's expression hardens. "Wolves don't talk."

I lift a brow. "And elves don't fly, yet look at you."

Eliyah's jaw bulges, and his eyes flash gold once more. "I'm. Not. An. Elf."

A second growl rumbles through the air. Then another.

My pulse spikes.

We're surrounded.

Dark figures shift through the wreckage, their glowing eyes blinking in and out of the smoke.

The train shakes as more of them land on the roof, claws scraping against the metal.

Then the first wolf moves.

It lunges. Straight for me.

I barely have time to yelp before Eliyah throws out his hands.

A shockwave of golden light explodes outward, slamming into the wolf mid-leap.

The beast is hurled back, flipping through the air before landing hard on the twisted remains of a train seat.

More shadows charge.

"Eliyah—"

"Hold on."

I don't even have time to protest before he grabs my wrist and pulls me into his chest.

Then... The wings move with thunderous power.

With a single powerful beat, we are airborne.

The force yanks my stomach into my throat.

Wind whips past me, icy, electric, impossible.

The wreckage falls away below us, a mess of

smoke and snarling shadows. The wolves' howls rise in a chorus, chasing us into the sky.

I clutch onto Eliyah's jacket, burying my face in his shoulder. I don't know how high we're going. I don't want to look.

"Kayla." His voice is steady.

I force myself to peek.

And—oh.

The world spreads out beneath us, an endless landscape of peaks and valleys glowing with colors I don't have words for. The mountains aren't just mountains, they're twisting spires of rock laced with glowing veins of silver and violet. The valleys ripple in impossible hues of pink and green, forming colors that shouldn't exist but somehow do.

"This is insane," I breathe, unable to look away.

The sky itself seems alive, shifting and shimmering with a strange, pearlescent light.

I blink, rubbing my eyes.

Am I hallucinating?

The air bends at the edges of my vision, like the whole sky is made of energy.

Ahead, a castle rises between two mountains, carved from the very rock itself.

Eliyah's breathing is heavier now as it huffs against my back. "We're almost there."

The steady rise and fall of his chest is growing uneven.

Then his wings falter.

We dip, just slightly, but enough to make my stomach drop.

"Eliyah?"

His jaw tightens. "Brace yourself. We're landing."

There's no time to argue.

We descend fast, skimming just above a river before Eliyah's wings give one final, powerful beat, then fold in.

We hit the ground in a burst of wind. Eliyah's knees bend on impact, absorbing most of the fall, but I still stumble and land with my face in a strange pile of something.

I really hope this is mud.

I pick up on the quiet snort from behind me, and now it's my turn to have burning ears.

I huff a deep breath and slump at the river's edge to wash my face. Then I take greedy slurps of water in my cupped hands.

The water is shockingly cool, and when it touches my tongue, it's like liquid energy sinking into my bones.

The exhaustion, the shock—it dulls, just a little.

Eliyah kneels beside me, dipping his hands into the river, but his gaze is distant.

I swallow hard.

My hands are still trembling. "Why did the wolf say I didn't belong?"

Eliyah stiffens.

For a second, he doesn't move. Then, slowly, he turns to face me.

"Wolves don't talk," he repeats.

"You didn't hear him...in your head?" I whisper.

His brows knit together. He stops drinking, his full attention on me now.

"I could only hear growling, as usual," he says carefully. "Are you telling me you heard a voice...in your mind?"

My throat tightens.

I want to say no. I want to pretend I imagined it. But the words are still ringing in my skull—low, deliberate, inescapable.

You don't belong here.

My hands clench into fists. "It said I didn't belong... And maybe it's right. This place is nothing like I've ever known before, and I have no special powers or wisdom. I always felt like the oddball in my old life in San Tan Valley, Arizona. But this... this place makes me feel like an alien."

Eliyah moves faster than I expect.

He grips my arms—not hard, but firm, his fingers pressing into my biceps until they ache.

His piercing eyes burn into mine.

"Listen to me, Kayla Prue Whitman." His voice is low but intense, like he's trying to press the words into my soul. "Dragons only choose the best. This realm may feel different to the one you're from, but you belong to the Dragon Rider Academy now. And no one—not even an arrogant wolf—can change that."

I want to believe him. I really do.

But in the back of my mind, that voice still lingers.

You don't belong here.

And somehow, I can't shake the feeling the arrogant wolf knows more about the truth than this not-elf-fairy-man.

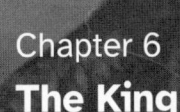

Chapter 6
The King

Eliyah and I walk in silence, but my brain is full of chatter as I take in the view.

The castle looms ahead, nestled between two jagged mountains like it was carved straight from a giant rock. It should look majestic but compared to the vibrant valleys and glowing pink sky we just left behind, it's... dull.

Colorless.

A gray husk swallowed by shadow.

I guess it makes sense I'm not going to a pretty school with rainbows and unicorns.

Of course, the one I'm summoned to looks more like a medieval prison than a magical school for the good guys.

I gulp.

What if Theridon Academy is a villain school?

The closer we get, the more the world loses its vibrancy. The lush scenery behind us fades, like someone turned down the saturation on reality.

I shiver.

The air is thick and humid, sticking to my skin. It's heavier here. Denser.

Then, as we reach the towering iron gates, the sky darkens all at once, clouds rolling in, swallowing the pink glow.

Rain begins to fall.

I gasp as the first drops sting my skin, little zaps of energy sparking through my fingertips.

"What is this magic?" I hold my palm out to catch the shimmering droplets.

Eliyah doesn't stop walking. "The school is protected."

"Protected?" I frown, watching the rain ripple in a puddle at my feet. "From what? It's like heaven out there..."

Eliyah pauses, just briefly, then glances at me with something unreadable in his expression.

"Have you already forgotten?"

A sharp pulse of dizziness washes over me.

And suddenly—I'm not here.

A flash of darkness.

Red eyes.

A voice.

You don't belong here.

I blink, my stomach twisting as I stumble forward.

The wolf.

I shake myself, trying to focus, but a strange haze clings to my thoughts.

I look up at Eliyah, and he watches me in a way

that makes me suspect he knows exactly what I just saw.

But he says nothing. Just presses his lips together and keeps walking. "We need to hurry, Siberious is waiting for you."

I don't argue, and there's no time to ask who Siberious is because we reach the front of the academy in seconds. I can only hope that Siberious isn't a Siberian tiger. I'm not sure how many more weird surprises I can take in one day.

We stop at the castle's entrance—a massive, intricately designed iron gate, curling into elegant spirals.

Eliyah presses his palm against the metal.

The air vibrates, and the ground trembles beneath my feet.

Rune-like symbols glow to life, tracing their way across the gate. Then, with a deep, resonant groan, the doors swing open.

I hesitate and look at the grandeur over my shoulder. The beautiful world I'm leaving behind.

Will I ever see it again? Will I even see the normal world again?

Or am I about to be trapped in the gloomy castle-prison forever?

Eliyah's cough draws me back and with a heavy breath, I follow him to my impending doom.

The moment we cross the threshold, the doors slam shut behind us, hitting my butt a little hard.

I jump forward with a wince.

The sound booms through the courtyard.

I spin, staring at the massive doors.

Something inside me twists. I can't tell if it's unease or finality.

I turn back, expecting a grand, bustling academy—students, torches, something alive.

But instead...

Silence.

A deep, unnatural silence.

No students laughing in the courtyard. No voices drifting from the halls. Not even the wind dares to move in this place. Everything is just still. Eerily still.

All I can hear is Eliyah's steady breath. And my own heartbeat.

I swallow. "Where is everyone?"

The air is so heavy I half-wonder if we walked into a tomb, not a school.

Eliyah's lips curve into the faintest of smiles. "It's orientation day."

That does not help my nerves.

He leads me forward through the courtyard, past tall, bronze pillars, each etched with unfamiliar symbols. With a flick of his wrist, an opening appears in one of the pillars, revealing a narrow, spiraling staircase.

I hesitate at the base of the stairs.

The air down here is cold, damp. The kind of cold that doesn't just settle on your skin—it seeps into your bones.

"After you," Eliyah says smoothly.

I exhale sharply and step forward, climbing the slick polished steps.

Golden lanterns glow on the walls, but they do little to warm the space.

The stairwell winds higher and higher, twisting so much I lose track of direction.

Just as my legs begin to ache, we reach the top.

A grand set of double doors stands before us, deep oak reinforced with golden carvings.

Eliyah pushes them open without hesitation.

The Headmaster's Office.

The office is grand, regal—yet cluttered.

Shelves overflow with old tomes, their spines worn with age. Floating crystals hover midair, pulsing with soft light. A dragon skull rests under glass, its hollow eye sockets eerily lifelike.

At the center of the room, behind an immense stone desk, sits a man. A small plaque is placed on the front of his desk with the words:

King Siberious. Lord of the Kingdom of Raina and Headmaster of Theridon Academy.

I stop breathing.

He looks like some kind of mythical warrior-meets-Santa-Claus.

His long white beard spills over his chest, nearly blending into the waist-length silver hair that falls freely around his broad shoulders. Several tight braids weave through the strands, keeping them out of his face.

He is stocky, barrel-chested, his velvet jacket stretched too tight across his broad shoulders. A pair of spectacles balances on the bridge of his nose, giving him a scholarly air that contrasts with his warrior-like build.

His piercing gray eyes flick to Eliyah.

Eliyah bows his head slightly, stepping forward to whisper something low in the King's ear.

Siberious's gaze shifts to me.

And immediately, my stomach knots.

The way he looks at me... it's not curiosity.

It's assessing.

Like I'm already in trouble.

I hug my arms around myself, a sudden wave of unease pressing against my chest.

I barely know where I am. I barely understand what's happening. And yet, I'm already terrified of losing the only person I know in this place.

Eliyah turns to leave, and panic rises in my throat.

I clutch his arm as he passes me. "Will I see you again?"

Eliyah stops.

For the first time, he falters.

His impassive mask cracks just slightly, something flickering across his face before he shoves it back down.

But his ears burn red.

A tiny smile flickers at the corner of his lips before he schools his expression.

"Good luck, Kayla Whitman." Then, he's gone.

The doors click shut behind him.

I turn back to King Siberious, my pulse still racing.

He leans forward, clasping his hands together.

"You have a young mind," he muses, his voice a

deep, rich timbre that fills the entire room. "Burning with endless questions."

His sharp eyes glint behind his spectacles.

"And I promise, in time, you shall come to know everything. But first..." He lifts a hand, holding up three fingers. His lips curl into something almost amused. "We shall start with three questions."

A flicker of something dangerous dances behind his gaze.

"Choose wisely."

Chapter 7
Questions

The silence stretches between us, thick enough to smother the air in the room.

I shift in my seat, the weight of his words presses on me like a tangible force.

Three questions. That's all I get.

My thoughts churn, desperate to make them count.

But the longer the silence lingers, the more my mind blanks.

I glance around the office, looking for something to ground myself.

Artifacts and relics line the walls, ancient books stacked in haphazard piles, and floating crystals hum with an eerie, pulsing light. But it's the clock in the corner that snags my attention.

Something about it feels...wrong.

At first glance, it's an ordinary grandfather clock—tall, ornate, its polished pinewood gleaming under the dim glow of lanterns.

But then I notice—it has no hands.

No numbers.

Just a face, ticking away the seconds of a time that doesn't seem to exist.

A cold prickle tickles down my spine, and a question tumbles out of me before I can hold my tongue. "Your clock...why is it blank?"

King Siberious hums, following my gaze. "Ah. Yes. You are from Earth. We do not follow time in this realm. I daresay it may take some getting used to, but once you do, there really is no better way to live."

I drag my fingers over the smooth armrest of the chair, my thoughts snagging on his words.

A life where time doesn't exist? How does that even work?

How do people... do anything in this realm? Without time, does no one age? Does anyone celebrate anniversaries or birthdays? How does a school run without it?

So. Many. Questions.

And my dumb mouth asks the lamest one.

"Then why have the clock at all?"

King Siberious smiles slightly. "Because I am particularly fond of the sound. *Tick-Tock. Tick-Tock.* It reminds me of a place I lived long ago."

Place. Not Earth? Maybe another world like mine.

That's not ominous at all.

A realm where time doesn't exist.

The words itch at the back of my mind, unsettling something deep inside me.

Riders and Hunters

My stomach knots as a suspicion I hadn't dared entertain begins to take root.

I swallow. "You said realm before," I begin, my voice tight. "So… if I'm not on Earth anymore, where am I?"

Siberious's brows pinch slightly, as if the question itself is strange to him. He tilts his head, studying me like I'm a puzzle piece that doesn't quite fit.

Then, with a thoughtful hum, he says, "Define Earth."

I blink. "What?" Swallowing, I try again, this time trying not to sound so rude. "Sorry, I mean, what do you mean?"

"Earth." He spreads his hands, palms up, as if presenting an open canvas. "Define it for me."

I open my mouth, but nothing comes out.

It should be easy. Earth is… well, it's Earth. But suddenly, my brain refuses to cooperate.

I scramble for something simple. "The planet… With humans. And technology. Where magic doesn't exist."

King Siberious leans back, his eyes gleaming. "Magic doesn't exist… Curious. And you are quite certain of that?"

I exhale sharply. "Of course, I'm sure."

His chuckle is deep, rich, vibrating through the space between us. "Tell me, Kayla Whitman…" He steeples his fingers together. "When you hold up a device—a phone, I believe you call it—and tap on the screen only to capture an image of yourself or your surroundings… what do you call that?"

I stare at him.

I know what he's getting at. And I don't like it.

I shift uncomfortably, my mind racing through every rational explanation I've ever known. Physics. Reflection. Light absorption. I don't know how exactly cameras work. But I know science explains things like technology.

Magic and technology are two very different things. One is undeniably real and explained. The other is a mystery. Stories told at bedtime.

And yet…

For some reason, my answer sticks to my tongue like glue.

Finally, I mutter, "Science."

King Siberious chortles, shaking his head as he rises from his chair. "Very well."

There's something in his voice—amusement, yes, but also something deeper. Like disappointment.

My chest tightens. Two questions wasted.

I should've asked something important. Why was I brought here? What the hell is going on? Why did a giant wolf attack the train? Does he know anything about giant talking wolves and why they might want me?

But no. I wasted a question on a clock and another on whether Earth is real.

I curl my fingers into my palms, frustration simmering under my skin. But then a sharp realization hits me. "Wait. You didn't answer my question."

"A-ha. Astute. Very astute." King Siberious rises to a bold stand, then moves to the arched window.

The glass is multi-colored, almost like a stained-glass window from an old church. But this one has no recognizable pattern or picture. Just swirls of iridescent color.

He pushes open the window, revealing a view so breathtaking, it makes me forget all my worries.

"You are currently sitting in the school of Theridon Academy, nestled between two lands. What you can see before you is Solmerys, or Sol, as we locals like to call it. The east mountain is Ormiris, where our beloved dragons reside. And to the west, we have Zerythia. None of these names will mean anything to you, of course. But Zerythia is ancient and holy ground. Very few of my students are permitted to go there."

My mind spins with names I cannot even try to spell while King Siberious moves to a nearby table.

He picks up a tall, glass jug, its shape elegant and unnatural, like a piece of sculpted crystal. The liquid inside shimmers, shifting between deep blue and glowing gold.

"Drink?" he offers, pouring the liquid into a cup.

My mouth is dry. I lick my lips.

It's probably a bad idea. There's no knowing what the strange drink will do to my human insides.

I take the cup anyway.

The moment the liquid touches my tongue, everything explodes.

I gasp, lowering the cup in my lap.

A rush of energy stretches from my chest to my extremities. Icy sensations soar through my veins at lightning speed and when it reaches my brain, I am flooded with perfect clarity.

No, something deeper than that.

The air sharpens. Every particle of dust catching the light looks like glitter now.

Not only that, but the glitter dances in a strange formation. Like each tiny speck is connected somehow.

But now I'm looking at the old leather books stacked haphazardly. The grain is so clear on the spines, and with such perfect sight, I am flooded with the strong leather smell.

My tongue flinches. As though I know exactly what it would taste and feel to have a book in my mouth.

My fingers twitch, and I straighten my back, sensing every nodule of my spine clicking into place. An ice-like invisible rod presses against my shoulders, forcing them to square, and my neck cracks in a way that feels just right.

Blinking rapidly, I stare at the empty cup in my lap, wondering how I ever existed without this...this power.

Is this magic?

Surely, this is what it feels like.

Even my genius friend Hollie could not explain any of this with science.

My thoughts come at me too fast, too loud, too clear.

And then, I see something.

The office burns away from view, like paper on fire.

A blackened sky, dipped in red.

Vast dragon wings.

A hand reaching for mine.

A voice whispering my name but not in a way I've ever heard before.

I choke, dropping the cup. It smashes into a million glittering pieces on the stone floor.

What the heck was that?

King Siberious watches, head tilted. "Ah. It would seem the elixir remembers you, even if you do not."

I barely register his words. I'm still reeling from the sensation buzzing through my veins, the feeling of something unlocking inside me.

But the weight of the moment settles fast.

I have one question left.

I want to know what it means. How can an elixir remember anything?

This is the first time I've ever been here, so how can I be remembered at all?

What is my purpose coming to the academy, and why is there a talking wolf out there hunting me down?

A flood of new questions washes over me faster than I can usually comprehend.

And suddenly, my mind is blank.

There's so much I should ask. There's so much I need to know.

But the only thing I manage—the only question I can force out of my mouth—is possibly the worst one I could've chosen.

"Why me?" I whisper.

The air shifts.

Something changes in King Siberious's expression.

He doesn't look amused anymore.

He looks... disappointed.

He exhales slowly, shaking his head like I just failed a test. "Ah. Such a waste of a valuable question."

My stomach drops.

"Why?"

"Because I already told you the answer," he says simply. "You just failed to recognize it."

My pulse pounds.

What does that mean?

Siberious rises to his feet, smoothing out the too-tight velvet jacket over his broad chest. "Come. It is time for orientation. Your classmates are waiting for you outside."

I don't move.

Something in me still wants to fight this. To demand answers.

"You never answered," I say. "*Why* me?"

King Siberious smiles faintly, but there's something sharp behind it.

"I did. Perhaps, with quiet contemplation, you shall remember."

Then he turns and walks away, leaving me with a shattered hope—not unlike the remnants of the cup at my feet—and the sinking feeling that my fate was sealed long before I ever stepped into this office.

Chapter 8
Orientation

The courtyard echoes with nervous chatter as students stand in neat rows, expressions ranging from excitement to outright terror. There are no children here, only young adults, each marked with an air of importance. The stern-looking teachers watch over us like silent sentinels, their gazes sharp and assessing.

There are stands surrounding the courtyard, and a sea of faces watch.

Judging from their gold and red uniforms, and the steely stares, they are students who have come to watch the newcomers.

I shift uncomfortably, scanning the gathered students around me.

They're all magical.

A blonde girl with pixie-cut hair flicks her wrist, conjuring a ribbon of water that dances between her fingers, shimmering under the morning sun. At least, I assume it's morning.

It's weak, and the day has just begun.

A boy beside her ignites a small flame in his palm, its glow casting flickering light against his sharp features. Another boy whispers something under his breath, and shadow-like tendrils rise from the ground. Several people back away in alarm.

I swallow, standing lamely and feeling out-of-place in all of this magic.

A smooth voice at my side pulls me from my thoughts. "You look like you're waiting for the executioner's axe. Relax, the first test rarely kills anyone."

I turn to find a charming, blond-haired man with pointed ears grinning at me. He looks vaguely familiar —like a younger, far less brooding version of Eliyah.

"What makes you think I'm worried?"

"Oh, just the sheer amount of existential dread in your eyes," he replies easily. "Name's Bovander. Fairy extraordinaire, future house champion, and professional charmer. My friends call me Bo, of course."

"Kayla," I offer, unable to stop the amused quirk of my lips. "Amateur human from planet Earth, and if I had any friends, they'd call me an idiot for signing up to this school."

Bo chuckles, and then, with a flick of his head, he tilts his neck slightly to show a black dragon mark curling along his skin.

"Like it? Stung like crazy for hours. But I think it's worth it."

I stiffen. The dragon tattoo ripples as Bo flexes his muscles and seems to come alive on his body.

I reach for my own neck, fingers brushing against the same dark ink imprinted into my skin. But as I look around, I notice something curious. Not all the tattoo marks are black.

Red. Gold. Black.

Bo seems to be following my thoughts, noticing my curiosity. He hums. "Three houses. The color of your imprint dictates where you belong. The black is Noctis. That's us." He grins, a little smugly, like that's the best one to be in. "Red is Ignis—fun at parties but careful, they're hot-tempered and can hold a grudge."

He points to a small group playing a game with fireballs emitting from their palms.

"Gold is Aurum. Siberious favors them. They're healers and, usually, wise. But I do wonder if some of the dragons made a mistake." He snorts, nodding to a lanky boy with ruffled black hair as he stumbles from group to group, seemingly unable to find a suitable spot to stand.

"They say the dragons decide based on... something." He waves his hand. "It's a mystery, really."

"What is black again?" I ask.

"Noctis." He winks. "Dark and brooding. Outcasts. Welcome to the club. Don't expect any favors from Siberious. He considers us the wildcards."

Before I can respond, King Siberious steps forward, and the chatter dies in an instant.

Everyone looks at him with a revered silence that puts my nerves on edge.

The elixir is still working. It's hard to ignore the sound of silence. The air hums with a light buzz. It tickles my eardrums, but as I cast my sights around me, no one else seems to notice it.

King Siberious clears his throat, and I focus my attention on him instead.

"For as long as ink has graced the parchment of history, there has been magic. A force neither born nor created but simply is. A breath woven into the fabric of existence itself. And at its heart—dragons.

"It is their ancient power that stirs the winds and sets the stars ablaze. Their very presence makes the air shimmer, the rivers whisper, the earth hum with life. Without them, the world would be but an empty husk, a hollow echo of what was meant to be.

"But as you well know, not all who walk this earth revere such wonders. There are those who see dragons not as guardians of magic, not as living embers of creation, but as threats to be vanquished, creatures to be conquered, relics to be erased. These are the Dragon Hunters.

"They do not seek balance. They do not seek peace. They seek dominion. And in their pursuit, they would see the skies emptied, the rivers silenced, the world stripped of its very soul.

"Make no mistake—these are not mere opponents. They are not rivals on a battlefield, nor wayward souls who might be reasoned with. They are our mortal enemies. And so long as breath remains in our lungs, so long as fire burns in our hearts, we must stand. Not for war. Not for vengeance.

"But for dragons. For magic. For the very essence of life itself."

A murmur ripples through the students. Some

exchange uneasy glances, while others stand taller as if absorbing the weight of his words.

Siberious continues.

"The Dragon Hunter faction has a settlement not far from the school. Therefore, it is strictly forbidden to leave the school grounds. Not only for your safety, but for the survival of magic itself. If dragons die, it will be the death of magic too."

He allows the silence to hang, his words sinking into the marrow of our bones.

Then, whispers fly from one end of the courtyard to the other.

"I heard they aren't just hunters. They're shifters too."

"My sister dated one, once."

A horrified gasp follows.

I crane my neck to get a better look at who is talking. It's the girl with the pixie-cut. "One of them seduced her. Luckily, her friends made an intervention and brought her back. King Siberious took pity on her and offered her another chance."

"That is lucky on both counts," the girl next to her muttered back. "I've heard Siberious can be cut-throat and doesn't offer second chances very often."

King Siberious raises his hand, signaling for silence. "Now, as dragon riders, you step into a bond beyond mortal understanding. This is not a duty nor a privilege—it is a sacred union, a merging of souls with the eternal forces that shape existence itself. You do not command a dragon; you become one with it, your fates entwined, your purpose undeniable.

"This oath is not mere words but a binding truth, woven into the very essence of who you are. To uphold it is to honor the magic that breathes through all things; to break it is to sever yourself from the world's lifeblood. So now, before the unseen forces that bear witness, raise your right hand and repeat after me."

The students lift their hands, murmuring in anticipation.

I follow suit, sensing a chill prickling the back of my neck. The air crackles as Siberious's voice deepens, and his next words echo around the courtyard with a resounding boom.

"I swear to protect the dragons, to honor their wisdom, and to stand against those who would see them fall. Their breath fuels the magic that flows through this world, and so I shall give my own to safeguard them. This is my duty. This is my bond."

The words feel heavy, ancient, like they belong to someone a lot more noble and put-together than me.

I try to keep up, but my tongue fumbles halfway through, and I'm pretty sure I just swore to *fondle* the dragons instead of honoring them.

Bo's snort confirms my suspicion.

Perfect.

Meanwhile, the other students chant in perfect harmony, their voices ringing out like they were born for this moment.

Then, just as the final syllable leaves my lips, the sky comes alive.

Riders and Hunters

Dark clouds twist and cover us all in a gloomy atmosphere.

I shudder.

It's like someone just snuffed out the sun.

A low rumble rolls across the sky—not thunder exactly, more like a warning growl from something big and not particularly friendly.

The school is surrounded by looming solid walls, surely too high for beast to scale.

But what if the wolves are here to attack?

I swallow and exchange a nervous look with Bo.

His brows are knitted together, and he looks just as puzzled as I am.

The air thickens, heavy and charged, raising every hair on my arms.

My hand is frozen at the square.

And then—because of course this is happening to me—a jagged bolt of lightning tears across the sky.

I barely have time to process the "*Oh, crap*" before a blinding streak of white-hot energy hurtles straight at me.

Pain explodes in my palm, sharp and searing, like I just high-fived the sun.

I let out a strangled yelp and stagger backward, clutching my hand against my chest.

The world spins, my ears ringing with static.

Somewhere in the distance, someone shrieks.

Probably me. Or maybe the other students, who have all taken a very respectable step away from me, like I've just been tagged by the universe, and they don't want to catch whatever I've got.

I squeeze my eyes shut, trying to get my brain to reboot. When I finally dare to uncurl my fingers, my breath catches.

A mark blazes in the center of my palm—glowing, shifting, alive. It swirls like a whirlpool, its light pulsing from blinding white to deep, endless indigo.

It should hurt, but instead, it just... is. Like it's sinking into me, settling, rewriting something I never knew was there.

I look up at the sea of confused faces aimed at me.

No one else is cradling their hand. In fact, everyone stares at me with their arms hanging limp at their sides.

Around me, murmurs turn into a full-blown buzz of speculation.

I don't need to hear the words to know what they're thinking.

That isn't normal. It wasn't supposed to happen.

Ever since graduation, wild and weird things keep happening to me. Am I cursed?

I don't know what it means. But judging by the way King Siberious narrows his eyes on me, he does. But he doesn't make a remark. In fact, when he looks away, his face relaxes. He spreads his broad hands and with a gentle wave, the dark cloud evaporates, letting in a beam of glorious sunshine.

"Welcome to the Dragon Rider Academy."

There's silence for a beat.

Then the students jump to their feet in the stands and cheer, clapping with gusto and hooting.

The newcomers look around, almost sheepish. Some of them wave. Before finally, everyone is celebrating. Stomping their feet. Whistling.

It seems that my new tattoo is all but forgotten.

"Can we have our three house captains on the stage, please?" King Siberious's voice booms, quashing the excitement. "All of you have been marked by a dragon. The color of your mark determines the house you shall be in..."

"Told you," Bo murmurs into my ear with a grin. "Come on. The boy with the dragon mark on his face is Felix. Don't stare. He might not be in Ignis, but he's got a royal temper on him."

I follow Bo through the crowd, frowning at the gold stitching on his red tunic. "How do you know so much already? Aren't you new, too?"

Bo cranes his neck to flash me another smile, but his eyes are dark. I sense a flash of something, something he's not quite ready to share with me. "Knowledge is the main currency in this realm. I make it my mission to gather as much of it as I can."

"So, you're a major gossip," I blurt, my lips quirking upward for a beat.

But Bo's brows lift with surprise. "Passing on what I know so freely would make what I know lose value. Why on earth would I do that?"

We pause at the back of the line of people in front of Felix. Up close, the dragon tattoo stretches from his cheek to his temple, like the dragon is crawling up his face.

His green eyes flash in my direction, and I avert my gaze quickly, remembering Bo's warning.

"Then why are you telling *me* so much?" I ask Bo, trying to ignore Felix's burning stare and hoping he didn't notice me looking at him.

Bo snorts again and lifts his palms. "I haven't told you anything."

But then he lowers his voice and leans in to whisper in my ear. "But there is something about you that makes me want to divulge all of my secrets. Is that your power?"

Before I can answer, King Siberious clears his throat. His gaze sweeps over us, settling momentarily on me before continuing.

"Before we proceed, allow me to introduce Ms. Mauve, the Deputy Head of Theridon Academy." He gestures to a regal woman standing to his right.

Draped in flowing chiffon and white robes, she exudes an air of quiet authority. Her presence alone demands attention, and the soft glow of fae magic shimmers faintly around her.

I mean, I assume it's fae magic. Her iridescent wings are a major give-away. They flutter, slow and deliberate, catching the sunlight and sparkling like glitter.

"She has served this academy for over a century and ensures that our traditions and values remain unbroken."

Frances nods, her piercing eyes scanning the gathered students with calm precision.

"Deputy Head Mauve will oversee your progress

and discipline. She has mentored generations of dragon riders and has an unerring ability to uncover potential where others see none. Trust her guidance, and you will find your place in our world."

He offers a knowing glance toward the teacher, who gives the faintest of smiles before stepping back into place.

"Your house captain will escort you to your common room shortly. But first..." King Siberious continues, his voice cutting through the last whispers of conversation. "We must begin the entrance test."

A murmur ripples through the students like a breeze stirring dry leaves. Some straighten, eager. Others shift uncomfortably, a few even exchanging wary glances.

I stiffen. "Test? Already?"

Bo smirks, the glint in his eyes downright smug. "What, you thought they'd ease us in? Welcome to Theridon, darling. They like to throw us into the fire and see who burns first."

Fantastic. Just fantastic.

I cross my arms, mostly to hide the growing terror slithering up my spine. I wasn't ready for this. I wasn't ready for any of this.

One by one, students step forward. And, one by one, they remind me exactly how much I don't belong here.

A centaur—broad-shouldered, with a gleaming bronze chest plate and hooves that could probably shatter bone— slams a single hoof against the ground, and the stone courtyard shudders beneath us.

A few students stumble.

I manage to keep my footing, but only barely.

Next, a girl with deep violet eyes and an eerie stillness lifts a row of books with a mere flick of her fingers. They hover midair, pages rustling in an invisible breeze, before spinning around her in perfect synchrony.

Psychic. Of course. Because moving books with your mind is totally normal.

Then there's the healer—a small, quiet girl with dark curls and a serene expression. She kneels beside a trembling rabbit, its tiny body marred by a fresh wound.

Soft golden light spills from her hands as she cups them over the injury, and, right before my eyes, the torn flesh knits itself back together.

The rabbit blinks, twitches its nose, then darts away as if it hadn't just performed a minor miracle.

The murmurs of awe deepen.

A fae girl steps forward, silver hair cascading like moonlight. She exhales, and her breath—her *breath*—shimmers into delicate frost, sculpting itself into twisting ice spires. They hover for a brief, breathtaking moment before shattering into a swirl of snowflakes that melt before they hit the ground.

There's also the tall one in crimson robes, eyes burning like embers. He doesn't even move—just wills a ring of fire into existence around his feet. The flames slither across the stone, licking hungrily at the ground, yet leaving nothing but unscorched rock in their wake.

And then Bo steps forward with an easy confidence, rolling his shoulders before extending his hands. A pulse of light bursts from his palms—orange and gold, forming intricate, shifting geometric patterns in the air, like a celestial dance. They shimmer, flicker, and fade just as quickly.

"Light magic," he explains, flexing his fingers. "Fairy-born. Comes with the sparkle package."

"Show-off," someone from the Ignis house mutters, their crossed arms doing little to hide the faint glow of their red-marked hand.

Bo, of course, grins. "Thank you," he replies with a mock bow. "I do try."

One by one, the line thins. Each display of magic is grander, more complex. The air hums with power, charged with the sheer weight of what's unfolding. Excitement crackles in every whispered murmur. Anticipation coils tighter with each passing second.

And way before I'm ready for it, it's my turn.

I step forward, every nerve screaming at me to turn around and bolt.

King Siberious watches, his expression unreadable, but there's something in his gaze—something calculating, sharp, like he's measuring something I can't quite grasp.

"Show us your powers," he commands.

I open my mouth. Close it. Swallow hard.

"Does crippling anxiety and a dry sense of humor count?"

The silence that follows is... profound.

A few students gasp. One actually snorts. A girl at

the back chokes on what I hope is a cough and not her attempt at suppressing laughter.

King Siberious doesn't react. Not even a twitch.

Tough crowd.

Instead, he gives a small nod to the woman at his side—Ms. Mauve, the deputy head.

She moves toward me, slow and deliberate, the weight of the moment pressing down on my chest.

Up close, she is... otherworldly. Not in the way the fae girl had been, but in a way that unsettles something deep in my bones. Her beauty is ageless, as if time doesn't quite know what to do with her. The flowing chiffon and white robes only add to the effect, making her seem like she's gliding rather than walking.

She places her hands on my shoulders. Her eyes slip shut.

The courtyard holds its breath.

My pulse hammers, loud in my ears.

The air thickens, charged, like the moment before a storm breaks.

A strange sensation crawls over my skin, like invisible threads wrapping around me, feeling through me, searching for something I don't understand.

Then the teacher's eyes snap open.

A hush falls over the courtyard.

Her voice rings out, clear and unyielding, each word striking the air like a chisel against stone. "For the first time in history, the dragons have chosen... a human. A primitive being with no powers whatsoever."

My stomach drops.

The silence that follows is deafening.

And then—

Chaos.

The whispers that follow cut through me like knives.

My cheeks burn. My stomach clenches.

"A human? That's impossible."

"She must have some hidden power, right?"

"Maybe the dragons made a mistake."

I don't need to turn around to know what the other students are thinking.

Bovander nudges me lightly. "Well. That's one way to make an entrance."

I force a breath out, my hands curling into fists.

All I can think about is that stupid wolf.

I *don't* belong here.

And now, everyone at the academy knows it too.

Chapter 9
The Mistake

"This has to be a mistake, right?"

"Isn't she the girl struck by lightning, though?"

"What does it mean?"

The questions crackle around me like fire, and I chew my lip, wishing that I could, for once, not be the weirdo with all the attention.

Bo looks at me triumphant. "I knew you were different, but this... this is something else."

"She doesn't belong here!"

The shout resounds like a banging drum sentencing me to death in the gloomy courtyard.

I glance up and flinch under the burning stares from the students in the stands above me.

That dang wolf was right. I don't belong at this school.

And now everyone knows it too.

Siberious lifts his hands. "Settle down, settle down."

But it's Mauve's descent into the sky that stops the mayhem.

She's suspended in the air, framed by the sun and looking more like an angel than a fae. But the expression on her face is one of thunder, not reverence. She waves her arms majestically, tendrils of golden light coil around her in a way that has us all transfixed.

She does not speak, I guess she doesn't need to. All eyes are on her now, and no one dares let out a breath, or even blink.

I marvel at her ability to command a whole school with something that I can only describe as feminine energy.

Siberious clears his throat, and his eyes twinkle. As though this is not the first time his deputy head has pulled this stunt.

"Thank you, Ms. Mauve. Now. Theridon Academy serves the dragons. All of you made a vow to serve them as well. So, it is in everyone's interest not to question the decision of our friends. They are ancient with scores of wisdom. I am most certain that there is a very strong reason for every person selected to be at the school. It is time for our house captains to take the new students to their common rooms. You shall find your possessions are already there, and you will also receive your class schedules. Rest up, we have a lot of work to do."

I rub the chills on my arms as I follow Bo through the crowd.

A chatter breaks out, and there's a mixture of

excited babble and a few suspicious stares in my direction again.

Meanwhile, my heart hammers, and my stomach swirls in a way that makes me feel on edge.

We march in organized lines back toward the castle.

At the center of the sprawling courtyard, a fountain in the shape of a dragon rearing up on its hind legs spews water that gleams like liquid silver.

My ankle twists on the cobbled stones, I hiss at the sharp pain but grit my teeth and move on.

As we reach the doors, I swallow, staring at the gargoyles perched on the roof. They seem to watch the students below with expressions that suggest they disapprove of everything happening at all times.

Relatable.

I risk another glance at the whirlpool-shaped mark burned into my palm. Still there. Still glowing faintly, like some kind of celestial prank etched into my skin.

How many more of these accidental tattoos am I going to collect? And, more importantly, why was I the only one struck by lightning during the vow?

Feels a little personal.

Bo keeps his stride smooth and easy as he leads me through a grand archway and into a spiral staircase so narrow and winding that I swear it's designed to weed out the weak.

My legs start protesting about halfway up, but the alternative is to collapse dramatically and risk being trampled by students who seem unnervingly comfortable scaling endless stairs like it's an Olympic sport.

By the time we reach the top, my thighs are on fire, my lungs hate me, and I'm seriously considering putting in a formal complaint about the lack of magical escalators.

We emerge onto a wide, open-air balcony overlooking the courtyard and, beyond that, the endless sweep of mist-drenched mountains.

The view is breathtaking in the kind of way that makes you forget, for just a second, that your life is spiraling into absolute chaos.

But then I hear a pointed throat clearing and turn to face my new house captain.

He towers over me, and his dark green eyes look like they see way too much. The dragon tattoo coils across his cheekbone, and I swear it's looking at me. Judging.

Honestly, it's very intimidating. Ten out of ten for terrifying first impressions.

Shoot. There I go again, staring when Bo specifically warned me not to.

He hands me a scroll—which, yes, is apparently how they do schedules here. Fancy.

I glance at it, and my brows shoot up. "Uh, yeah, quick question. This says I have classes in Elemental Manipulation, Draconic Lore, and Combat Training. Just one tiny problem—I'm not magical. I can't do half of this stuff."

He gives me a look that suggests he's torn between amusement and the overwhelming urge to throw me off the balcony.

"Isn't that the point?" he says, voice dry. "You're at a school. To learn."

I narrow my eyes. "Magic can be learned?"

"Yes. Here anyone can wield magic. Even little humans like you."

Little. Humans. Like. Me.

Oh, this guy is asking for me to accidentally set something on fire in protest.

Before I can come up with a suitably scathing reply, he gestures toward a door marked with the number 3.

"That's your room," he says, and with that, he's done with me.

I barely take a step before I'm ambushed.

A group of students from my dorm descend on me like a pack of nosy, overexcited wolves.

"How did a dragon choose you?"

"Show us the mark!"

"Was it painful?"

"What does it mean?"

They crowd closer, eyes gleaming with curiosity, and the walls start closing in.

Before I can decide whether to answer or make a break for it, Bo steps in, his towering presence enough to make them pause.

"Back off," he says, calm but firm. "She just got here."

There's a murmur of disappointment, but they obey, backing up just enough for me to breathe again.

I should thank him. A normal person would.

But when Bo turns to me, probably to ask if I'm

okay or try to talk, something about all of this is too much.

I hug my arms around myself and blurt, "I'm tired," before making a beeline for my room.

When the door shuts behind me, I exhale.

I lean against it for a second, the events of the day crashing over me like a tidal wave.

A school of magic. A lightning mark on my hand. A dragon choosing me. Magic can be learned?

I glance down at my glowing hand.

Yeah. Sure. What could possibly go wrong?

Chapter 10
Roommates for Life

Soft, golden light filters through the arched window, pooling on the stone floor in gentle patches. The walls are a muted gray, worn smooth by time, and two simple beds sit against opposite walls, each draped with heavy, navy-blue quilts. One of the beds is decorated, while the other sits plain and sad.

The room is small, but cozy. It's not much, but it definitely beats the attic over the laundromat.

A flurry of motion behind one bed catches my eye.

I edge closer to get a better look at my roommate.

A girl with a cloud of copper curls is on her knees, wrestling a bulging suitcase that looks ready to burst. Clothes—bright, mismatched, and unapologetically chaotic—spill across the floor.

"Oops!" She giggles to herself. She hasn't seen me yet, too lost in her mess.

I clear my throat and force a smile.

She glances up, cheeks flushed, her amber eyes are as bright as gemstones.

"Oh! You must be Kayla!" She springs to her feet.

She brushes dust from her skirt and bounces on her toes, her energy so contagious I'm almost winded just standing near it.

"I'm Marigold, but everyone calls me Mari. Or Goldie. Or 'Hey, you, Hot Mess'." Her accompanying laugh sounds like church bells on a summer's day.

She thrusts her hand toward me, fingers splayed wide.

Her enthusiasm is disarming.

I reach out, and before I know it, her hands wrap around mine, warm and earnest. I get a waft of her scent—it's fruity, like strawberries and cream.

"Nice to meet you," I manage, my voice soft against the backdrop of her vibrant energy.

Then I bite back a tear.

This is the most tenderness I've experienced from another human being in a very long time.

Mari lifts a lock of hair from my shoulder and inspects it with an expression of wonderment. "I love your hair, it's so unusual. So cool! How did you make the ends so red. And is that a hint of orange?"

"Hair dye," I reply with a nonchalant shrug.

After the crash, I needed a new identity. And everyone was calling me the girl who didn't burn. I wanted my hair to look like fire.

I avert my gaze, staring at nothing as I lose myself in thought. But my focus snaps back to Mari who has her head tilted and big, round eyes boring into me.

"Ahh," she says, her voice hushed now.

Did she hear my thoughts? Or maybe my body language gave me away. I guess grief isn't easy to hide. If it was, my friends wouldn't have dropped me after the crash.

A familiar pang hits me again.

"Isn't this place incredible?" Mari twirls, her arms wide.

I can't decide if she's changing the subject on purpose or just caught up in her excitement again. Either way, I'm glad for it.

She stops moving for three seconds to give me a beaming smile, and I can't help but return one.

"We're going to be roommates! Can you believe it? I was so worried I'd get someone who'd hate my plants or worse!" She leans close. "Wait. You're not a swamp witch, are you?"

She whispers the last part, her eyes comically wide, as if the walls could listen and share secrets.

I settle on the empty bed, and stare at my duffle bag peeking out from under it. The weight on my chest is a stark contrast to the whirlwind that is Mari.

"No, I'm not a swamp witch. Just... human. A pathetic human with nothing of value and no powers or friends to speak of."

My shoulders slump under the pressure.

But Mari is having none of it. She claps, snapping me out of my sorry state.

"Well, now you've got me. And..." She darts back to her suitcase, pulling out a small potted flower with delicate purple blooms.

"Now you've got Gerald, too. He doesn't talk much,

but he's a great listener." She sets the plant on the windowsill, patting its leaves like it might purr under her touch.

I glance around the room, taking in the patchwork quilt, the string of twinkling lights already woven around her bedpost, and a collection of trinkets—stones, feathers, and what looks suspiciously like a dragon scale—lined up on her nightstand.

"How did you manage to bring all of this?" I ask, unable to hide my surprise.

I didn't get to pack. Who knows what's in my duffle bag. I can't imagine Eliyah was very careful to collect anything sentimental. I'll be lucky if I have a pair of clean socks without holes in them.

Mari winks, her grin mischievous. "Just a little levitation spell. Don't tell the professors, though. I'm still supposed to be practicing restraint."

She flops onto her bed, her feet kicking in the air, chin propped on her hands.

"So, tell me everything. Where are you from? What's your story? Do you think the cafeteria food here is as bad as they say?"

A lump rises in my throat, but the room feels so warm—so safe—that words slip out before I can stop them.

I tell her everything that happened in the orientation. The crazy lightning strike during the vow, the different powers our peers presented. And Mauve's announcement to everyone that I'm basically a freak.

I exhale and flop back against the pillow, rubbing

my temples. "Ever since I got on that train, people keep telling me I don't belong here."

Mari watches me for a moment before scooting closer, her curls bouncing.

"So... you were struck by lightning, huh?" she says, not unkindly, but definitely curious.

I groan.

Of course that's the part she'd cling to. "Ugh. Don't remind me."

But I hold up my hand anyway, letting her see the swirling mark glowing faintly in the candlelight.

Mari's eyes widen.

"Whoa," she breathes, reaching for my wrist like she can't help herself. "That's amazing."

I snort. "Yeah, amazing is one word for it. I'd personally go with 'terrifying'."

"Well, magical marks have meaning."

Mari twists her arm and pulls back her sleeve, revealing her own mark—a black dragon curled nose to tail.

I stare, then yank my collar down to show her my dragon mark.

Mari traces it with her index finger, her breath steams my cheeks. "I'm glad we got put into the same house. Maybe this one on your hand means you have special powers buried inside you."

I shrug. "Yeah. No. I don't think so."

Mari pulls back and tilts her head as she studies me. "Well, it must mean something. People don't just walk around getting zapped from the skies and not have something cool happen to them..."

I roll my eyes. "Great. So, I can expect to wake up tomorrow with mega powers? Or turn into a shapeshifting monster?"

Mari laughs. "Only if you're really lucky."

Her smile dims slightly, and she twists her sleeve back down, fingers tapping against her knee.

"You know, I didn't even get to say goodbye to my parents."

I pause, the words sinking in.

"They sent you here without telling you?"

She hesitates. "Not exactly. My parents are non-magical. Librarians, actually." Her fingers move from her knee and now drum anxiously against the bedpost. "They didn't even know *I* was magical until I got accepted here."

I frown. "How does that even work?"

She shakes her head. "No clue. I just... showed signs one day. And now, I'm here. Just like you."

That's not comforting.

Mari must sense my mood because she suddenly leans forward, her expression serious.

"Do you remember yet?"

I blink. "Remember what?"

Her face creases in confusion. "No one told you?"

"Told me what?"

Mari hesitates, then drops her voice to a whisper. "We're here to remember something. Something big about our past, I suppose. Or maybe our future." She crinkles her nose. "The cycles are different in this realm, so that kind of thing confuses the heck out of me."

I stare at her.

There's a whole other reason we're here? One that no one bothered to mention to me?

Something big?

I should ask more questions. I want to.

But Mari's gasp stops me.

"Oh! I can't believe I missed the whole ceremony! Siberious will be so mad."

I blink. "Were you here all this time?"

Mari springs up and grabs a stack of papers from her bed, holding them against her chest like a precious treasure.

"I was catching up on my story, and I guess I just got sucked in and forgot!" She sighs dreamily and flops back onto her pillows, waving the pages in the air.

I raise a brow. "Story?"

"Oh, it's amazing. It's about a wolf shifter and a dragon rider who fall in love—but they're forbidden to see each other. It's amazing!"

I snort. "So, like Romeo and Juliet... Let me guess. They both die at the end."

Mari freezes, and an awkward silence hangs in the air.

Her lips part. Her eyes widen. A slow horror creeps across her face, her hands clutching the pages like I just told her the meaning of life and also that it's terrible.

"You've read it? I'm only half-way through," she whispers, voice trembling.

Oh. Oh, no.

"You-—just now—you—you said it like you knew the ending!"

I wave my hands frantically. "No! I didn't mean—I mean, I was just guessing! It's a tragedy, that's what tragedies do! It's the classic star-crossed lovers die horribly trope! But maybe—maybe in this one, they—uh, they fake their deaths! And live happily ever after! Maybe the dragon rider pulls some last-minute, totally unexpected magic and—resurrection!"

Mari's lower lip trembles.

"That... doesn't sound like where it was going..." Her voice cracks.

Shoot. I ruined the ending.

I, Kayla, professional foot-in-mouth disaster, just spoiled the tragic romance of Mari's beloved story, and I have no idea how to fix this.

I flounder for a distraction and latch onto the first thing I see.

"So, uh—what's with this?" I gesture wildly to the angry, prickly mistake of a plant perched on my nightstand.

Mari sniffs, blinking rapidly as she drags herself out of her heartbreak. "That? Oh, it's a Bloodthorn Sprout. It's supposed to bond with its owner and grow based on their emotions. I usually keep mine on my shoulder."

I squint at it. "So, you're saying... this thing is basically a mood plant?"

"Yes."

"And it looks like this because of... me?"

Mari tilts her head, appraising it with a sudden,

entirely unfair amount of amusement, considering she was crying two seconds ago.

"Well, you've had a day."

I glare at the plant.

It glares back.

"Great," I mutter. "I'm so happy I get to sleep next to a passive-aggressive cactus."

Mari snickers and flops back onto her bed.

"Welcome to Theridon, Kayla."

Chapter 11
Purgatory

The dining hall at Theridon Academy is not what I expect.

I'm braced for floating chandeliers, enchanted goblets, and steaming plates of food that refill at will. Instead, I step into a vast, moody cavern of a room, where the only source of light comes from a row of iron chandeliers that drip candle wax like slow-moving tears. The ceiling arches high above, its beams twisted like gnarled tree branches, and the entire space hums with an eerie kind of stillness, as if every sound is absorbed into the very stones of the castle.

It's echoey, vast, and imposing.

And definitely not Hogwarts.

I sigh, slumping into a seat at one of the long wooden tables. "You know, I really thought a magic school would have more of a... I don't know. A welcoming vibe?"

Mari plops down beside me, already making herself at home. "Oh, come on, it's not that bad. It's historic."

"More like, haunted." I wave a hand toward the gargoyle-like statues carved into the pillars, their expressions permanently locked in varying degrees of disapproval. "It's kind of terrifying."

Before I can complain further, pitchers of water and steaming bowls of... something are placed in front of us.

I stare down at my bowl.

It's oatmeal.

No fruit. No honey. No sugar.

Just pure, unflavored, mushy oatmeal that looks like it might taste like regret.

I feel like I've stumbled into Oliver Twist, only I'm pretty sure no one is desperate enough to be asking for more of this slop.

Mari hums happily as she grabs her spoon. "Yum."

"Yum?" I squint at her. "Are we looking at the same thing?"

"It's nutritious."

"It's punishment."

I glance around, hoping for something, anything, to make up for the fact that this is what's passing as dinner. But all I see are identical bowls of blandness and pitchers of plain water. No magical elixirs like the one Siberious gave me. Nothing even remotely exciting.

"What happened to the drink from earlier?" I

mutter, pushing the oatmeal around with my spoon like it might morph into something edible if I glare at it long enough.

Mari tilts her head. "Oh, Siberious only gives those out when needed. Normally, we eat simple foods to keep our blood sugar levels steady and our minds clear."

I blink at her. Then at my sad bowl.

I drag a hand down my face. "We're in purgatory."

Mari giggles, nudging me. "Oh, stop."

"I'm serious. If I designed purgatory, this is exactly how I'd do it. Dreary gothic halls, a never-ending staircase to nowhere, and oatmeal. Lots and lots of bland oatmeal."

Mari full-on cackles, almost knocking over her water.

"Well, at least there's good company in purgatory." She winks.

I snort but take a bite anyway. It's as tasteless as expected.

The rubbery texture sticks like glue on my tongue. It takes physical effort to swallow.

I cover up my gag with a cough.

Across the table, a group of students has gathered around Bo, who is deep into one of his stories. His voice is low and rich with the kind of confidence that makes people hang onto his every word.

"...riding through the Shadowed Woods, where the trees whisper warnings and the air is so thick with magic even the horses can sense it. It takes skill to navigate through them. And guts to make it out alive."

The group leans in, captivated, and I don't even realize I'm staring until his eyes flick to mine.

For a second, there's nothing but the weight of his gaze—sharp, assessing, almost amused. Then, with the slow ease of someone who knows exactly what he's doing, he winks.

My brain short-circuits.

Mari makes a high-pitched sound beside me and grabs my arm, leaning into my ear. "Oh, my gosh. He winked at you. Bovander just *winked* at you."

I wave her off, trying to act like my face isn't heating up. "He winks at everyone. It's probably, like, his thing."

Mari isn't listening. "He's so cool." She sighs dreamily. "Did you know he once found a secret treasure hoard in the ruins of Eldrath Keep? He didn't even keep it. He gave it to the villagers. Who does that?!"

"Someone who likes treasure hunting but doesn't like taxes?" I suggest.

Mari giggles. "Either way, he's perfect."

Before I can tease her, the heavy doors at the front of the hall slam open with a tremendous bang.

The entire room freezes.

A girl with a pixie cut stumbles inside, her cheeks rosy, her expression flustered. She rushes forward, her breath coming in quick bursts.

"I'm sorry, Your Highness," she gasps, her voice trembling. "I tried to stop her. But... there's something wrong with Char."

The moment she says it, a second figure storms into the hall.

Her presence is like a lightning strike.

Literally.

Electricity crackles from her fingertips, tiny arcs of light snapping between her hands. Her eyes are wild with fury.

"You're all frauds."

Her voice rings through the air, slicing through the silence like a blade.

Siberious rises slowly, his usual smirk fading.

The tension in the room tightens like a bowstring.

Mauve moves next, rising gracefully to her feet.

But unlike the rest of us, Char doesn't back down.

She locks eyes with Mauve, her chest heaving.

"Your mask doesn't fool me. Not anymore." Char snarls. "I know everything. I know *exactly* what you're doing here, and it makes me sick."

Before anyone can react, two centaurs appear, moving swiftly to her sides.

They each grab an arm, but Char thrashes wildly.

"They're lying to you!" she screams, desperate, unhinged. "Don't listen to anything they say! Get out now, while you can!"

As the centaurs seize her, the torches lining the hall sputter. A harsh wind whips through the room, even though there are no open windows.

Electricity crackles from her fingertips, sparking against the stone floor.

Siberious takes several slow steps forward, his expression unreadable. Then, with an easy chuckle, he says, "And this is why we have a strict no-drinking policy."

Nervous laughter ripples through the hall.

But Bo isn't laughing.

And for the briefest moment, I swear I see him exchange a worried look with Siberious.

Something is very, very wrong.

Chapter 12
Secrets and Shadows

If Char's meltdown had been a little less dramatic, maybe I'd be able to breathe right now.

But no. Instead of having a normal first night at Theridon Academy—like, I don't know, quietly panicking in my room—I get a front-row seat to a conspiracy-laden freak-out and a public arrest.

So, yeah, not ideal.

Siberious smooths a hand over his fancy robe like he just wrapped up an evening lecture rather than watched a girl get dragged out by centaurs.

"The moons have shifted," he says smoothly, as if he wasn't just accused of high-level scheming. "Off to bed. You need to be rested before your classes."

And just like that, the crowd dissolves into nervous chatter.

The students shuffle toward the dorm halls, whispers sparking like tiny brush fires as we go.

Mari, to absolutely no one's surprise, does not keep her voice down.

She nudges me as we walk, whisper-yelling in my ear. "Okay, but seriously, what was that? Where did she even get a drink? She must have bathed in wine to be that detached from reality."

I huff out a laugh, even as unease curls in my gut.

Char didn't look drunk. She looked desperate.

A shadow moves beside us, and I nearly trip when Bo materializes out of nowhere.

"She wasn't drunk," he mutters, his voice low and unreadable.

Mari and I both freeze.

I frown up at him. "What do you mean?"

Bo's jaw tightens. "Nothing. Never mind."

Without another word, he turns and strides ahead, disappearing into the crowd.

Right.

Because that wasn't suspicious at all.

I stare after him, considering whether I should, you know, maybe demand some actual answers.

But Mari lets out a tiny, strangled squeal and grabs my arm so suddenly that I almost fall over.

"Oh. My. Gosh," she breathes, practically vibrating. "Bovander Siberious was RIGHT NEXT TO ME. His arm hairs touched my elbow. I felt them. Now I'm tingling from head to toe!"

She does an inward squeal, jumps in place, and clutches her own face like she's trying and failing to contain her joy.

I, meanwhile, am stuck on a far more important detail.

My brain lags.

"Siberious?" I repeat. "As in..."

Mari stops mid-bounce, blinking at me like I just told her I've never heard of gravity.

"Wait." She gasps. "You didn't know?"

"Know what?"

Her jaw drops, and her eyes bulge.

She smacks my arm and throws both hands into the air. "Gosh, Kayla. Hasn't anyone told you *anything* about this place?"

I fold my arms, feeling defensive.

"Apparently not."

By the time we reach our dorm, Mari throws herself onto her bed like a fainting damsel in distress.

"Bovander." She sighs dreamily, hugging a pillow to her chest. "He's King Siberious's youngest son. The golden boy. The darling of the kingdom. He's a total celebrity where I'm from."

I sit on my bed, dazed.

And suddenly, everything about Bo makes sense.

His arrogance.

His magic.

The way he knows everything about this school like he built it himself.

The look he shared with King Siberious in the hall.

I exhale slowly, my head spinning with it all.

What were the chances that Prince Bovander introduced himself to me? Of all people.

I grit my teeth, wondering if Siberious is using him to spy on me.

I sit up again, turning to look at Mari.

"What do you think Char means?" I keep my voice

quiet. "What do you think they are they lying to us about?"

Mari opens her mouth to answer—then pauses.

I narrow my eyes. "And don't tell me she was drunk."

Mari closes her mouth with a shrug. "Does it matter? We're here to be dragon riders, Kayla. Not investigators."

I don't respond.

But something doesn't feel right.

I glance toward the window, where the night stretches deep and endless.

The inky sky has a deep maroon shade to it with streaks of purple. A red moon shines high in the sky. It's fascinating. Almost interesting enough to distract me.

Almost.

I force myself to curl up in bed and wait for sleep.

The unease in my chest festers, and after an hour of tossing and turning, I give up.

I stare at the ceiling, my mind spiraling.

The wolf on the train.

The warning in his eyes.

The glowing mark on my hand.

What am I missing?

Because it feels like every answer leads to five more questions.

A huff from across the room yanks me out of my thoughts.

Mari throws her blankets off, swings her legs over

the edge of the bed, and stands with purpose. "I can't take it any longer."

I blink. "What?"

She's already reaching for her boots.

"Where are you going?" I ask warily, watching as she wraps herself in a dark shawl.

Mari ties her curls back into a ponytail, securing them with a ribbon. "To the market."

I push myself upright. "Wait—what?"

She fastens her boots, completely unbothered.

"I need to know what happens next in my story. I can't cope."

For a second, my brain struggles to keep up.

I'd assumed she meant the chaos of the night—Char's outburst, the weird way Siberious handled it, the secrets of Theridon.

But she means her magazine story.

"Hold on." I rub my temples. "Aren't the markets closed? It's the middle of the night."

Mari pauses mid-lace-up, looks at me, and then bursts into laughter.

"Ohhh, that's right." She smacks her forehead playfully. "You come from Earth."

I squint at her. "What does that have to do with anything?"

Mari beams. "You've got so much un-learning to do, my sweet, confused friend."

I cross my arms. "*Un-learning?*"

She grins mischievously and extends a hand toward me.

"Come with me, and I'll show you."

Chapter 13
The Market Beyond Time

We slip through the castle corridors like shadows, Mari leading the way with practiced ease. I try to memorize every turn, but the paths never seem to stay the same.

One moment, we're in a narrow stone passage, the walls lined with iron sconces dripping wax. The next, we step into a grand hallway lined with mirrored arches, reflecting a thousand versions of ourselves sneaking through the dark.

"Uh, Mari?" I whisper. "Are the hallways moving?"

She grins over her shoulder. "Theridon doesn't believe in fixed architecture."

"Oh, of course not," I mutter. "That would be way too normal."

Mari chuckles and tugs me forward. "Don't worry. Magic finds its own path. You just have to trust where it takes you."

Trust.

Right.

Because trusting strange sentient castles always ends well.

After a series of turns—some of which I'm certain should have led us in a circle—Mari stops in front of a heavy wooden door at the end of a dimly lit corridor. It looks... normal. Which instantly makes me suspicious.

She places a hand against it and whispers something in a language I don't recognize.

There's a faint shimmer, like heat rippling in the air, and then the wood melts away like dissolving ink.

Beyond it?

Nothing but a pitch-black void.

I reel back. "Nope. No. Absolutely not. I am not stepping into a void, Mari. That's rule number one of horror stories."

Mari grins, unfazed. "It's just a passage."

"It's a void."

"It looks like a void. But it's a shortcut." She grabs my hand.

Before I can argue further, she pulls me through.

The second we step out, the air changes.

One minute, we're in dark, dreary Theridon, where the sky is nothing but endless, murky gray.

The next?

A rush of warmth and color bursts around us, like someone painted over the world in golds and violets and swirling ribbons of pink. The sky is alive, shifting and humming. It's like I just stumbled into a Monet painting.

I gasp, spinning on the spot. "How is this possible?"

Mari waves a hand, and the colors brighten, shimmering like stained glass catching the sun. "Siberious likes to keep things dull at the academy. So, he has a spell to keep the weather gloomy. He controls when it's night or day there."

I stare at her. "You're telling me the sky at Theridon is fake?"

Mari shrugs. "Not fake. Just... curated."

I blink. "And people are just... fine with that?"

"They don't really think about it." She twirls, letting the colors swirl around her. "Days stretch much longer in this realm. Not that it matters, time is just a concept made up by humans. Probably to control people."

I think about it for a second. "Is it like when you're having the best day of your life, time flies. And when the world is out to get you, it drags?"

Mari beams like a proud parent. "Exactly. That is our notion of time here. Measured by how you perceive it instead of by machines and conventions."

My brows quirk up. "So, your day and mine can have different lengths?"

Mari shrugs. "No idea. But Siberious likes us to have a time when all of us sleep at Theridon, so he kind of 'curates' us as night and day sort of cycle that matches our class schedule. You'll see what I mean when classes start."

· · ·

I stare. "What?"

She smirks. "You poor thing, I can see your brain melting over this."

I rub my temples. "I just don't get how anyone functions without time. How do you know when to eat? Sleep? Show up for things?"

Mari laughs. "The world still moves, and people age. We chart what you call "time" in cycles. Cycles of the moons."

She points up at the inky sky.

I follow her line of sight and frown. "Well, I guess I'm an idiot, because I only see one moon."

Mari snorts. "Of course, you do. They shift."

That sounds insanely vague and impractical, but okay. Besides, two moons? That's confusing.

Maybe the magical train somehow transported me from Arizona to Mars. Mars has two moons, right?

Mari links arms with me, steering me forward. "Don't worry. I'll ease you into all the other secrets gently."

I narrow my eyes. "There's more?"

"Oh, so much more." She squeezes my arm. "But for now, just wait until you meet your dragon. I can't wait to bond with mine!"

I pause mid-step.

"Right. Dragons." I sigh. "Mine will need to be beyond patient with me."

Mari giggles.

But I'm not done.

"And just wait until my dragon finds out I'm afraid of heights."

Mari stumbles to a stop, gaping at me. "You're what?"

I groan. "Yeah. Apparently, I wasn't informed about flying on the back of mythical beasts in my future when I developed that particular fear."

Mari bursts out laughing. "Oh, Kayla, your life is going to be so fun. I'm so excited."

That makes one of us.

The path winds downward, and soon, the trees thin out, revealing a village unlike anything I've ever seen.

The buildings are woven into nature itself—stone and ivy, twisted vines supporting wooden beams, rooftops thatched with what looks suspiciously like shimmering dragon scales.

The streets are alive with magic. Witches, warlocks, fae, and centaurs stroll through cobblestone walkways, their conversations a mix of languages both ancient and new.

Glowing lanterns float above twisting alleyways, casting shadows that don't quite match the people beneath them.

A fountain in the center of the village bubbles with liquid silver, reflecting the sky like captured starlight.

It's loud, chaotic, bursting with energy, and yet perfectly balanced, like an ecosystem that thrives on its own rhythm.

I slow my steps, taking it all in.

Mari grabs my sleeve, pointing. "Look, Kayla! More Bloodhound plants!"

I follow her gaze to a row of market stalls where bright, blooming crimson flowers sit in woven baskets.

The second I pass, the petals shrink, their vibrant reds bleeding into withered browns and grays.

Mari pouts. "Oh, too bad. They looked so pretty before."

I glare at the nearest plant. "Yeah, well, I'm starting to think I have a bad reputation in the botanical world."

Mari tugs me toward a market stall, where a man sits slouched in a wooden chair.

At first glance, I think he's asleep. Then I notice his eyes—thin, slitted pupils, flickering with an odd, golden sheen.

His goat-like hooves rest lazily on the edge of the counter, and he has curved horns peeking through his wild mess of silver-streaked curls.

A satyr.

Mari claps her hands on the counter. "Master Zevi! I need my next installment."

The satyr jerks awake with a snort, nearly falling backward.

I stifle a laugh. Guess that answers the question of whether he was sleeping or just being dramatic.

He blinks blearily at Mari, then groans, rubbing his face. "Gods above, child. Did no one tell you it is dangerous to wake an old satyr?"

Mari tilts her head, all innocence. "Good thing you're not old, then, Zevi."

He grumbles something under his breath, then waves a hand, and a stack of papers materializes on the counter.

Mari squeals in delight, grabbing them instantly.

Meanwhile, I lean against the counter, eyeing him.

He raises a brow.

I raise one back.

"You look like you have questions," he drawls, voice raspy with sleep.

"Yes," I say. "But let's start with an easy one. Why does this place feel like I stepped into an alternate dimension?"

He smirks, then studies me with a keen eye. "Hmm. You're not from here, I gather."

I shake my head.

He hums again. "Well, then, I suppose the obvious answer is that you did...but I'll let you in on a secret." He leans close and lowers his voice. "Most people here are not from this realm."

Before I can demand further explanation from the smug satyr, the ground beneath us trembles.

A deep, guttural roar splits the night air, rattling through my ribs like an earthquake.

I flinch. "What was—"

"Uh oh," Mari says, her voice just a little too edgy for my liking.

She drops a gold coin on the table and snatches a magazine in a wildly un-Mari-like frantic motion.

Something between a roar and a sqwark shakes the sky.

And suddenly, a chill rushes over me—sharp and unnatural, like the moment before a storm breaks.

The market reacts instantly.

Stall owners scramble into action.

Some flick their fingers, and tables fold themselves, and items whirl into enchanted satchels.

Others dump everything on carts, wheels screeching against stone as they flee.

A few just drop everything and run.

Panic crackles through the air like wildfire.

I stare, alarmed. "WHAT THE HECK IS THAT?"

Mari doesn't answer.

She's shoving her magazine into her bag with shaking hands, her fingers unsteady.

Her face has gone pale.

And that's what finally makes my stomach drop.

Because Mari doesn't get rattled.

I grab her arm. "Mari."

She looks up, startled.

Before she can say anything, a third sqwark-roar rips through the air, closer this time.

A shadow moves over the rooftops.

And suddenly, the sky isn't a swirl of color anymore.

It's dark.

Suffocating.

And whatever just arrived?

It's huge.

And it's hunting.

Chapter 14
The Hunter in the Sky

"RUN!" Mari shouts.

I run.

Or, at least, I try.

But my legs feel like lead from climbing a thousand staircases today, and my feet—traitorous, useless things—trip over absolutely nothing.

I hit the ground hard.

Pain bursts across my chin as I slam against the cobbled stone, the impact rattling through my skull.

For a second, I just lay there, stunned. My temples throb, but the rest of me is numb.

Then I taste blood.

It drips hot and wet down my chin, pooling in my palm, staining my fingers.

I blink at my hand while my mind slowly catches up.

Huh. That's... a lot of blood.

Mari's gasp rips me back to reality.

"No, no, no, no," she whispers, eyes wide with panic. Her face twists in horror.

She rips a piece of her shawl, balls it in her hands, and thrusts it against my chin.

"Press hard on it and get up." Her voice quivers. "We need to move. Fast."

Something in her tone, something raw, terrified, makes my heart stutter.

I don't question her. I just follow orders.

But just as I push myself up, something huge swoops down from the sky.

A black blur slams into Mari, knocking her sideways.

She crumples to the ground.

I hold my breath, waiting for her to stir. To scramble to her feet again, but she doesn't move.

A scream rips from my throat.

I stagger to my feet, my body no longer numb but screaming in protest.

After a couple of awkward steps, I drop to my knees beside her.

"Mari?" I pat her face, and shake her shoulder, panic coursing through me.

Wake up. Wake up. Wake up.

She doesn't stir. Doesn't groan.

I lean in close to her mouth.

She's breathing.

Barely.

No, no, no—she's okay. She's fine. She has to be. Right?

I lift my head, my vision swimming, just in time to see it.

A monster of a bird is circling back.

The thing is massive. A hulking, feathered nightmare blotting out the moon. Beady, devilish eyes gleam in the dark. A curved beak snaps open and shut, hungry.

Its wings stretch wide, each feather sleek and sharp like blades.

A bald eagle.

But ten times the size. And to my horror, the eagle-like bird monster has hooves and a tail. My brain scrambles to put together the pieces. Half-horse, half-bird.

My Potterhead cogs start to spin.

A hippogriff?

Only this one is not friendly and it's a thousand times more terrifying.

The marketplace is empty now.

Everyone else fled while I'm frozen here.

It's just me and Mari.

And that thing.

I inwardly yell at my body, "Get up. Move. Move, dang it."

I throw Mari's arm over my shoulder and try to drag her away.

Turns out?

Moving an unconscious body is not as easy as TV makes it look.

Especially when you're bleeding, exhausted, and very much about to die.

I grit my teeth, dig my heels into the cobblestones, and pull.

Mari's body shifts, barely.

I make some progress, but my movements are too slow. Agonizingly so. And it's not enough.

The bird shrieks, a sound so sharp it splits the air like a blade.

I wince as a shadow falls over me.

The beast is diving straight for us.

And I—

I'm not fast enough.

Not strong enough.

Not ready for this.

So, this is it?

I always figured I'd go out in some ridiculous, embarrassing way—like tripping off a ledge or choking on a peanut.

Not by being ripped apart by a giant bird.

I guess it would make a funny story in the afterlife.

I squeeze my eyes shut, waiting for the inevitable.

The air shifts across me and something moves.

Fast.

A black blur streaks past me, cutting through the night like a shadow come to life.

A crash. A snarl. A blur of movement.

I whip my head up just in time to see two monsters collide.

The bird shrieks in fury, claws slashing, beak snapping.

The creature that intercepted it?

Not a creature.

A wolf.

A huge, four-legged beast, bigger than any wolf should be.

It's fast, a blur of shadows and muscle, striking and dodging with a predatory grace that shouldn't even be possible.

The wolf lunges, teeth flashing in the weird moonlight, claws raking against the bird's chest.

The bird snaps back, its razor-sharp beak grazing the wolf's side.

But despite the impact, the wolf doesn't even flinch.

Instead, it twists and latches onto the bird's wing with its teeth. An ugly ripping sound floods the air.

The bird screeches as feathers explode into the air like shrapnel.

They tear at each other, claws and teeth, shadows and wings, in a twisted, primal battle.

And me?

I crouch over Mari, frozen and unable to look away.

My brain is on fire, trying to make sense of what I'm seeing, and how any of this is possible.

Because I know that wolf.

Even through the chaos, the dust, the wildness of its movements, I know it.

The piercing, intelligent eyes.

The way it moves.

The energy rolling off of it, powerful and ancient and terrifying.

I have absolutely seen it before.

On the train.
A cold chill snaps down my spine.
Is it... following me?
And if so...
Is it here to save me?
Or to claim me?

Chapter 15
The Wolf in the Shadows

The battle ends in a blur of feathers and shadows, the night air thick with the scent of blood and the sound of ragged, dying screeches.

The giant bird convulses, wings flapping in one last, desperate attempt to regain control, but the wolf —massive, powerful, utterly relentless—clamps its jaws around its throat and does not let go.

A final, choked cry pierces the air.

Then silence.

The marketplace is quiet and empty, the cobbled streets empty but for the oozing blood running like a river from the dead hippogriff's neck.

Then there's Mari and me.

I should run. I should be scrambling to my feet and sprinting as far as my aching legs can carry me, but my muscles are locked in place. Because the wolf has turned to me.

The golden eyes glow eerily in the darkness,

locked onto mine like I'm something to be studied. Or hunted.

My breath sticks in my throat as the tension in the air tightens, wrapping around my ribs like a vise.

Then, the air around the beast begins to ripple.

A strange energy crackles, coiling in smoky tendrils, curling around the massive creature's body and pulling inward, shifting and twisting, like ink bleeding into water.

The wolf's form shrinks, reshaping itself, and before I can even process what's happening, the wolf is gone.

And in its place stands a man.

He is tall, broad-shouldered, clad in black body armor that gleams in the moonlight. A sword is strapped to his back, its hilt barely visible beneath the tousled strands of raven-black hair that frame his face.

He should look regal, a knight from some lost era, but there's nothing noble in the way he moves.

His shoulders rise and fall as his puffs come out short and fast. His movements are confident, controlled, and undeniably strong.

This is a predator in human skin.

And he is marching toward me.

His golden eyes, no longer those of a wolf, but somehow still just as wild and unrelenting, stay locked on me, his gaze sharp and intent.

My body tenses, my stomach twisting with the same primal fear I felt back on the train.

He doesn't blink.

And he does not stop.

I should run.

I should move.

But I still can't.

I glance at the swirl on my hand. If there was ever a good time to spontaneously develop mega powers, now would be it.

But nothing happens.

Something roots me in place, as if the very air around us has turned heavy, dragging me into this moment like a fly caught in a web.

My mind is screaming at me to move, to do anything but stand here like a rabbit frozen before the jaws of a wolf.

Then Mari stirs.

A small, pained groan leaves her lips as she pushes herself up weakly. The spell breaks, and I burst into action.

"Mari," I whisper.

Mari's lashes flutter as she looks around, and then her gaze locks on our incoming doom.

Before I can fill her in on the situation, she flings out her hand, slicing the air open with magic.

A void rips open behind us, shimmering with dark, pulsing energy.

"Come on, quick!"

This time, I don't hesitate.

Oh, sweet, sweet void. I've never been so happy to run into one.

I grab Mari's arm as she drags me backward. Together, we dive into the void.

The last thing I see before the portal snaps shut is the man's golden, unreadable eyes.

Watching me.

The moment we stumble into the dormitory, Mari collapses onto her bed, gasping.

I double over, hands braced on my knees, my breath coming in short, unsteady bursts.

The silence stretches, broken only by the rapid beating of my heart in my ears.

My chin stings, and when I reach up, my fingers come away wet.

Great. More blood.

Mari sees it at the same time and bolts upright.

"Oh, Kayla... You're still bleeding."

She scrambles through her bag.

I sit down on the edge of my bed, blinking down at my hands, only now processing the sticky warmth seeping into my skin.

I should have felt it before. Should have noticed the sting.

But all I can see is that man's face.

The way he looked at me.

Like he knew me.

Mari thrusts a small glass bottle into my hand. "Here. It's a healing tonic. It won't get rid of the wound completely, but it'll stop the bleeding."

I eye the vial suspiciously. "What's the catch?"

Mari sighs, exasperated. "It'll leave a small scar. But nothing too noticeable for class."

I make a face. "Oh, fantastic. Love that for me."

I dab the tonic onto my chin, wincing as it sears against the open wound. There's a faint shimmer, and then the pain fades to a dull throb.

Mari flops onto her pillows, rubbing her face.

"So..." she says, voice muffled. "Are we gonna talk about what just happened, or are we pretending that was a totally normal night?"

I exhale sharply, rubbing my temples. "We were attacked by a hippogriff."

Mari sits up so fast she nearly falls off the bed.

"What?"

"A *huge* one." I exhale shakily. "We are so lucky to survive that."

Mari shudders, wrapping her arms around herself. "Lucky?" She scoffs. "We should be dead."

I nod, feeling my stomach turn. "Yeah. We would've been."

Mari frowns. "What do you mean?"

I press my hands against my knees, staring at the floor.

"A wolf fought it off."

Mari gasps.

I nod, throat dry. "Otherwise, we wouldn't have stood a chance."

Mari shakes her head, eyes wide. "A wolf?"

I press my lips together, heart hammering.

Then, I tell her everything.

The wolf on the train.

The warning it gave me.

The fact that it was the same one that saved us tonight.

And then, finally...

"That wolf..." I hesitate. "It talked to me."

Silence.

For a second, Mari just stares at me.

Then she screams.

I flinch at her sudden outburst and clamp my hands over my ears. "MARI—"

She claps her hands over her mouth, eyes impossibly wide. Her entire body vibrates like she's just been plugged into an electrical current.

Without a word, she dives for her bag, rummaging wildly.

I watch, confused and slightly alarmed, as she yanks out a magazine and waves it in my face.

She jabs a finger at me, bouncing on her knees.

"Kayla," she whispers, like she's unveiling the secrets of the universe. "Don't you know what this *means*?!"

I blink.

She waves the papers even more aggressively.

"The wolf," she breathes, eyes gleaming. "He's a shifter."

I nod slowly. "Yeah, I know I'm slow, but I got that part."

Mari shakes her head wildly. "No, no, no. Not just *any* shifter."

She leans forward, grabbing me, her nails dig into my shoulders.

"He's *imprinted on you*."

I just stare at her wide, glassy eyes while my stomach plummets.

"Uh...Excuse me, he's what?"

Mari grins like she's just uncovered the greatest mystery of all time. "You. Have. Been. Imprinted. On."

I stare at her, mouth dry, brain officially broken.

There's a very real chance I'm going to pass out.

Chapter 16
The Water Listens

The next morning, I am exhausted.

Mari is still buzzing about the whole imprinting thing, but my brain is stuck on the wolf, the hippogriff, and the man with golden eyes.

I barely slept, because every time I closed them, I saw him—watching me, moving toward me, like he was claiming something he already owned.

Now, I'm sitting stiffly at a desk in my first class, trying to pretend I belong here while my mind is still whirling from last night.

The classroom is odd, and nothing like the ones in my old high school.

Instead of rows of desks, the space is circular, lined with natural stone, the ceiling high and domed like an observatory. Vines and roots creep along the walls, woven between glowing runes that pulse faintly in rhythm with the flickering torches. The air is thick with something invisible yet alive, like a whisper waiting to be spoken.

The students settle in, chatting in hushed excitement as they take their seats at carved wooden desks arranged in a crescent.

I slide into a seat next to a centaur from another house. His long, black hair flows like silk to his waist, and when he turns to look at me, I swear his green eyes hold the weight of a thousand ancient books.

He gives me a small, polite nod. "I am Lior."

"Kayla," I reply, relieved that at least one person isn't glaring at me like I'm an anomaly.

Before I can say anything else, the class hushes as our instructor glides into the room.

Mrs. Lightbringer.

She is nothing like Siberious or Mauve.

Her strawberry-blonde hair is loose and wild, cascading down her back in waves. Her clothes are simple, soft cotton—nothing grand or fae-like, but she wears them with an elegance that makes her glow. Even the air around her seems brighter, softer.

She smiles warmly at the class and clasps her hands.

"You entered this school because you were chosen by a dragon based on the unique gifts and qualities you have." Her voice comes out like a gentle wind.

I try not to squirm at that statement.

Chosen.

Someone from the back snorts.

"Not everyone," they mutter, just loud enough for the whole room to hear.

Every head turns toward me, and the hair on my arms prickles.

I ignore them, but my pulse hammers anyway, as if my fifth sense can feel the weight of their stares on me, sinking into my body like daggers.

Mrs. Lightbringer, to her credit, doesn't acknowledge it. She simply continues with grace.

"But thanks to dragons, magic weaves through the very air you breathe. And here at Theridon, you have more power at your fingertips than anywhere else in existence."

I inhale shakily, suddenly feeling like I shouldn't be breathing at all.

I have no magic. And yet, I was still chosen.

Why?

Mrs. Lightbringer walks to the center of the room, gesturing to the glowing runes embedded in the stone walls.

"There are many types of magic," she explains, her voice soft but commanding. "Elemental—the control of wind, fire, earth, and water. Light—the manipulation of electricity and energy. Psychic—magic through words, thoughts, and vibration."

She pauses, then looks around the room, her expression turning almost... reverent.

"And then there is the rarest and most powerful magic of all..."

The air in the room seems to shift, the torches flickering.

"The magic of dragons."

A murmur ripples through the students.

Lightbringer's voice lowers, as if speaking too loudly might disturb some ancient force.

"This is a combination of all core magic properties along with something so ancient, so rarely seen, that it has turned to legend."

She lets the words settle, then straightens with a smile. "But today, we focus on the first—elemental magic."

With a graceful wave of her hand, goblets of water appear on each of our desks.

"Your task is to transform the water in any way you wish. A centaurian ice sculpture, a perfect snowball, or even a puff of steam. The only limit is your imagination." She gestures toward the goblets. "Go crazy."

I watch as the other students immediately set to work, as if they've been doing this for years.

Lior, the centaur beside me, lifts his hand calmly over the goblet. The water inside ripples once, then spirals upward like an elegant ribbon, twisting and hardening into a delicate tower of ice.

A student across from me sculpts a tiny bird from water, the liquid hovering midair before freezing in a burst of frost.

A fae girl at the next table claps her hands, and her water instantly erupts into a swirling steam dragon, curling around her head before vanishing into mist.

Even Mari sighs, bored. "This is too easy."

I turn to her just as she lifts her goblet, tilting it.

Instead of spilling, the water hangs suspended in the air, shimmering. Then, in a blink, it shifts into solid ice—a perfectly sculpted ice wolf, teeth bared, standing on nothing but air.

Mari grins at me. "Oh look. It's your boyfriend."

I groan. "Hilarious."

I stare at my own goblet.

Nothing about this feels instinctive.

Nothing inside me hums with magic, the way it seems to for everyone else.

I lift my hands and concentrate on the goblet of water in front of me.

It has a slight sparkle to it, catching the stream of sunshine pouring in through the stain glass windows.

My lip stings as I chew on it fiercely, willing the dang water to move. To shift. To do...something.

*Any*thing.

Nothing happens.

I try again.

Still nothing.

I swirl my fingers over the surface, whisper something—everything I can think of.

"Abracadabra. Shazam. Bibbitty-something-boo."

The water stays stubbornly still.

Finally, frustrated, I raise my hand.

Lightbringer glides over, smiling gently.

"Yes, Kayla?"

I hesitate, then gesture helplessly to my goblet.

"How do I...use magic to change the water?"

The room goes quiet.

I feel every set of eyes on me again.

Lightbringer blinks, momentarily caught off guard.

It's a simple question, but something about it makes her expression shift—just slightly.

Then she recovers, her smile brightening.

"Ah, well..." She tilts her head. "Thinking too much can hinder you. Magic isn't about logic. It's about will. Just imagine what you want it to be, then make an action that feels natural. The water will hear you and obey."

I frown. "Hear me?"

"Magic is alive, Kayla. It feels your intent. The more you force it, the more it resists. But if you let it flow, it will respond."

I glance at my goblet again, feeling doubt creep in.

It's not just about imagining something.

It's about feeling it.

But I don't feel anything.

Not yet.

Chapter 17
Mystic Botany & The Perils of Talking Plants

The air outside is thick with the scent of damp earth and blooming greenery, and for the first time since arriving at Theridon, I actually feel a little lighter. Maybe it's the open sky, the crisp breeze, or the fact that we're not inside a stuffy stone room filled with judgmental stares.

Or maybe it's just Mari, who is positively vibrating with excitement.

"Oh, you're going to love this class, Kayla." She practically skips beside me, her copper curls bouncing as she gestures wildly to the overgrown expanse of green ahead of us. "Mystic Botany is one of the most fascinating subjects in the whole curriculum! The plants here aren't just plants. They're alive-alive. With thoughts. And personalities. And—"

"Wait." I eye a cluster of thick grass that shudders as we pass. The blades ripple like a wave, whispering with breathy giggles.

I stumble back. "Did the grass just laugh?"

Mari nods enthusiastically. "Oh! That's Ticklegrass. Careful, their pollen is a mild skin irritant."

Just as she says it, a deeper voice chimes in. "That is correct, Marigold."

We turn as our teacher, Mr. Pinewood, strides forward.

He is tall and lean, with bark-colored skin and eyes the soft green of fresh spring leaves. His hair is a wild mess of dark curls, dotted with tiny flowers and bits of moss. He looks as if he spends more time with plants than people.

He gestures to the giggling grass.

"Ticklegrass is one name. But here, it is more commonly known as Flusterweed," he corrects. "And yes, they are highly ticklish. Their pollen can cause mild itching, but here's a little-known fact: if inhaled, it may also result in spontaneous rhyming."

I blink. "Rhyming?"

"Yes. A student once had an unfortunate incident where they spoke only in couplets for an entire week."

Mari bursts into laughter. "Oh, I love this place."

Before I can respond, an agonized scream shatters the air.

We whip around just as Lior lets out a choked noise, his face red with shock.

He lifts his hoof—a delicate purple flower crushed beneath it.

Pinewood rushes over, his expression grave.

"Careful!" He kneels beside the wilted plant.

I stare, dumbfounded. "Did that flower just scream?"

Mari nods, her eyes wide, face flushed. "It's a Wild Thornock. I read about them. They have over twenty-five million neurons and are actually more sensitive to touch than we are!"

Lior stares down at the flower, his expression somewhere between horrified and apologetic.

"I didn't mean to— I'm so sorry—"

The flower grumbles, its petals twitching as it slowly uncurls itself from its flattened state.

Lior steps away like he's just committed murder. His hands tremble as he looks at us, his voice low with disbelief.

"I... I just talked to a flower."

There's a brief silence. Then, a few students snicker.

Lior's face darkens.

But Pinewood straightens, casting a sharp glare across the class.

"All life is precious," he says, his voice firm but calm. "All life is intelligent. You think it's funny to speak to a flower?"

His gaze locks onto the group of snickering students. "Why?"

The laughter dies instantly.

One of the boys clears his throat. "Well... because flowers are—"

"Are what?" Pinewood's voice is dangerously quiet now.

Lior, now beet red, mutters something under his breath, rubbing the back of his neck.

Pinewood sighs, shaking his head. "You think

because a thing cannot walk or speak as you do, that it does not think? That it does not feel?"

The students remain uncomfortably silent.

Lior swallows hard, then bows slightly toward the now-ruffled Wild Thornock. "My deepest apologies."

The flower ruffles its petals in what might be forgiveness.

Mari squeals quietly beside me. "Isn't this place amazing?"

* * *

The next day, or moon switch—or whatever they call it here—Pinewood leads us further down a winding garden path, toward a row of tall, familiar-looking trees.

"These," he says, gesturing to the trees, "are—"

I cut in before I can stop myself.

"We have these back home!" My voice rushes out too fast, my excitement bubbling over before I can contain it.

Everyone turns to look at me.

I barely notice.

My chest tightens as I take a step forward, memories rushing in.

"My old home... my parents' house. It was surrounded by these palms." I swallow hard. "They grow like crazy and need to be pruned all the time. And they're full of scorpions."

The words taste bittersweet on my tongue. And my heart bleeds as memories of summers past come rushing back. If I close my eyes, I can almost see my dad doing yard work, while my mom sits in the swing on the porch, working on her latest crochet project.

Meanwhile, my sister and I ride our bikes up and down the drive. Palm fronds brush my hair and back as I ride underneath the giant palm tree outside my house.

When I open my eyes again, they burn, and a single hot tear rolls down my face, leaving a sting in its path. I swipe it away with my sleeve.

With my heart flooded with mixed emotions, I lift my hand, reaching toward one of the long, sweeping fronds—but to my shock, the tree actually leans away from me.

As if... avoiding my touch.

I blink, pulling my hand back. "Uh."

Pinewood folds his arms. "I highly doubt you have Wingo Palms on Earth."

I frown, glancing back at the trees. "What makes them different?"

"These are nasty," Mr. Pinewood says simply. "Get too close and—"

"Ouch!"

The class whips around just in time to see Bo staggering back, his usual confident smirk replaced with a deep frown.

A long, thin needle is lodged in his forearm, and thick, purple blood glistens at the puncture site.

Bo scowls, snapping the needle off and yanking it free.

Pinewood nods knowingly. "That happens."

I stare. "Bo bleeds purple?"

Bo glares at me. "Yes. Problem?"

I lift my hands. "Nope. Totally normal. Completely unremarkable."

Mr. Pinewood gestures toward him. "I suggest you go to the medical center to have that looked at. Will anyone assist him?"

The moment the words leave his mouth, Mari's hand shoots up so fast that the wind literally whooshes past me.

"We will, sir." She beams, grabbing my wrist.

I blink at her. "What? What are you—"

"Perfect! Off you go, then," Pinewood says without hesitation.

Bo raises a single brow. "You? Helping me?"

Mari flashes her brightest smile. "Consider it charity work."

I groan as Mari drags me forward, her grip firm and full of dangerous intent.

"What are you doing?" I hiss under my breath.

Mari leans in just enough to whisper, "This, my dear Kayla, is called an opportunity."

I glance at Bo, who's watching us with suspicion and mild amusement.

Somehow, I'm not convinced this is the kind of opportunity I want.

Chapter 18
The Wolf and the Prince

Bo walks ahead, his long strides forcing Mari and me to practically jog to keep up.

The medical facility isn't far, but the air between us is thick with unspoken words, making the distance stretch longer than it should.

The weight of the conversation that hasn't even started yet presses against my chest, and by the way Mari keeps stealing glances at Bo, I know she's about to start poking at it.

"So," she says at last, her voice light, as if she's making casual conversation rather than prying for information. "You seem to know a lot about wolves."

Bo glances at her, one brow lifting in amused suspicion. "I know a lot about everything."

Mari scoffs. "No, I mean, you tell stories about them. About the settlements. You've been to one, haven't you?"

At that, Bo stops walking. He turns slightly, looking

down at Mari with an expression that is equal parts curiosity and caution.

"Why do you ask?" His voice is smooth, but there's a sharpness beneath it.

Mari hesitates for half a second too long.

"Because a wolf—"

"Attacked me." I finish quickly, shooting Mari a warning look before she can even think about saying anything else.

Her mouth snaps shut, though I can see the frustration flickering behind her eyes.

She might love a good story, but I don't trust Bo enough to let him be part of this one.

Bo watches the exchange closely, and even though his expression remains unreadable, I can tell he's filing that little detail away for later.

"A wolf attacked you?" he asks, voice carefully neutral.

I nod, keeping my expression calm, controlled. I won't let on that the wolf saved me. That it spoke to me. That it imprinted on me.

Bo doesn't press further, but the tension in his jaw tightens just enough for me to notice.

"Are all wolves dragon hunters?" I ask, hoping to shift the subject away from me.

For a moment, he doesn't answer.

Then, his voice lowers. "Wolves," he says, "are notoriously unpredictable."

It's not exactly an answer, and that bothers me more than if he had just said yes.

We reach the medical facility before I can push him further.

The healer on duty is a young fae with golden curls, and the moment she catches sight of Bo, her entire demeanor shifts. Her face brightens, and she practically floats over to him, her voice soft and melodic.

"Oh, hello Bovander." She practically sings his name, tilting her head in a way that makes her hair cascade over her shoulder like she's been practicing it in a mirror.

Bo gives her one of those easy smiles, the kind that probably has half the student body writing terrible poetry about him.

"It's just Bo," he corrects smoothly, his tone warm but detached.

The healer giggles.

Mari leans closer to me, whispering, "I bet she's going to find an excuse to touch him."

I stifle a laugh, and sure enough, the healer extends her hand and presses gentle fingers to Bo's forearm, inspecting the wound with a level of care that I'm pretty sure is unnecessary.

"You poor thing," she coos, one hand going to his chest. "A Wingo Palm? That must sting."

Bo shrugs, unconcerned. "I barely felt it, honesty."

She lets out another small, delighted giggle, like he's just recited poetry instead of downplaying an injury. Her fingers linger a little too long as she bandages him, the golden glow of her magic sealing the wound as she murmurs a soft incantation.

"There," she says sweetly. "Good as new."

Bo thanks her with a charming smile, but the moment she turns and flutters away, the ease in his expression fades.

His attention shifts back to me, the warmth gone, replaced with something much more serious.

I gulp.

"You shouldn't go looking for wolves," His voice is lower now. "Especially if you've been attacked by one."

I hold his gaze for a second longer than I should, lost for words.

I don't want to go looking for wolves. I'll be perfectly fine if I live out the rest of my life never seeing so much as a small dog again. Let alone a wolf. It was Mari's dumb idea to ask questions anyway.

But something inside me keeps my mouth shut. I'm not sure if it's the fact that Bo is staring me down like a concerned parent that makes me pause, or loyalty to my only friend.

I grab Mari's wrist, tugging her toward the door before she can start asking more questions.

"Well, you should go get some rest and... we better head back to class. I've got loads to learn!" I force my voice into something light and breezy. "Or... to the next class. Maybe if we're really lucky, classes are over and now we get to eat more oatmeal goo? I'm still figuring out how time moves so differently here, it's hard to keep up."

Bo's frown twitches at the edges, as if my words

have managed to amuse him. Just for a second at least. Then, without another word, he turns and strides off in the other direction.

Mari watches him go, a dreamy look on her face, sighing dramatically.

I groan. "You are ridiculous."

She just grins, hooking her arm through mine. "And you're avoiding something."

The moment we step inside our dorm, I let out a sharp exhale and turn to face Mari, arms crossed. "What the heck was that?"

Mari blinks at me innocently. "What was what?"

I narrow my eyes. "You tried to get Bo involved."

She shrugs. "Of course, I did."

"Mari, we don't need him involved!" I throw my hands up.

She flops onto her bed, crossing her arms over her chest. "Why not? He obviously knows things about the wolf settlements. He could help us."

I rub a hand down my face, trying to keep my frustration in check. "You don't understand, Mari. No one can know about the wolf. Not Bo. Not the teachers. No one."

Mari tilts her head, considering me. "Why?"

I hesitate.

Because the wolf imprinted on me. Because I don't know what it means. Because the wolves are supposed to be the enemy.

Mari sighs, a little deflated.

"I didn't mean to put you in a weird spot," she says, more sincere now.

I nod, letting the tension ease slightly. "It's fine. Just... be careful. I keep getting the feeling that not everything is as it seems and... and..."

I can't finish the thought aloud. It's too terrible.

What if the wolves are up to something? Maybe they're trying to root out the weakest link and break them so they can infiltrate the academy and take the riders out?

Knowing that I'm the only one without powers, it's pretty obvious that's me.

The weakest link.

Mari hums softly, and we fall into a troubled silence. Then she shifts, sitting up with her legs crossed beneath her. Her fingers play with the edges of the magazine she grabbed from the market, the corners of the pages slightly crinkled.

"It's just..." She glances at me hesitantly.

I raise a brow, snapping out of my spiraling thoughts. "Just what?"

Her grip on the magazine tightens, and she leans forward to give me a wide-eyed stare.

"My story," she whispers.

I blink. "Your story?"

Mari meets my gaze, something vulnerable flickering in her expression. "It's why I wanted to know about the wolves. Why I got excited."

I take a slow breath, bracing myself. "Mari, your story—"

"It's about a wolf shifter imprinting on a rider. Just like you. Maybe it—"

"Is only a story," I press before she can finish.

"And we don't know if that one even has a happy ending."

Mari looks at me then, really looks at me, and something about the way she does it makes my stomach twist. There's no defiance in her gaze, no anger, just a quiet kind of belief that feels too big for the room.

Then her gaze lowers to the magazine in her arms.

"I still have hope," she mumbles, her shoulders sloping.

I don't know what to say to that.

Chapter 19
The Vow of a Wolf

If I had known "dragon academy" actually meant "flunking twelve kinds of magical gym classes while being humiliated in front of your peers," I might have wished that I stayed unconscious in the San Tan mountains. Or lived out the rest of my days in that moldy apartment above the laundromat.

It starts with Spell Theory.

I sit in a classroom that looks like someone cast *Explosion* on a library and then politely swept it into piles.

Floating quills zip around, scribbling notes midair. Books flap like birds, hurling themselves off shelves when they get bored.

The professor, an elderly woman named Madam Hexley, wears robes so tattered it looks like she lost a fight with a raccoon.

"Magic is energy," she says in a tone that implies we're all deeply stupid. "It flows through everything. You, me, that chair you're slouching in, Kayla."

I sit up straighter, cheeks flushing.

"You must channel it through focus. Intention. Emotion. *Try not to sob while casting,* but feel something. Let it move through you."

When it's my turn to try a basic flame spell, my fingers twitch.

I whisper the words. I try to *feel* something.

Nothing happens.

Hexley sighs so loudly I'm surprised the windows don't crack. "Didn't a dragon choose you, Kayla?"

"Yes? I think so," I say, more like a question than I mean to.

"Well," she says dryly. "Let's hope it wasn't out of pity."

Ouch.

* * *

Next is Combat Drills.

"DAGGERS OUT!" Commander Vorn is a man so wide and strong I'm not convinced he's neither warlock nor fae.

We stand on a stone platform ringed with fire. Real fire. Spells shimmer around the edge like invisible tripwires.

I'm handed a dagger with a blade the length of my forearm and told to spar with a third year named Enza who looks like she's already murdered three people today and is eager for her fourth.

I try to remember Bo's advice—"Elbows in, don't hesitate"—but I barely lift my blade before Enza knocks it from my hand and kicks my knee so hard I spin.

"Gotta be quicker." She smirks, offering her hand to help me up.

I glare at her and mutter, "In the real world, we settle fights with passive-aggressive texts."

* * *

Potion Alchemy is... messy.

And very, very wet.

It *should* be straightforward. Add ingredients. Stir clockwise. Heat gently.

But my toadstool essence bubbles over, reacts with my moonroot wrong, and suddenly the cauldron belches a cloud of pink smoke that smells like burnt marshmallows and shame.

"You made a love-sneeze potion," says the professor as students start giggling and rubbing their noses. "That's not even in the syllabus."

I stare into the bubbling mess, wondering if I can just crawl inside it and disappear.

* * *

The only place I *almost* don't fail is Magical History, and that's because the teacher, Master Lorin, mostly lectures while pacing dramatically in a long cloak and speaking like he's in a Shakespeare play.

"Thousands of years ago, the bond between dragons and riders was sacred," he intones, sweeping around a floating map of Theridon. "But what happens when that bond is broken?"

A chill sweeps through the room.

I glance around at the students, all focused and spellbound.

Me? I'm doodling a cartoon wolf chasing a fire-breathing pigeon in my notebook. The pigeon is winning.

* * *

Flying 101 is the worst.

They take us up to the sky docks, which is just a fancy name for "giant circular death trap on top of the highest tower." There are no guardrails. There is no mercy.

Mauve hands out enchanted dummy dragons for us to practice on until we bond with our actual dragon.

The first challenge is to get on.

A simple concept, sure. But for me?

I may as well be climbing Mount Everest.

I try to scramble onto the dummy dragon's back with the grace of a goat learning ballet.

Mauve rolls her eyes. "Put your weight on your thighs, not your knees, unless you want to plummet to your demise. No one will save you here."

"Great pep talk," I mutter.

"What was that?" Mauve narrows her eyes at me.

My face grows hot under the firm stare.

"Nothing. Sorry."

I shuffle onto the dummy, ignoring the fact that the scales are razor sharp and digging into my inner thighs. If I didn't have leathers on, I'd look like I ran a mile with a cheese grater between my legs.

Mauve waves her hands, and we take off.

The wind slams into me.

I scream. Not out of fear—okay, a little out of fear—but mostly because I accidentally let go with one hand and nearly hurl myself off the side.

When the dummy dragon lands, I fall off into a crumpled heap on the ground.

Mari on the other hand, glides down and hops off her fake dragon like she's getting off a bike.

I sigh, but then a shadow covers me, and I look up at Mauve.

She lifts her brows at me. "Miss Whitman, you have no powers, no discernible talents... if you are to have any hope of success here, you best work on your center of gravity and at least become a proficient rider. Or else, I fear your dragon..."

She doesn't finish the sentence, but my mind finishes it for her.

My dragon will realize I'm only useful to carry as a light snack.

* * *

In Magical Creatures, I'm supposed to tame a feathered serpent named Cyril. The reward: if we do, we get to keep it as a pet.

Cyril hisses the moment I approach.

I resist the urge to hiss back.

The professor, a bubbly woman with moon tattoos across her cheeks, claps cheerfully. "Oh, he likes you! He only hisses when he's considering swallowing someone whole!"

Charming.

I reach out, trying to project calm energy like she taught us.

Cyril spits venom at my boots.

I shake my fist at the snake. Forget keeping this thing as a pet, it will probably strangle me in my sleep.

We stare at each other like mortal enemies who will one day duel at dawn.

* * *

By the end of the week, I am getting used to the way time works here.

There are two moons, and everyone talks about time in cycles. So, time does exist after all. But no one applies numbers or names to it.

And not all days are equal.

But it feels so much more complicated and random.

It's like the moons have a mind of their own, and sometimes the red moon just isn't feeling it and doesn't show up when it's supposed to.

Life at Theridon is hard.

Siberious was not joking when he said we'd be tested to the max.

My arms are sore, my uniform is singed, my pride obliterated, and my mood plant is a shriveled brown twig that has turned its pot to face the wall like it's given up on life.

Mari floats into our dorm one night, still humming from her elemental magic class. "I made a tornado today! A little one, but it *was so cute!* What about you?"

I stare at her blankly. "I made the classroom smell like a bakery and got tackled by a flying ferret."

Mari winces. "Ah. Progress."

"Yeah, if the goal is comedic death."

* * *

Still, I keep showing up. Every day. Failing with style.

I burn scrolls. I drop weapons. I nearly fall off my enchanted dummy dragon twice more. The professors start giving me *the look*—that half-pity, half-*you sure you want to stay here?* expression that makes my throat close up.

And the other students?

They whisper. Some of them even point at me.

"Isn't she the human girl?"

"Why'd a dragon pick *her*?"

"You'd think getting struck by lightning would give her some powers. She can't even levitate a pebble."

But at night... in the dark... I remember.

The feel of fire around me.

The weightlessness as the plane fell.

The red dragon—gold-eyed and wild—pulling me from the flames.

The necklace burning into my collarbone.

Eliyah saving me from the wolf.

I remember the feeling of being chosen.

Even if I don't understand *why*.

And that keeps me going.

Even when I feel like a fraud, with dirt on my face and a wand that occasionally sneezes glitter.

* * *

After yet another draining day of failure and humiliation–something I'm becoming accustomed to at the school–sleep comes, and my dream starts the same way.

The roar of wind and fire. The gut-wrenching screech of metal tearing apart. The chaos of the plane breaking in half, people screaming, seats ripping from the floor. The plunge.

The suffocating weight of gravity pulling me down, down, down...

And then, the dragon.

It emerges from the firestorm, its wings blotting out the sky, its massive body twisting through the wreckage like it was always meant to be there.

Its golden eyes lock onto me, and for a split second, I feel safe.

But the dream always ends with the dragon flying away, leaving me on the ground in the middle of the San Tan mountains.

Riders and Hunters

Not this time.

This time, I'm in a place I don't recognize.

Not a desert, or a mountain.

A forest.

The smoke is thick, curling around my legs like living tendrils.

I stagger forward, coughing, my hands shaking as I try to get my bearings.

Everything feels far too real to be a dream, but too foreign to be a memory.

The sky is the biggest giveaway. Peeping between the trees overhead are swirls of pink and violet. The air is thick and alive with an energy that I've only experienced since leaving Earth and ending up in this bizarre new realm.

Confused, and oddly awake, I continue to stagger forward.

It feels like a thread is tugging on my midriff, telling me where to go as I navigate the winding path.

Then I see him, and the reaction is bold and instant.

A man stands in the distance, his broad figure emerging from the haze. Dark hair. Warrior's clothing. And eyes—piercing, molten gold.

I freeze as a sense of knowing and something I can't describe rushes over me.

Somewhere, deep in my bones, I know who he is.

The wolf shifter from the market.

His chest heaves, and he stands strong and fierce, his hands balled into fists.

He doesn't speak. Doesn't flinch. He only stares at

me, his gaze burning into mine with something raw, something primal.

It's familiar.

And I pause.

I'd managed to throw Mari off the topic of this wolf-shifter-imprinting-thing, but here I am, dreaming about him.

A snapping twig has me turning on the spot, I lock eyes on a deer before it staggers back and jumps into the overgrowth.

I find the man again, and that's when I realize he wasn't looking at me.

He was looking *through* me.

My nerves settle.

Slowly, he turns and walks away.

I don't hesitate.

A rush of curiosity forces me to follow. I have to know what it is about this guy who makes me feel... I don't know.

Serious. Alert. Like every atom in my body is vibrating at an unimaginable speed.

The smoke fades as I move deeper into the dense, endless jungle.

The trees loom high above, ancient and twisted, their roots thick and gnarled. The air is heavy, filled with the scent of damp earth and something darker—a presence that lurks in the shadows, watching.

My ears are on edge.

A faraway owl hoots softly to my right. Something snuffles to my left, hidden under the brambles, digging.

The air grows crisp, and a strange sense of foreboding claws its way up my spine.

I don't know why I keep going.

All of my senses are screaming at me to turn back. And usually, I would be the first to run in the face of danger. But not this time.

I can't stop. It's like my brain is no longer connected to my body, and it's moving on autopilot. I guess this is what sleepwalking is like. Only, I'm still asleep.

*Dream*walking? Is that even a thing?

The deeper we go, the darker it becomes. The trees seem to breathe, the vines slither like snakes, and the shadows move on their own. They whisper against my skin, pulling, curling, urging me to turn away. Go back.

But I don't.

Because ahead of me, the man stops.

Without a word, he turns to an old, gnarled oak in the center of a clearing.

And...after a few heart-stopping moments of tension, he starts punching it.

I flinch, watching this guy pound the tree like he's Rocky taking out a decade of frustration on an old oak tree.

His fists collide with the bark in a brutal, merciless rhythm. Again and again and again, until his knuckles split, blood smeared across the rough wood.

My stomach knots, and a metallic taste fills my mouth at the sight.

Yet, I can't seem to look away.

And he doesn't stop.

He grits his teeth, snarling under his breath, his entire body shaking with barely-contained agony.

A figure appears beside the tree. A hooded stranger.

The man with bleeding knuckles turns to it. "I need to find her."

His voice is rough, desperate. And my heart jolts at the urgent tone.

"I won't stop. I can't."

The hooded figure steps from the shadows, standing just at the edge of the clearing. Their face is hidden, their form cloaked in deep gray robes.

A murmur too quiet for my ears to discern has the man finally turning away from the bloodied tree.

Crimson drops slide down the bark, pooling at the roots.

"I vow to you," he says, taking a knee and lowering to the ground. "She *will* be one of us."

A pulse of power ripples through the air at his words, as if something ancient and binding just took shape.

I take a step closer, my heart slamming against my ribs.

He stills.

Then, his head snaps around. And his golden eyes lock onto mine.

This time, I know he's not looking at a deer or whatever else might be behind me.

The way his eyes claim me is too raw, too invasive to be a coincidence.

Everything inside of me shatters.

He dips his chin, and his eyes blaze like two golden suns, burning my very soul.

I take a step back, aghast.

A surge of something rushes through my veins, like an unseen force is trying to drag me toward him.

My breath catches, my vision blurs, and for one soul-searing moment, I know—I know—

What *do* I know?

My thoughts are slipping like water between my fingers as the world begins to swirl and rush around me.

Then it all fades.

I wake up.

I sit up gasping, my body slick with sweat.

The room is dark, except for the faint glow of Mari's bedside lamp.

She's curled up under her covers, snoring softly. Even her mood plant lets out a soft, whistling snore.

I press a trembling hand to my forehead, trying to steady my breathing.

That was different.

That was real. I mean, it felt real.

But then my sight flickers over to Mari's sleeping figure, and a memory rushes back to me. A wolf imprinted on me, or so she said.

Was that dream just my brain's way of processing Mari's crazy theory?

I reach for the pitcher of water beside my bed, my hands still unsteady as I pour a drink and take a deep gulp.

The cool liquid soothes my throat, but it does nothing to settle the wild panic racing through me.

Who was he?

And why did it feel like I already knew him?

Something inside me twists, an aching kind of certainty taking root in my chest.

Everything—the dragon, the wolves, the academy, the vow in the jungle—is connected. And somehow, it feels like I'm the center of it all.

I just don't know how. Not yet, anyway.

My brain is spinning so much I can't figure out if I'm going to pass out or puke. When sleep does not take me, I slip out of bed and pad silently toward the door.

The hallway outside is eerily quiet, the castle's usual hum of life muted in the dead of night.

As I walk, I let my mind wander, piecing things together.

The wolves are the enemy. That's what they've told me. But the wolf in my dream—the man with golden eyes—wasn't just a monster.

He was desperate. That makes him even more dangerous.

And that kind of desperation only comes from one thing.

Loss.

I shiver, wrapping my arms around myself as I turn down another hallway.

That's when I hear it.

A hushed conversation.

I press myself against the wall, holding my breath

as I peek around the corner. One of the voices is unmistakable.

The dimly lit corridor illuminates the faces of two troubled faces.

One is of a young girl, one of the new students with psychic magic. And the other is none other than Ms. Mauve.

I strain to pick up on their conversation, but the voices are too faint to carry over the sound of the girl sobbing.

I can't make out what they're saying, but something in the way they lean in close, the way Ms. Mauve's needle-like fingers tighten around the student's arm, makes my skin crawl.

I freeze, questions running through my mind.

Should I say something?

Is the girl in danger?

Then I hear the student's words. "I'm sorry, it won't happen again, I promise."

My body relaxes. It's just a student being reprimanded by a concerned teacher for being out of bed. That must be it.

I exhale the tension in my chest and slip past them unnoticed and figure that's my sign to go back to my room. I round a corner, and a gasp catches in my throat as my gaze lands on something between two gargoyle statues.

A figure on the ground.

At first, my brain refuses to process what I'm looking at.

A trick of the light, maybe. A shadow?

Upon closer inspection, it's a person. Maybe a student who's simply collapsed from exhaustion. After all, I can't be the only person struggling to scale the inhumane number of staircases in this school.

But then a scream rings out, and my blood turns cold.

There's no one else around, so maybe it's mine.

The hairs on the back of my neck are on end and saliva builds in my mouth as I pull on the person's shoulder and roll them onto their back.

Skin waxy and white as marble. Two soulless eyes stare back at me, and a blue pair of lips form an O.

Alarms explode through the castle, shattering the quiet as doors slam open, and students pour out, flooding the halls.

Shocked faces turn from me to the body, then back at me again.

My stomach clenches.

This isn't good.

"Move aside. Let me through. What happened?" The deep voice cuts through the noise like a blade, and I turn just as King Siberious steps into view.

His red nightrobe billows behind him, his white hair is ruffled, and for some reason, his feet are shoved into a pair of brown fluffy slippers.

"Stars above..." Siberious mutters, his eyes bulging. Without skipping a beat, he clears his throat and turns official. "Back to your rooms. Immediately. Any student found out of bed in five minutes will be expelled."

For a second, the entire crowd pauses, collectively

processing the sight of their disheveled king. Then a rush of movement as everyone scatters.

I'm still frozen on the spot, too stunned to do anything.

But then someone whispers a name.

Char.

And my entire world tilts.

The girl who had made a scene. The one who had screamed that we were all being lied to.

Was dead.

Chapter 20
Dreamwalking

The hall is crammed with whispering students, and I shoulder my way through the people, trying to make myself as small as possible.

Once free, I bolt down the corridor. My bare feet slap against the cold stone floor as I round the corner, my breath coming fast.

Mari's door creaks open just as I approach.

She steps out, hair a frizzy mess, her eyes bleary and confused. Her mood plant glows a groggy shade of mauve, the little leaves still curling like it's in bed.

"Kayla? Where have you been?"

I grab her by the arm, pulling her into the common room just off our hallway.

The fire has burned down to glowing embers, casting long shadows on the stone walls. The massive hearth, carved with depictions of ancient dragon battles, gives the room a grandeur that feels out of sync with the panic knotting my stomach.

"Char's dead."

That gets her attention. Her whole body stiffens. "What?"

Her tone is serious for once, and her eyes dance as she studies my face.

I guess she's wondering whether I'm joking or if this is another sarcastic remark.

I wish it was.

Shock freezes my arms in place, but I just about manage a grave nod.

"I found her. Just now. She was lying in the corridor like...like a statue. I think she'd been dead for a while."

Mari covers her mouth, eyes wide. "Do you think it was the wolves? Do you think they got into the castle somehow?"

I sink down into the oversized armchair near the fireplace and shake my head. "I don't know. But it doesn't make sense. There were no wounds. No sign of a fight. She was just... gone. Like a shell of a person."

Mari lowers herself slowly onto the couch across from me, her legs folding beneath her. Her eyes are wide and unfocused as she takes it in.

For a moment, we just sit there in stunned silence.

The fire crackles softly, filling the room with a strange, tense warmth.

"We need to tell someone," she says, her voice small.

I shrug. "I'm pretty sure the whole castle knows by now. Alarms were blaring. The king showed up in fluffy slippers."

Riders and Hunters

Mari blinks. "Slippers?"

"Yep. Brown. With bear faces."

Mari's frown cracks, and she lets out a snort, then quickly claps a hand over her mouth in horror. "Sorry. That's not funny. I just... I pictured a war horn blaring and the king waddling in wearing teddy bears on his feet."

I almost laugh, but manage to hold it in. I can't stop a smile, though.

Mari returns a sheepish one.

We both fall into silence again, but it doesn't last long. The heavy door creaks open, and we both jump like we've been caught sneaking out past curfew.

Bo strides in, wearing dark joggers and a long-sleeved black tee. His hair is damp, like he's been running. Or fighting. His expression is neutral until he sees us huddled by the fire. Then his brow furrows.

"What are you two doing still up?"

"You're one to talk." I eye him.

He shifts his arm slightly, and I can't believe what I'm looking at—three long, jagged, red marks trailing down the side of his forearm, half-hidden under his sleeve. One of them weeps purple.

I stare.

They're too deliberate to be scratches from a tree branch.

Bo notices my line of sight and pulls the fabric down quickly, but Mari and I exchange a loaded glance.

"Where have *you* been?" Mari asks, too casually to sound convincing.

Bo shrugs. But his shoulders remain high and stiff.

"Out," his voice is curt. There's an edge to it.

I blink. "Wow. Incredible. So specific. I feel almost like I was there."

He rolls his eyes and cracks his knuckles. "I don't need to explain myself to you."

My brows lift.

This side of Bo is a stark contrast to the cocky, jovial show off that I'd seen before.

"No, but we'd prefer it to the cryptic, murdery vibes you're giving off right now." I fold my arms.

Bo sighs and runs a hand through his hair, clearly irritated. "What's going on?"

Mari and I share another look.

I nod for her to tell him.

"Char's dead."

Bo's face goes pale.

He doesn't sit down. Doesn't react dramatically. But I notice the tight clench of his jaw, the slight twitch at the corner of his mouth. His chest puffs out. Then he lets out a huff and ruffles his hair. "It's already happening."

I sit forward. "What was that?"

"Nothing," he says quickly. *Too* quickly.

"Bo," I press, my voice firm.

He stands abruptly, knocking over a stool near the wall. "You two don't understand what's going on. And if you had any sense, you'd stop asking questions and go back to bed."

Mari recoils slightly. "That's kind of harsh."

"Harsh is better than dead," he snaps. "You want to end up like Char? Keep asking questions."

Mari and I exchange a shocked look.

Is that a threat?

Bo walks to the door but pauses, his back still to us. The firelight dances across his silhouette, making him look taller, broader, more dangerous somehow.

"Just... be careful. Okay?" he says, voice lower now. Almost pleading.

And with that, he leaves.

The silence that follows feels heavier than before.

Mari hugs her knees to her chest and stares into the fire.

"Do you still think he's the darling of the kingdom?" I mutter.

Mari glares at the door. "No."

I bite my tongue. I guess her crush has fizzled out already.

I lean back in my chair, letting the embers warm my bare feet. "There's something he's not telling us."

"Obviously. The whole 'I'm fine' thing only works when you don't look like you've been mauled by a demon raccoon," Mari says darkly.

"Those scratches," I murmur. "They looked deep. Like claw marks."

Mari shifts. "What if he's... what if he's not just hiding something? What if he's part of it?"

I turn to her, startled. "Part of what?"

She shrugs helplessly. "I don't know. Whatever's going on. The murder. The secrecy. The wolves.

Maybe he's one of them. Or—worse—maybe he's caught in between."

I hate how plausible that sounds.

"You think he could be working for the dragon hunters?"

The thought turns my blood to ice. Before we can continue speculating, the door to the common area opens with a bang, and tired students come streaming in.

Mari and I take the opportunity to jump up and head for the privacy of our room again.

My insides tangle as I wrestle with the thought of whether to tell Mari about the other mysterious events of the night.

I start pacing, the stone floor cold under my toes.

"I had a crazy dream tonight," I blurt after a long pause. Keeping this to myself is too hard.

Mari perks up. "Is it about your dragon?"

My curiosity piques at the question, but there's more pressing matters to discuss, so I let it go.

"Not exactly. There was this man. In a forest. And it wasn't Earth. It felt... like here. Like the forest on the edge of the academy grounds. But older. Wilder. He saw me. I mean, *really* saw me. And then there was this whole blood-oath thing. It was so intense."

Mari frowns, and her eyes flash at me in a way that has me on edge.

"Blood oath?" she whispers.

The words hang heavy in the air like a noose over my head.

I swallow.

"Yeah. He made a vow. That 'she'd' be one of them. Whatever 'them' means. And then he looked at me. Like... like he knew me."

I chew my tongue.

What if Char was who the wolf was talking about?

Mari wraps her blanket around her tighter. "This is starting to sound less like a dream and more like a memory. Or maybe it was a vision. Maybe you can dreamwalk."

I give her an incredulous look. "Wait...that's actually a thing? What is dreamwalking?"

Mari drags both hands over her face with an exhale. Like a tired parent who has been asked one too many questions at the end of the day.

"When you sleep... you... you leave your body somehow and...walk."

"So, like my soul is sleepwalking?" I try and fail to hide the amused tone in my voice.

Mari's glare hits me square between the eyes. She's not impressed.

"This isn't a joke. Dreamwalking is dangerous. Really dangerous."

I blink several times, taking it all in.

"Is it even a thing?"

For the first time since the slippers comment, Mari laughs.

"Kayla. You're living in a dragon rider academy, in a world with talking wolves, mood plants, and magic. Of course, it's a thing."

I snort. "Fair point."

Mari hugs herself and sighs. "You should speak to

King Siberious. He will want to know about the wolves, and he can offer some advice on the dreamwalking thing. Until then, I think it's better you try not to do it again."

I throw my hands in the air. "I didn't do it on purpose, Mari. It's not like I wanted to see a weirdo punching a tree and making a blood oath."

We fall silent again, there's a faint murmur of voices on the other side of our door. It's obvious that no one is getting anymore sleep tonight.

"So, what now?" Mari finally asks.

The weight of her words presses on my chest. It's hard to breathe.

I stop pacing. "Now, we wait, I guess. We stay alert. We ask questions quietly and watch who's acting weird."

Mari snorts. "So... everyone?"

I let out a breath, a little tension leaving my chest, but nausea rises from my stomach instead. "Exactly."

I fall onto my bed and bury my face in my pillow.

A storm is coming. I can feel it in the air, in the ground, in my bones.

Something has shifted.

Char's death wasn't random. Someone wanted her silenced.

I'm starting to think maybe the dream was a warning.

And somehow, Bo is tangled in the web the dream tried to warn me about. I just don't know if he's the hunter, the prey, or the one setting the trap.

Chapter 21
Trust

Breakfast is usually chaotic—clinking cutlery, spells gone wrong, someone summoning a spoon from across the hall like they're too elite to reach for it. But this morning, everything feels... muffled.

Muted.

Like the castle itself is holding its breath.

The moment Mari and I step into the Dining Hall, I feel it in my bones.

Students sit in tight clusters, speaking in whispers like the walls are listening. Plates are barely touched. Even the lame food looks extra sad—porridge congealing, eggs rubbery and untouched.

Mari's mood plant droops pitifully on her shoulder, leaves curled in on themselves like a turtle retreating into its shell.

"Yikes," she whispers, eyeing the long room. "Did someone cast a depression charm in here or what?"

She elbows me with a wry smile. "Makes you wanna ask... 'who died?'"

Mari winces under my glare. "Too soon?"

I nod solemnly. "Too soon."

There are a million inappropriate jokes I can laugh at. But death is not one of them. Never.

We slide into our usual seats near the middle of the hall.

The chatter here is quieter, but a few familiar faces glance up as we pass.

Tasha, a girl with hair like blue fire, leans in toward a group of wide-eyed first-years and whispers, "I heard she was drained. Like, magically. Nothing left inside."

"That's not what I heard," mutters a boy beside her—Jonas, maybe?—His mop of sandy hair completely covers his eyes, but his pointed ears peep out between the greasy strands. "My roommate said she was in her astronomy class and asked Mr. Helman to talk about dreams. And the difference between a dream and a vision."

"She was unstable," someone else adds. "Always talking about conspiracies. Maybe she finally snapped."

The words bounce around like pebbles in a tin can. But they sit at the bottom of my stomach like boulders.

No one sounds like they really believe what they're saying. Everyone's just trying to fill the silence. At least, that's what I'm telling myself. It's better than the alternative.

Mari gives me a furtive look, and I know what she's thinking.

I jerk my head, giving her a warning look back.

But despite my reaction, Mari leans in to whisper in my ear, her mood plant's leaves tickle my neck. "Told you dreamwalking is dangerous."

I glance toward the staff table to avoid her judgy stare and instantly feel the prickling sense of something wrong.

"Where's Ms. Mauve?" I murmur, half-trying to change the subject, and half-curious.

Mari's brow furrows as she looks up. "That's weird. She's always here early. First to glare at your outfit, last to leave."

It's true. Ms. Mauve practically lives in that high-backed chair, sipping tar-black coffee and staring everyone down with a mixture of wisdom and condemnation.

Especially at me. Ever since the orientation, she's always been cold and particularly interested in watching me be completely ordinary.

Every day, she's been a constant reminder of how much of a disappointment I am.

But today, her seat is empty.

And that... that feels off.

Before I can voice it, a silver goblet clinks loudly against the edge of the High Table.

The murmuring dies down like someone flipped a switch.

King Siberious stands tall in the center, his crimson robe sweeping behind him like fire trailing on water. He doesn't look angry. Or sad. Or even disappointed.

He looks... carved from stone.

Stoic.

Eyes sharp. Mouth grim. Hands folded calmly on the platform before him.

"I know you are all feeling the weight of last night's tragedy," he begins, his voice low but rich, echoing around the hall without the need for magic. "And there are many rumors milling around, so I believe it is appropriate for me to set the record straight."

He pauses just long enough for the tension to build.

"Charlotte Felden, known to many of you as Char, passed away suddenly during the red moon cycle."

A ripple of discomfort moves through the crowd.

Someone across the room stifles a sob.

The mood plant on Mari's shoulder lets out a weak, mourning trill.

"We believe the cause to be a heart attack," Siberious continues. "It is not uncommon here. The strain of the training. The change in environment. The pressure."

He pauses, letting the words settle like dust. But instead, they seem to float like ash over all of us.

I swallow against the uncomfortable lump growing in my throat.

"This academy is not for everyone."

His voice hardens—not cruel, but unyielding—as he sweeps his gaze across the room. No one is whispering now. All eyes are locked on him.

"The training you are undergoing is intense. It

will test your mind. Your body. Your will. And while some will thrive under this pressure... others will break."

Silence. Unforgiving. Cold.

King Siberious's hard gaze softens—just barely.

"This is not said to frighten you," he continues, "but to prepare you."

He lifts a hand, fingers splayed slightly, as if inviting silence to linger longer.

"To honor Charlotte's memory—and to remind each of you what is truly at stake—you will be placed into groups of three for a very special challenge. It will not take place in the safety of these castle walls. Instead, you will journey into the forest. Should you fail, you will leave this school with immediate effect. But should you succeed...your dragon is waiting for you on the mountain."

A few students gasp audibly.

Someone near the front drops their fork with a loud clatter.

Siberious allows the reaction to ripple through the room before pressing on.

"Now a word of caution... The forest surrounding Theridon is old. Ancient. It holds more than trees and shadows. There are trials within—puzzles, dangers, truths—that will test you in ways the classroom cannot. These are all designed to make certain you are worthy of your bond with a dragon."

He begins to walk slowly behind the staff table, each step deliberate.

"You will need your wits."

A flicker of movement in his fingers—magic?—vanishes before I can be sure.

"You will need your stamina. There are paths that twist and shift, that will demand your strength, your resilience, and your trust in one another."

He returns to the center of the platform.

"And you will need your power."

The way he says it sends a chill down my spine.

"There is something waiting for you at the end of your path. An adversary. One that cannot be overcome by brute force alone. You will need to stand together, not as classmates—but as one."

A pause.

His next words are soft, almost whispered—but they cut like a blade.

"If you fail to trust each other... you will not make it back."

Siberious exhales slowly, then lifts his gaze across the hall.

"Take care of yourselves," he says. "Take care of each other. The dragon does not fly alone."

With that, he lifts his goblet and drinks.

A hum of murmuring fills the space again, nervous and unsteady.

"Okay, I'm officially not hungry," I whisper, pushing my bowl of oatmeal slop away.

Mari frowns. "Did he just casually imply we'll die if we don't play nice in group work?"

"Pretty much. I guess he thinks Char died from... lack of trust and poor communication skills."

Mari blinks. "He really said 'collaborate or die'."

I shrug. "Honestly? On brand."

King Siberious begins moving down the aisles, speaking quietly to clusters of students, assigning teams. It's like watching the Sorting Hat with less sorting into cute houses and more threat of violent death.

I slouch in my chair, hoping he passes us by.

He doesn't.

He stops just behind our table, and I feel him before I see him. His presence is like a pressure system, making my bones ache and the air thicken.

"You two." His eyes lock on Mari and me. "Together."

Mari lets out a little breath of relief and gives me a hopeful smile.

I manage a half-smile back. At least we know each other. Being with Mari gives me a pretty solid chance that maybe, just maybe, we can pass this test.

After all, despite my only powers being sarcasm and clumsy footing, she's a powerful witch and doesn't hate me. So, there's definitely potential.

Then King Siberious turns. The shift of his long hair wafts a musty smell over to me, and I don't know if it's the scent or the word that leaves his mouth that takes my breath away.

"Bo."

My insides freeze.

I cough.

Bo, sitting two tables over, doesn't look surprised. He stands without comment, grabs his tray, and starts walking toward us.

I'm half-surprised he has a casual smirk on his face, his shoulders pulled back and chest puffed out. His strides are long and confident. The cocky mask is back on, but this time, I'm not fooled.

I groan, slumping in my seat. "No. No no no."

"This feels intentional," Mari whispers, matching my energy for once. "Like we're being punished."

Bo catches our words and must pick up on our lack of enthusiasm because his smile vanishes. He drops onto the bench across from us with all the joy of someone preparing for their own execution. His tray contains only black coffee and a chunk of stale bread. It's the brooding breakfast of champions.

He doesn't speak. Doesn't even look at us. Just stares into the distance like he's the main character in a sad indie movie.

"You good?" I ask, cocking my head.

Nothing.

Mari leans over the table. "Bo. Say something, or we're reporting you to the Drama Queen Committee."

He blinks slowly. "You two can talk. You both look like you'd rather be paired with an ogre than me. What do you want me to say?"

I shrug. "I don't know. Maybe acknowledge the fact that you're suddenly on Team Trauma with two girls who know you're hiding something sketchy?"

He sighs. "This isn't the time."

"It literally is," Mari says. "He said we have to trust each other or die. That feels very time-sensitive."

Bo runs a hand through his already-messy hair,

clearly debating whether to argue or just walk out and accept his inevitable doom.

I lean closer, lowering my voice. "Look. You don't have to tell us everything. But if we're doing some kind of life-or-death obstacle course today, it'd be great if we knew whether or not you're going to sprout fangs and betray us halfway through."

His eyes flick to mine.

For one moment, I see a crack in the mask—exhaustion, fear, something ancient and heavy. For a flash, I'm reminded of Eliyah on the train. Maybe that look is an elf thing.

My jaw tightens. Not elf.

Then it's gone.

"I'm not going to hurt you," he says quietly. "But I can't promise someone else won't try."

I blink.

Mari frowns. "That's not comforting."

Bo leans back. "Wasn't trying to be. And I'm not making any promises to protect you either. So, you both better pull your weight, or we're all doomed."

Chapter 22
The Forest of Trials

We're not even in the forest yet, and I'm already sweating.

Not from heat. From nerves. From the way Mari keeps sneaking worried glances at me. From the truth unraveling too fast.

I tug on the sleeve of my training gear, trying not to look like I'm coming apart at the seams.

"So," Mari says, not looking at me, her tone deceptively casual as she smooths her black-and-red tunic. "Do you think Char was having dreams? Like yours?"

The question lands like a punch to the chest.

I stare at the floor.

My mind flashes to the vacant look in Char's dead eyes, the way her body had seemed more statue than human. Empty. Like she never used to be alive.

"I don't know," I murmur, voice tight. "Maybe."

Mari sits on the edge of her bed, pulling on her

boots. "How long have you been having dreams that vivid?"

I glance up.

The question is simple.

The answer isn't.

I rake my fingers through my hair, gathering it into a high bun. It gives me something to focus on. Something to twist and tie and control.

"Since the crash, I guess."

Mari's head jerks up. "The crash?"

I freeze and hold my breath.

Oh, shoot, is that bad?

Judging from the way Mari is looking at me, I'm guessing it is.

"You've been having dreams since *before* you got here?"

I nod slowly. Then I make the mistake of adding, "Ever since the plane went down and I lost my family."

Mari gasps. A sharp, open-mouthed, full-body inhale. Her eyes go round, shimmering with emotion. "Your whole family died?"

I flinch. The words hit like a slap, blunt and too loud, even though she barely whispered them.

"I—can we not—?" I stand too fast. My boots aren't even on yet. "Let's just get ready."

It's a terrible disappointment that my mouth has a mind of its own. I had planned to keep that information to myself. No one needs any more reasons to pity me.

But the damage is done.

Mari is staring at me like I'm a war orphan. Like

she's one second away from launching into a sympathy monologue or hugging me until I can't breathe.

"Mari." My voice is firm. "Don't."

"But, Kayla..."

"No."

She presses her lips together, clearly swallowing back more questions. More feelings. Her mood plant droops dramatically on her nightstand, a soft purring whimper echoing from its pot.

She leaves it behind without another word, and I follow suit. Mine's curled up in its little clay bowl like it's bracing for an apocalypse. Its color is no longer blue or green or even purple.

It's... gray.

Still.

That can't be good.

I glance at it one last time, trying to shake off the dread curling in my stomach.

"Don't be symbolic," I mutter at the plant. "Stay alive."

I yank on my black boots and adjust the leather straps across my chest.

The gear they gave us is sleek—black and crimson with silver buckles, snug in some places, flexible in others. There are hooks and loops for weapons or wands or whatever magical doom we'll be expected to face today.

As we step into the common room, Bo is already waiting.

And looking far too comfortable.

His training leathers fit him like a tailor designed them specifically for his brooding hero aesthetic. The red accents make his blond hair seem even paler. His sharp jawline is dusted with the barest trace of stubble, and he's standing like someone who knows he looks good.

Like the perfect fae prince.

Because he is.

A cluster of girls loiter nearby, whispering and giggling like this is a perfume commercial instead of a death march.

Bo doesn't acknowledge them. He just looks at me. His gaze lingers, slow and unreadable.

For the first time... I get it.

I get why people stare.

Why they want to get close, and why they shouldn't.

Mari lets out a tiny sigh beside me.

I elbow her gently and lean close. "Should we get his autograph? It might be worth at least another magazine at the market?"

Normally, Mari would snort. Maybe roll her eyes. Something.

But today, she just gives me a haunted look.

"How can you be so cool," she mutters, "when we're about to face our deaths?"

I blink, taken aback. "How can you be so doom and gloom when going off on kamikaze adventures is totally your kind of thing?"

Her expression wavers.

She opens her mouth, then shuts it again.

Riders and Hunters

We fall into step behind Bo as we make our way toward the castle's outer gates.

Students are already filing into lines, grouping up with their assigned trios. Some look confident. Some are clearly on the verge of vomiting.

I spot Madame Hexley chatting with a group by the weapons rack, laughing a little too cheerfully for the occasion.

The sky is a cool, pale silver overhead. No sun. Just clouds. Like even the heavens aren't sure how today's going to end.

Ahead, the forest looms.

And loom is the only word for it.

I stop walking.

It's not just that the forest is huge. Or dense. Or that the trees are twisted like ancient giants with gnarled fingers and moss-covered spines.

It's that I've *seen* it before.

Every shadowed glen. Every vine-covered root. Every fog-draped path.

This is the forest from my dream.

The one where the golden-eyed man made his blood oath.

My breath catches.

Mari steps up beside me, noticing my reaction. "You okay?"

I nod stiffly. "Yeah. Totally fine. Just... déjà vu."

Bo's voice comes from behind us. "You've dreamwalked in this place?"

I twist around to face him. "What makes you say that?"

His lips tilt upward, just a little. Not quite a smile. More like the ghost of one. "Because I have, too."

My heart skips a beat. "What?"

He doesn't elaborate. Instead, he walks past us, toward the mouth of the trail, where two professors stand with clipboards and serious expressions.

Mari and I follow, both of us suddenly far too aware of how quiet it's gotten again.

Bo glances over his shoulder at me once more. There's something unspoken in his eyes—something ancient and knowing.

"Yes. I've been here before." He lowers his voice just enough that only I can hear. "Yes, you can be eaten by your own shadow if you're not careful. And no, I'm pretty sure a lot of us won't make it out alive."

A beat.

Then he says, almost gently, "But we will."

I don't know if it's the certainty in his voice, or the flicker of something like concern behind his bravado—but somehow, my pulse slows.

Just a little.

Chapter 23
Runes and Logic

We don't get far into the forest before the trees swallow the light.

The path behind us disappears into the mist like it never existed. The air thickens, cool and damp. Ahead, flickering torches float in midair, no poles, no brackets. Just free-floating fire, pulsing like a heartbeat.

Mari inches a little closer, her eyes darting. "Okay. This is less enchanted forest and more cursed-by-an-ancient-queen-who-eats-souls."

I snort. "That's very specific."

Bo glances back at us, unimpressed. "Are you done?"

"Are you ever fun?" I shoot back.

He shrugs. "Fun is for people who die in these situations."

I blink.

That's not the Bo I remember—the one who smirked and flirted with anything that breathed. The one who practically sparkled with smug, sunny confidence.

"What happened to you?" I ask, only half-teasing. "*You* used to be fun."

He doesn't answer at first. Just keeps walking, the shadows slanting across his face like war paint.

"Things change," he mutters eventually. "People change."

Mari gives me a look behind his back—yikes—but I just frown, watching Bo's shoulders tense as he leads the way.

Now I get it.

There's a difference between time here and time on Earth. My brain thinks it's only been a couple of weeks since I got to the academy. But days stretch long like weeks. All the while moments pass by like ordinary seconds.

Yet, somehow, it feels like I've been Mari's friend for an eternity, and I've known Bo long enough to sense he's grown since orientation.

The carefree, smug attitude is gone. In place, is a troubled soul, trying and failing to convince everyone around him that he's not terrified about what we're going to face.

I finally get it. The kind of time I know about doesn't exist here.

The idea melts my brain, but for once, I'm not totally rejecting it.

We keep moving in silence, the woods pressing closer with every step. Our boots crunch across dead leaves and brittle twigs.

Mari rolls her shoulders.

"You good?" she asks me.

I hesitate. Bo's words from earlier still echo in my head.

You've dreamwalked in this forest, haven't you?

"Just thinking."

Bo doesn't look at me, but I feel the weight of his attention like a second shadow.

Mari squints. "Are you thinking about your dream again?"

"Yeah," I say quietly. "All of this is looking eerily familiar, and I'm not sure how."

Bo finally speaks. "Dreams at Theridon... they're not always yours. And they're not always safe."

Mari frowns at me.

But I stop walking to give Bo a pointed look. "What does *that* mean?"

"It means..." His, eyes scan the trees. "This world is saturated in magic. Dreams can be shaped. Warped. Used."

"Used by who?"

He looks over his shoulder at me. "By whoever wants to get inside of your head."

The silence that follows is thick.

I kick at a root. "Cool. So, nothing in my brain is real and strangers can get inside my head. Love that for me."

Mari makes a face. "So comforting to know, thanks."

Bo doesn't respond. He just starts walking again, more tense than before.

We round a bend where a rack of weapons stands gleaming beneath a tree whose bark is nearly black.

A hovering sign pulses above it in fiery red script: "Choose your weapon. Choose your fate."

A dozen options glint in the dappled light—bows, swords, staffs, daggers, crossbows, whips, and things I don't even recognize.

Bo doesn't hesitate. He grabs a massive two-handed sword like he's greeting an old friend.

I'm amazed at how his biceps bulge as he waves it around like a twig.

Mari picks a silver wand, sleek and thin, with a copper-colored crystal embedded at the tip.

"Obviously," she says with a smirk.

I stare at the weapons, thinking.

A sword's too heavy and awkward to carry. A bow and arrow? Let's not repeat the one disastrous archery class I had in '21.

I somehow hit a water trough instead of a target.

And it was behind me.

So, I go for a simple knife. The handle is worn smooth and looks nothing special. It's small, sharp, balanced.

Close combat's terrifying, but if something's trying to kill me, I'd rather be close enough to fight dirty.

Weapon chosen, we move toward the sound of murmuring voices ahead.

Students gather in front of a narrow archway formed by tree branches, where Ms. Mauve stands in ceremonial robes and holds a staff with a glowing blue orb.

"That explains where she was at breakfast," I mutter to Mari.

"You think she was setting this up?"

"Who else? With her powers, I'll bet she's created the challenges single-handedly."

Bo remains silent.

The crowd settles, looking at Ms. Mauve, waiting for instruction.

"Enter the forest to begin your challenge," she says. "Find the right path and thrive... or lose your way and die."

I resist the urge to roll my eyes.

Cheery pep talk.

The students ahead of us walk through the arch and vanish into fog.

Bo adjusts his sword on his back.

Mari fiddles with her wand.

I adjust my bun... like that's going to help.

Then it's our turn.

We step through the arch... And the world shifts.

Suddenly, we're alone in a clearing surrounded by silent trees. In front of us stands a massive stone wall with a grid of symbols. Next to it, a pedestal holding a small box.

"Well, at least it's not another hippogriff," I mumble.

Bo shoots me an inquisitive look, and my cheeks flush.

I shouldn't have said that, especially after giving Mari such a hard time when she wanted to tell Bo about our trip to the market.

Luckily, no one seems interested in continuing the conversation.

"What now?" Mari whispers.

Bo hums in thought, inspecting the scene. "It looks like a door. But there's no lock. No handle. Maybe you need to cast the right spell to open it?"

Mari steps forward, squinting. "Let me see..."

She makes a flourish with her wand and mutters something under the breath.

But nothing happens.

Mari tries again. And again.

Finally, she frowns, deeply, and her cheeks redden. "No. Not a spell."

Bo clears his throat. "Maybe it requires light magic."

His hands glow as he stretches them out. But even after he makes dramatic movements that reminds me of a man doing Tai Chi while holding glow sticks, nothing happens. Nothing except Bo giving us a dazzling light show.

Soon, Mari and Bo are both standing, defeated. Frowning deep and skeptical.

Meanwhile, I open the box.

"I think it's a puzzle," I suggest, pulling out a small scroll.

Bo and Mari join me, their brows lifted as I unfold the paper.

Sure enough, it's a riddle:

The path is hidden, not with might,
But in the choice to choose what's right.
Pick the signs that match the tale,

Or be trapped forever behind the veil.

I make a beeline for the wall and brush away the dust, revealing pictures—animals, moons, stars, runes, flames.

Bo scratches his head. "Well, that's interesting. Any of this make sense to you?"

Mari frowns. "They remind me of the runes I've seen in divination class. But I don't recognize these ones."

I grin, a bubble of hope rising in me for once. "Time for some room-escape logic."

They both stare at me like I've just grown two more arms.

Bo rests a hand on his right hip. "Room what?"

"Room escape," I say. "It's like... a game. Back where I'm from. You're locked in a room and have to solve puzzles to get out. This feels exactly like that."

I crack my knuckles and inspect the markings.

Mari makes a sound that is something between a gasp and a laugh. "You... willingly walked into locked rooms?"

"It was fun!" I protest. "And nerdy. But mostly fun."

Bo snorts. "And you survived that? I'm shocked."

I ignore him and point at the symbols. "It's not random. The riddle says 'match the tale', right? So, we're supposed to find the symbols that match a story. Look."

"What story?" Mari asks.

"Look around, there's got to be a book...or more writing somewhere."

We begin to search the clearing, when Bo

retrieves something from under a pile of dead leaves. "Or another scroll?"

Heartened, I take it from him. I unravel the damp parchment and hold it out for the three of us.

I read aloud:

"In the time before dragons, the wolf watched the stars.

The owl gave him wisdom, the flame gave him fire.

But it was the moon that taught him to wait."

"*Time before...*" I say.

Mari raises her palm.

"I swear, Kayla. If I hear one more joke about time--"

"It's a clue," I correct her. "I guess if you're not familiar with the concept, this would be really hard to figure out. But it's actually simple."

Bo and Mari exchange a confused look.

"What's simple?" Mari asks.

I laugh, it's refreshing to feel like I have an idea what is going on for a change.

"*Time before*...it's talking about the order. The order we press the runes. Like a passcode."

They continue to give me blank stares.

I sigh. "We're supposed to pick the wolf, the owl, the flame, and the moon. In that order."

Bo glances at the wall. "What happens if we pick wrong?"

I point to the fifth symbol: a skull.

Mari shudders. "Probably... not a badge and a hug, that's for sure."

With shaky hands, I reach for the wolf symbol, but Bo grabs my hand.

"Hold on. Let's just think about this."

I lift my brows at him, surprised by the strength of his grip on me. A heat pulses from his palm, burning my skin.

"What is there to think about?"

Bo drags his other hand through his hair in frustration. "If you are wrong, we all might die. So, I just want to make sure."

I cock my head to the side. "Got any better ideas? I'm all ears."

Bo drops my hand like I zapped him. "You really think it's that simple? Just pressing the symbols in the correct order and...what? A door will magically open, letting us through?"

I press my lips together and look at the wall. There's an energy surrounding it, like it's humming. And my instincts propel me forward.

I nod.

"I've not been sure about a lot of things since I got to this place. Heck, I've not been sure of anything since I lost my family in that stupid plane crash. But this? This I know I'm right. I just *know* it."

I say the last few words with as much fervor as I can muster and give Bo a hard look.

He glances at Mari, who shrugs back.

Then he steps aside. "Very well. I can't believe I'm placing my life in the hands of a human with no powers. But...go ahead."

The words sting more than I expect.

It's not just what he said. It's how he said it—like he's already resigned to me being the weakest link.

A rush of annoyance swells in my chest, hot and sharp.

I bury it.

Not because he's wrong. But because now I have to be right.

I step closer to the wall, feeling the ancient energy vibrating off it.

The massive stone slabs are carved with glowing symbols—etched so deep it's like they were clawed into the rock by something with talons. The surrounding trees have gone still, like the forest is watching. Waiting.

I reach out, my hand steady now, and press the four symbols in the order I remember from the riddle: wolf, owl, flame, moon.

Each one pulses with soft golden light beneath my fingers. For a split second, nothing happens.

Then the stone wall groans, low and deep, like the earth itself is exhaling.

The symbols flare, light streaking between them like veins, and a seam splits down the center of the wall.

Dust swirls up as the stone doors slide open with a shuddering boom, revealing a shadowy corridor lined with moss-covered columns and flickering blue flames hovering in midair. It smells of wet stone and old secrets.

Cold air brushes past us like a whisper: *Enter if you dare... or turn back while you still can.*

Riders and Hunters

Mari steps up beside me, her eyes wide. "I'm never mocking your Earth hobbies again."

I flash her a grin. "Room escape for the win."

Bo lingers at the threshold, gaze sweeping over the opening with narrowed eyes. For once, he doesn't say anything smug. He just follows us inside.

We walk shoulder to shoulder, boots echoing softly across the smooth stone. The blue flames seem to pulse in time with our steps, lighting the way as the corridor curves forward into darkness.

I should be scared.

But for the first time in a long time—I feel capable.

Powerless? Sure.

But underestimated? Absolutely.

We emerge from the corridor to find ourselves once again in the forest, only this time, the trees are taller, thicker, the light dimmer than before.

But before we can enjoy our victory, we come to a screeching halt.

The path ahead ends in a vertical rock face, towering into the fog like the wall of a fortress. An obstacle course has been rigged up the cliffside—ropes hanging at odd angles, rotting ladders nailed into the rock, narrow ledges that barely deserve the name.

Mari lets out a strangled sound. "You've got to be kidding me."

I stare up at the climb, dread pooling in my gut.

"I am never complaining about the castle stairs again."

Chapter 24
The Sky Watches

"I take it back." Mari squints up at the cliffside. "I take *everything* back. The training, the challenge, my enthusiasm for adventure, my respect for ropes—*all of it*."

The rock face looms above us like a sleeping giant. Ropes dangle like vines. Narrow planks form shaky ladders at weird angles. There's even a section that looks like it was cobbled together with old bridge pieces and regret.

Bo frowns. "It's passable. If we move fast and don't look down."

"Thanks, coach," I mutter. "That's *super* reassuring."

Mari twirls her wand, lips pressed together. "No way are we doing this raw. Hold on."

She mutters something under her breath, soft syllables in a language I don't recognize.

Her wand glows silver, and a trail of magic snakes

up the ropes and ladders, reinforcing them with shimmering lines of light.

"There," she says, a little breathless. "That should help keep everything stable."

"Define 'help,'" I say.

Bo gives the rope ladder a hard tug. It doesn't wobble.

"It'll hold," he says, and starts climbing without waiting for us.

We follow, Mari going second, me last.

The rope creaks under our combined weight, but it holds. Barely.

We climb in silence for a long time, the forest falling away below us.

My fingers burn. My arms ache. Sweat drips into my eyes.

But we're doing it.

We're making progress.

Mari glances down and flashes me a tired grin. "Not bad, huh? Little magic, little teamw—"

And then Bo slips.

It happens so fast I barely see it.

His foot misses a rung.

The rope groans.

He swears, loud and sharp, as his grip loosens, and he plummets downward...

On instinct, I swipe the air, my fingers brushing his shirt.

The world moves in slow motion as I reach again, fisting the cotton over his arm.

This time, I keep a grip.

My knife drops from my belt and clatters down the cliffside, but my hand closes around Bo's wrist. The sudden weight yanks me hard against the ladder, my arms screaming.

"MARI!" I shout.

She's already reacting, wand glowing as she reinforces the nearest rungs with a hiss of magic.

Bo dangles in midair, feet scrabbling against the rock.

"I've got you!" I say through clenched teeth.

He looks up at me, surprised. "You shouldn't be able to—"

"Less talking, more *climbing*!"

Mari mutters another spell, and the ladder glows brighter beneath Bo.

He finds his footing, and with a grunt, scrambles up to the next ledge.

We collapse there, all three of us gasping.

Mari looks pale.

"That's on me," she says, staring at the ropes. "The spell—I didn't anchor it deep enough. It's my fault."

"It's not," Bo says gruffly. "I was careless."

"I'm the witch," Mari snaps. "You two rely on me to keep you from falling to your deaths. If I screw up, we *all* die."

I rub my sore arms. "Well, not to be that girl, but I *did* save him."

Bo looks at me, unreadable. "You did."

And just like that, the silence returns.

We climb the rest in tense quiet, every step deliberate, every muscle screaming.

When we finally haul ourselves over the top, we collapse onto the ground in a heap, panting, filthy, bruised, but alive.

The sky above is clear now, the clouds finally drifting apart.

For one blissful moment, it feels like relief.

Then shadows sweep across the sky.

Long. Massive. Swooping.

We blink up at them, breath still ragged.

Mari shields her eyes. "What is that?"

Bo pushes up onto one elbow, squinting. "Are those... birds?"

No.

No, they are *not* birds.

I sit bolt upright, heart slamming against my ribs.

"Oh, no," I whisper.

They circle above us slowly, their massive wings casting long shadows that drift lazily over the treetops.

The shapes are unmistakable. Elongated bodies. Wings like sails. Tails that cut through the air like blades.

And gold—faint glimmers of gold reflecting off the sunlight as one of them dips low enough for the light to catch its scales.

Mari gasps.

Bo's jaw clenches.

But I'm the one who speaks.

My voice is barely audible, hoarse with fear and recognition.

"Dragons."

Their wings slice silently through the sky, graceful and menacing. The sun glints off scales—some bronze, others black, one shimmering blue—and their slow, lazy rotations feel more intentional than random.

Like they're waiting for something.

Watching.

Mari shields her eyes with her hand, squinting. "Do you think our dragons are up there?"

Bo narrows his gaze skyward, mouth tightening. "No doubt. But they're keeping their distance."

I frown. "Why aren't they coming down?"

Mari hugs herself. "It's like they're studying us. Judging us."

I don't say what I'm thinking, because the thought has been clanging around in my head since we spotted them: they're not just watching us—they're waiting for someone to fall behind.

We start moving again, trudging across a rocky outcrop that offers little in the way of cover.

The path ahead curves into a dense grove of low-hanging trees. Mist curls between their roots, thick and slow, like oil in water.

The kind of place you'd lose your footing—or your life—if you're not careful.

Bo walks ahead, eyes sweeping the tree line. His sword rests across his back again, and though his gait is relaxed, I can see the tension in his shoulders. He's listening. Waiting.

Mari mutters, "What do you think's next? We had riddles, and a near-death climbing experience... now what?"

"A giant?" I offer. "Cyclops?"

"An enchanted statue," Mari adds. "Or a hydra. Those are in season."

I shudder. "Why are you like this?"

She grins, but it's short-lived. Her gaze flicks upward again. "They haven't stopped circling."

"I know," I say. "It's creepy."

"Creepy is an understatement." Bo slows his pace until he falls in beside me. "It's like they know we're not ready."

"That or they're placing bets on who's going to die first," Mari calls over her shoulder.

Bo chuckles, and it surprises me. The sound is rare lately—less polished than before. Less performative. Like something he forgot he was allowed to do.

We come to a narrow strip of path carved between two massive boulders.

Mari takes the lead again, ducking between them.

Bo slows slightly, and then—

His hand clutches my waist.

I freeze.

It's not a grab or a shove. It's gentle. Steadying. Warm.

"Wait," he says, voice low.

I turn toward him, heart tapping a little faster. "What?"

He's looking at me differently now. Not with his usual amusement or judgment. Something softer. His eyes are clearer here, in the filtered light—pale blue with streaks of silver. Like frost that remembers fire.

"Back there. On the cliff," he murmurs. "Thank you."

I blink. "For what?"

"For saving me."

"Oh." I shrug like it's nothing, but my pulse is thudding in my ears. "I'm stronger than I look, I guess."

I try to smile, to make light of it, but his expression doesn't shift.

He's not laughing. He's not teasing.

"I knew there was something special about you," he murmurs.

His hand is still resting gently against my side, and I get butterflies.

"I don't know how you held me," he says, almost to himself. "I'm not exactly small."

"No, you're not." I laugh.

We stare at each other for a moment too long.

Then his gaze dips briefly to my mouth.

Something stirs low in my stomach—something unfamiliar and dangerous.

His eyes are zooming in, and my brain is scrambling to figure out what's going to happen next.

Mari screams.

The sound slices through the forest like lightning.

Bo's hand drops instantly from my waist. He spins toward the path, already withdrawing his sword.

I bolt forward, dodging between the rocks and tearing after Mari's voice.

We find her standing in the clearing beyond, rigid as stone.

"What happened?" I gasp, heart hammering.

She doesn't answer.

Her eyes are locked on something ahead.

I follow her gaze, and I stop breathing.

"This is a problem."

Chapter 25
Shadows and Fears

Mari is frozen.

Bo and I rush to her side, our eyes locking on the thing standing in the middle of the clearing.

It's massive.

Not in the typical monster way—no exaggerated horns or glowing red eyes or gnarled claws. No. This creature is wrong because of its stillness.

It stands upright, humanoid in shape, but its skin ripples like ink spilled underwater. It has no face. No features.

Only a hollow in the center of its chest, like something has carved out its heart and replaced it with a swirl of glowing, purple-black smoke.

"What is that?" I whisper, my face twisting.

Bo's grip tightens on his sword. "A shadow revenant. I've only read about them."

"Oh, yeah? And what have you read?" Mari hisses.

Bo doesn't answer.

The thing moves.

It tilts its head slowly, like it's sniffing the air—though it has no nose, no mouth, no eyes.

I shudder.

Then it lunges.

Mari screams again, seemingly forgetting that she is a witch and can totally wave that wand of hers and make this freaky monster disappear.

Bo steps in front of her, sword flashing up just in time to block a tendril of black smoke whipping toward us like a spear.

"Split up!" he barks.

Mari rolls left.

I dart right.

The creature slams into Bo, but he's ready.

His blade flares with light, and he whips it in a clean arc, slicing through one of the creature's tendrils.

It screams—not with a voice, but with a sound that rips through the air like glass breaking inside your head.

I stagger back, hands over my ears.

That's when it turns to me.

A stench floods the air as it approaches, I mean, it is the worst kind of body odor I've ever smelled.

And something inside me shifts.

Suddenly, I can hear everything—the rush of blood in my veins, the pounding of feet in the dirt, the soft hiss of Mari's magic, the strain of Bo's breath.

The world sharpens.

Let's also not forget—smell. The thing reeks of rot and static and iron.

My stomach clenches, but I don't recoil. I understand now. I can track it.

And it's coming for me.

"KAYLA!" Mari launches a volley of glowing blue orbs from her wand.

They slam into the creature's side, exploding in bursts of frost.

It staggers.

I run—straight at it.

Its tendrils lash out, but I duck low, slide across the mossy earth, and come up hard with my borrowed dagger slashing across what I think might be its leg.

The blade sinks in.

It doesn't bleed, there's not even a mark, but it shudders like it felt it anyway.

Mari flicks her wrist and mutters a spell.

A column of wind slams into the revenant, driving it back.

She leaps across a low bolder, nimble as a deer, firing blasts from her wand like a magical action hero.

Bo charges from the side, his sword now glowing white-hot. With a growl, he snaps his wrist, and the light erupts into a ribbon, whipping through the air and lassoing the revenant's middle.

He yanks hard.

The creature crashes into a tree, snapping the trunk like a twig.

"Nice trick," I pant, ducking another lashing

tendril. "You'd be popular with the cowboys back where I'm from."

Bo grunts. "Focus!"

The three of us move like we've been training together for years.

Bo holds the revenant's attention, slicing and lashing with light.

Mari darts in and out, casting spells of distraction and disorientation.

And me?

I wait.

I feel.

My senses burn.

I track the shift of air, the twitches of its muscles, the direction of its strikes before they land.

Then I strike back.

I launch off a bolder and bring my elbow down hard on its upper back.

It roars again, staggering.

Mari sends a searing bolt of fire right into the hollow of its chest.

The smoke flares purple.

"Keep hitting the center!" she yells.

Bo snarls something in a language I've never heard before.

I want to say Elvish, but Eliyah's words set me straight.

I'm not an elf.

And whatever Eliyah is, Bo is too.

My thoughts fizzle as he lashes his whip-blade again. It wraps around the creature's arms.

He twists, yanking it to its knees.

"Kayla, now!"

I run.

My boots pound the ground, but my body buzzes with adrenaline, and something else. Only, I can't put my finger on what.

I jump, eyes locked on the ugly beast.

I bring the dagger down hard into the hollow in its chest. And the blade sinks.

The revenant reacts. Not a sound per se. Not a scream either.

It's a pulse.

A shockwave blasts outward.

Mari flies backward into the brush.

Bo stumbles.

I'm thrown off the creature's chest, landing hard on my back with a grunt.

For a moment, just a second, it's still. Like a haunting sculpture at a low budget summer camp.

Then it leans over with a groan and collapses in a pile of dust.

A black mist floods my vision and when it fades, I blink at the empty space where the monster had been.

It's gone.

Leaving nothing behind but a burning stench and the sound of my own heartbeat.

We lie there, gasping, chests heaving.

Bo rises first. He offers me a clammy hand.

I take it.

My body aches in places I didn't know I could feel.

Mari limps over, her braid half undone, clothes smudged, and for once, no snark on her face.

We won.

We *actually* won.

"I can't feel anything," Mari wheezes, dropping onto a rock.

Bo plants his sword in the dirt. "Remind me why we signed up for this again?"

I stagger forward, still feeling the phantom thrum in my hands from where I stabbed the creature. "Because it's fun," I say hoarsely. "Clearly."

We laugh—tired, shaky, almost-delirious laughter.

Maybe we are ready for our dragons. We faced all of the challenges and lived to tell the tale.

I'm just about to congratulate us all when something wraps around my ankle.

Cold. Wet. Strong.

I screech.

Bo and Mari whip around.

Another tendril of black mist has slithered up from the earth. It coils tight around my leg, then yanks.

Hard.

I hit the ground with a cry, dirt in my mouth, my fingers scrabbling for purchase.

Mari shrieks my name.

Bo shouts something—magic bursting in the air—but it's too late.

I'm dragged, fast, into the trees.

Branches whip past. Leaves slash at my face.

Riders and Hunters

My body bangs against roots and rocks and cold moss.

The light fades.

Bo's voice echoes once, then is gone.

Mari's scream is swallowed by the forest.

And I am gone with it.

Chapter 26
The Wolf in the Firelight

The plane is falling again.

Same roaring wind. Same screeching metal. Same screaming.

My heart slams against my ribs as the cabin lurches, tilts, breaks apart.

And I fall.

But this time, I know what's coming.

There's no panic, just... inevitability. Like I've dreamed it so many times my body's given up on fear.

I brace for impact.

And then I land.

Only, it's not a crash.

It's soft. Earth. Moss.

The forest again.

The dream forest.

Everything's dim and unnaturally quiet, like the world is asleep.

Smoke curls through the air, thick and lazy, and the trees stretch so tall they block out the sky.

My feet crunch on charred leaves as I step forward.

And there it is.

The monster.

The same one from the challenge.

Only now, it's dead.

Slumped on its side, twisted and unmoving. Giant claw marks slash across its torso—deep, clean gouges. Like something massive shredded it.

Okay. Creepy forest? Check. Dead evil creature? Check. Weird sense of déjà vu and dread? Check and check.

But it's what I see next that really throws me.

There's a man crouched by a fire in the clearing. Like... an actual campfire. With glowing embers and everything.

He's just there. Tending it. As if roasting marshmallows next to nightmare creatures is a totally normal Tuesday activity.

I freeze.

He's wearing dark hunting gear—leathers, layered tunic, buckled straps, and a cloak tossed over one shoulder. There's a massive broadsword propped beside him.

His hair is jaw-length and dark, wind-ruffled and just messy enough to be annoyingly good-looking. Strong jaw, sharp cheekbones, and I hate that I even notice that he's, like, hot in a tortured anti-hero kind of way.

Then the scent hits me.

Not smoke. Not pine. Something else. Wild. Raw. Like iron and earth and—steak?

My stomach grumbles.

What the heck? Is that his scent, or am I just ravenously hungry? Maybe both?

I can't remember the last time I ate anything juicy, like a steak.

My body reacts without my permission—heat flares under my skin, and my chest tightens like I've just sprinted a mile.

Before I can process that delightful wave of hormones, pain explodes through my leg. A sharp, blinding stab just above the knee.

"Ughhh," I groan, slamming back into the ground as my vision blurs.

The guy looks up.

His eyes glow faintly amber in the firelight.

"Wake up," he says.

And I do.

I jolt upright, sucking in a breath, except this time —it's real.

The trees are still here. The fire's still crackling. The monster really is dead. And, oh yeah, my leg is twisted at an angle it absolutely should not be in.

Blood soaks through the tear in my leathers. My shirt is ripped, my arms are scraped, and I look like a dragon chewed me up and spit me out.

Excellent.

The mystery wilderness man stirs the fire with a stick like he's got all the time in the world. Like he didn't just kill a monster the size of a small house.

"Don't move," he says without looking at me.

I scowl. "Yeah, thanks, I hadn't figured that out from the whole bone-screaming pain thing."

"You're lucky I was nearby," he mutters.

"Oh please," I snap. "I had it handled."

That gets a reaction.

He turns, raises a brow, and gives me a look so dry it could soak up the ocean.

"You were unconscious. Bleeding. Your leg's twisted like a broken wand. Sure. Totally had it handled."

I roll my eyes. "I've had worse."

He snorts. *Actually* snorts. "Doubtful."

I open my mouth to fire back, but he says one word that turns my blood cold.

"Kayla."

I freeze. "How do you know my name?"

There's a pause.

His jaw tightens. Something flickers behind his eyes.

"You don't remember?"

I blink. "What?"

"You *really* don't remember?" he presses, and for a second, he looks hopeful.

Okay. This is officially weird.

I squint at him.

That voice. That stare. The way he moves. It's familiar in the way dreams are—blurry but intense.

Wait.

The train. The wolf. The hippogriff. The dreams.

"You," I whisper. "You're... I've seen you before."

He looks back at the fire. "Saved your life, twice now. You're welcome."

I stare at him like he's sprouted a second head. "Who are you?"

He doesn't answer. Of course, he doesn't.

"Ugh," I groan, trying to sit up again.

My whole body screams.

"I need to find my friends. Bo and Mari. They're gonna be freaking out—"

"You're not going anywhere," he says flatly. "Your leg's broken. You're vulnerable. And there are other things in this forest that'd love a bleeding dragon girl snack."

"I'm not vulnerable," I grit out. "I'm a dragon rider."

His head tilts, and now there's definite amusement behind that unreadable expression. "Oh, yeah? Then where's your dragon?"

I glare.

My fingers fumble with my torn collar, and I tug it aside to show the mark—the curled, glowing tattoo on my collarbone.

The bond.

The proof.

He looks. Blinks once.

"Cute. But anyone can get a tattoo. Doesn't mean anything."

I want to throw a rock at him.

"It wasn't a tattoo! I was chosen."

He snorts. "By Siberious?"

"Yes!"

He lets out a low whistle and shakes his head. "An enchanted necklace has really given you a superiority complex, Kayla."

I snap my head toward him. "Stop saying my name."

"Why?"

"Because it feels weird. I don't know who you are, and you keep talking to me like we're old friends."

He stiffens.

The firelight flickers between us.

"I could talk to you like we're enemies, if that's more your style," he says, voice low.

"Isn't that what we are?" I shoot back.

He lets out a breath like I've tired him by merely existing. "Your ignorance is exhausting."

"Then explain something for once!"

Silence.

The fire crackles.

Finally, he looks at me. The glow dances in his eyes, and something stirs in them—something tired and dangerous and deeply sad.

"My name," he says, "is Ajax."

The name echoes in my head, and my heart stops for a beat.

I know that name.

Not from school. Not from stories.

From somewhere deeper.

From dreams.

From something I've forgotten.

Chapter 27
The Enemy Has a Face

The firelight dances across his knuckles.

Scars. Deep, raw, and permanent. Faded in places but unmistakably earned. Some are jagged. Others are almost clean, like they were burned in rather than scraped.

For a moment, I wonder how many fights he's been in. How many creatures he's killed.

How many people.

But then he leans down and scoops me into his arms like I weigh nothing. Not like someone with a twisted leg and several hundred layers of emotional baggage.

"Put me down," I protest, instantly squirming.

"You can barely breathe without wincing. Save your energy," Ajax says flatly, already walking.

"This is humiliating," I mutter. "And unnecessary. I can limp."

"You'd bleed out before we made it two feet."

"Oh, good. I love optimism."

We move through the trees, the forest dappled in red moonlight now.

Ajax walks like he's memorized every root and curve of the land—fluid and silent, his arms steady. His chest is solid beneath me, and unfortunately warm.

My heart flutters.

Stupid traitorous body doesn't know this man is allegedly the enemy.

"I'm not going to be one of you," I blurt.

His brow twitches. "What?"

"I heard what you said. In my dream. That I'd 'be one of you.' Not happening."

He stops and slowly, lowers me onto a mossy rock.

Then he looks at me. *Really* looks at me.

"You remember?" he asks.

My stomach flips.

"I don't know what you're talking about," I lie.

He lets out a dry laugh, not amused. "You're unbelievable."

"Excuse me?"

"How many times have you been shown the truth?" he snaps. "How many times have you looked it straight in the eye—felt it in your bones—and still, *still,* you cling to whatever version of reality is easiest to swallow?"

"That's not fair," I say through gritted teeth. "Believe what, exactly?"

Ajax opens his mouth, but something snaps behind us.

A low growl follows.

Then comes the sound.

Heavy footsteps. Branches breaking. Wet snorts.

Bears.

Big ones.

And I'm pretty sure they're not here for berries.

Ajax turns toward the sound, and something ripples through him.

Bones shift. Limbs stretch.

And right in front of me, he changes.

Fur erupts across his skin. His body expands, his legs thickening, arms reshaping. His face elongates into a muzzle, and glowing amber eyes flash from the wolf's massive head. His body is colossal, sleek and deadly.

I gasp.

Okay. Definitely not your average golden retriever.

One of the bears charges.

Ajax meets it mid-air.

They crash with a roar, fangs flashing.

The other bear moves for me, and I stumble back, adrenaline taking over.

My hands scramble for something, *anything*.

I find a stick.

It's not sharp.

It's not even sturdy.

If anything, it's a twig pretending to be helpful.

The bear roars again, but before it can reach me, Ajax finishes the first and lunges at the second, claws tearing.

The bear howls in a way that twists my stomach, then it vanishes into the trees.

I'm left panting, holding my sad little stick like it's a powerful wand.

Ajax shifts back, panting, blood on his arms and chest—not his, I think.

I hope.

He looks at the stick. Then at me.

"What exactly were you planning to do with that?" he deadpans.

I toss it to the ground and glare at him. "I don't know. Whittle a spear. Distract them with interpretive dance. Hypnotize him. Something."

The corner of his mouth almost twitches.

He walks toward me again.

"No," I say. "Seriously. Don't even think about it. I'm not some lost princess you need to rescue."

"Oh, I know you're not a princess." He chuckles dark and low. "But you're bleeding."

He lifts me again like it's the easiest thing in the world. "Don't worry. I'll take you back to your beloved school. But only after you're healed."

"That'll take weeks!"

"Ah," Ajax says, his voice light with amusement. "Weeks. That's a good one."

I blink. "What's that supposed to mean?"

But he doesn't answer.

* * *

We arrive sometime before the next moon cycle.

At first, I think Ajax has brought me to a village. But it's not that organized. More like a loose-knit community—canvas tents and rough wooden cabins nestled deep in the trees, smoke curling into the pale sky. A scattering of lanterns glow like fireflies. Somewhere, someone's playing a lute.

Children run past us, giggling. One of them has twitching wolf ears poking out of her tangled hair.

I blink.

Another tosses a carved stick like it's a spear and lets out a howl before chasing after her friends.

Ajax strides straight through it all with me in his arms like an oversized sack of potatoes.

"Put me down," I mutter. "I'll hop."

He snorts. "I've seen you 'hop,' Trouble. You tripped over your own legs trying to escape your own shadow."

"That was *once*."

"Not taking the risk."

I hate that he's right.

My pride smolders while the rest of me sags in relief. Still, it's hard to act tough when you're being carried like a damsel in a woodland fairytale gone sideways.

As we pass the campfire, heads turn.

"There he is!" someone shouts. "The brooder returns! This time, with a *treat!*"

I gulp.

"You're not cannibals, are you?" I whisper.

Ajax gives me a look that's half disgusted, half bewildered.

"No," he says flatly. "We are not *academy staff*."

Someone laughs. "Wow. Has he said more than five words? Alert the Elders, he's not our Ajax!"

"Maybe he got hit in the head."

"Maybe he likes her."

Ajax ignores them all. His jaw tightens, eyes fixed forward.

But me? I stare like an idiot.

These people—these wolf shifters—aren't the monsters I expected. No dragon-skin cloaks. No glowing red eyes. Just regular people. Laughing. Cooking. Sharpening weapons and telling jokes.

Ajax lowers me to a sit on a huge log by the campfire, a dull ache spreads over my leg as I shift it, and the log is so lumpy it would be more comfortable to sit on the ground.

A dark-haired woman appears at my side and hands me a steaming wooden mug. The scent is earthy and rich, something like herbs and honey.

Another woman—old, with a friendly smile and short cropped, white hair—hands me a plate of actual food. "Here you go, love. You look half-starved."

I look at the bowl in my hands. Real food.

A slab of roasted meat.

Tough, rich, possibly venison. A handful of roasted nuts. A smear of something savory and tangy on the side.

I don't ask questions. I just bite in.

The flavor explodes on my tongue—smoke, salt, garlic, something wild and gamey and good.

I groan softly before I can stop myself.

Ajax raises an eyebrow. "Better than the glue they feed you at the Academy, isn't it?"

I wipe my mouth, trying to look indifferent even as I shovel in another bite.

"It's edible," I say, around a mouthful.

He smirks. "That's your second helping."

"It's... protein. I need fuel."

He doesn't push it, just sits next to me, cupping his own bowl of food.

When I'm done, I gulp down my drink and sit back. I nearly melt from relief.

My legs throb. My head buzzes. But my belly is full and warm.

"Who *are* these people?" I murmur.

Ajax motions lazily to an old man with his black hair tied in a knot at the top of his head. The lights of the flames dance across his weathered skin and illuminates a kind smile. "That's Darnan. Veteran tracker. He could find a ghost in a blizzard."

The man gives me a nod, his pale eyes crinkling at the corners.

"The girl with the silver braid is Selah. She's a healer. Best one we've got."

Selah raises her mug in greeting.

"And the guy covered in rings?"

Ajax grimaces. "That's Ryn. He's a thief. He has the fastest hand and can make himself invisible."

Ryn grins and winks at me.

I let out a breath. "They're not what I expected."

"What did you expect? A pack of dogs?" Ajax asked, with a dark laugh.

I pause.

I hadn't thought much about the dragon hunters.

They were the enemy. Dangerous. People or... things to avoid.

"I don't know," I reply, honest.

We sit for a while, listening to the crackle of the fire.

The warmth seeps into my skin. The lute music floats through the air like a lullaby, and a sleepiness washes over me, relaxing my muscles.

I don't realize I'm swaying slightly until someone speaks.

"You've come from Theridon, haven't you?" Darnan asks, his voice gruff.

I nod, guarded.

He glances at Selah. Something unspoken passes between them.

"Poor girl," she murmurs. "They never tell you what it really is, do they?"

I lean forward and rest my elbows on my knees. "What do you mean? It's a dragon rider school."

"Sure. Sure." Darnan leans forward, hands out to the flames. "Did they tell you about the first humans who bonded with dragons? About how it twisted them?"

Ajax is silent beside me.

"*What* twisted them?"

"The magic," Darnan says. "They went in full of hope. Young. Brave. When they came back... they weren't human anymore. Sure, they had powers, but it made them evil."

Riders and Hunters

I open my mouth, then close it.

No one at Theridon talked about the first riders like that.

"We believe it's a curse," Ryn pipes up, fiddling with one of his rings. "A curse from the dragons. It spreads. Infects. And the only way to break it?"

"Kill the dragons," Selah finishes softly.

I stare into the fire, heart thudding. "That's why you hunt them."

They all nod.

"But Siberious said you're—"

"Ruthless? Terrorists?" Selah cuts in. "He would. He'd say dragons are to be protected. He's got his own plans."

I look at Ajax. "Plans?"

His eyes glitter in the firelight. "Control. He doesn't train riders. He *breeds* them. Fattened calves for the dragons."

"No," I whisper. "I don't believe that. I *can't*."

Besides, if they did want to fatten us up for dragons, they'd feed us better.

Darnan leans closer. "Has anyone gone missing lately?"

"No," I say slowly. "But..."

I chew on my lip. "A girl died. They said it was a heart attack."

My chest tightens.

I hadn't let myself question it, not really. But now?

I can't shake the memory of Char's pale, lifeless face. The blankness in her eyes. The way her body was untouched. Like nothing ever happened... Except everything had.

"She didn't have any injuries," I murmur, more to myself than anything. "There was no sign of a fight. No blood."

"Dragons don't leave a mark," Ajax says. "They don't eat flesh. They consume *souls*."

The fire cracks and spits.

My breath hitches.

"No," I say, but the word rings hollow.

Because I *remember*.

Char's eyes. Vacant. Not a scratch on her.

Just a shell.

And it happened not long after her public outburst.

Was she really drunk, or was she trying to warn us all of the terrible truth?

And something icy curls around my spine.

For the first time since arriving at Theridon, I wonder if I've been standing on the wrong side of the war.

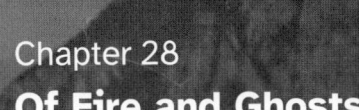

Chapter 28
Of Fire and Ghosts

The fire is down to glowing embers now, and the wolf shifters have long since retreated to their tents and cabins, their laughter and stories fading into the hush of the night. The forest has gone still again, so still it's like it's watching.

Ajax and I are the only ones left by the fire. Me, broken and half-baked, lying on a fur blanket with my leg splinted and my pride somewhere under a tree. And him, brooding, quiet, moonlit—like a statue carved from regret and forest shadow.

He crouches beside me, checking the bindings on my leg, and I can't help but notice the scars on his knuckles.

Deep. Raw.

Not the kind you get from one unlucky punch. The kind that comes from survival. From bare-handed fights. From years of rage with nowhere to go.

"What happened?" I ask before I can stop myself. "To your hands?"

Ajax doesn't look at me. "Life."

Oh, well. That clears everything up.

He adjusts the splint, and I wince.

"You'll want to bite on something," he mutters.

I raise an eyebrow. "What are you planning to do, kill me quietly?"

He holds out a thick stick. "I need to set the bone. Unless you want it healing twisted."

I glare at him. "I hate this."

"You'll hate walking worse if it heals wrong."

Ugh.

I bite the stick.

And then everything explodes.

White-hot agony tears through my leg, up my spine, and into every nerve in my body. Stars bloom behind my eyes.

I can't even scream—the stick is jammed too tight between my teeth.

My hands claw the blanket, my vision blurs, and for a horrifying moment, I think I might actually pass out.

When it's over, I'm sweating. Trembling. My breath comes in gasps.

Ajax doesn't say anything. He wets a cloth and presses it to my forehead. The coolness makes me want to cry.

"You're strong, Kayla," he says quietly. "You'll get through this."

And I don't know why, but that breaks me more than the pain. Because I haven't heard someone say that—not since Mom.

Not since the crash.

I shove the thought away before it can wrap around my throat.

He continues wiping my face gently, his calloused fingers warm against my clammy skin.

"How do you know me?" I whisper.

He's silent for a beat too long.

"You don't want the answer."

"Try me."

He sits back on his heels, tosses more wood on the fire, and watches the flames catch.

"I want to tell you a story," he says.

I fold my arms. "Why does everyone in this forest insist on telling me bedtime stories?"

"Because stories help simple minds like yours to listen to the truth without breaking them," he replies.

Fair.

He looks into the fire. "There was once a little wolf pup. Wild with a short temper. He had a brother—smaller, softer. They were everything to each other. For many moon cycles, they explored the forest going on adventures."

I lie still, watching his profile.

His voice is low, smoky, like he's whispering secrets to the flames.

"One day, the pack was attacked. Magical folk with pointed ears, men who were half-man, half-horse. Other creatures too. Were they there to hunt the wolves? Or did the wolves just get in the way of their plans? No one knows. Everything burned. The pups were separated. The little wolf found his brother again... just in time to watch him die."

I suck in a breath.

Ajax doesn't blink.

"The wolf's brother was his whole family. He buried him alone. And the pack didn't come back. He was ten."

My chest aches in a way that has nothing to do with my leg.

The fire frames Ajax's face in a golden glow, and long shadows cast over his troubled face.

I'm an absolute sucker for a wounded soldier. I resist the urge to take his hand.

But Ajax isn't done, he takes a swig of his drink.

"For a long time, the little wolf boy hated the world. Thought it had taken everything. But eventually... he found something. Not someone. Just... something. The way the wind moved through the trees seem to echo the past. The way certain places triggered moments long passed. He realized... his brother wasn't truly gone."

He finally looks at me. The firelight flickers in his eyes.

"The magic in this world carries memory. Echoes. If you listen long enough... sometimes, it speaks back."

He holds my gaze and gives me a pointed look, as if this cryptic story was supposed to unlock something inside of me.

But I'm just as clueless as before.

He's the wolf boy. That much I got.

And like me, he's all alone. I lost a sister. He lost a brother.

Maybe we aren't so different after all.

I stare into the flames, feeling hollow.

The colors converge together in swirls of red, black, and yellow. When the wind drifts, the flames flicker and...

I see her.

A flash of flaming red hair.

A girl, running between the trees on the other side of the camp.

I sit up straight, a thought hitting me square between the eyes.

No. No, that's not—

"Shelby?" I whisper.

The girl disappears into the tree growth.

I push myself up, panic crashing over me. "Shelby!"

The pain in my leg spikes so hard I nearly black out.

I fall back with a yelp.

But I land on Ajax's chest. His arms are around me in a second, bracing me.

"Easy. You really are trouble, aren't you?"

"I saw her," I gasp, heart hammering. "My sister. She was right here."

His jaw tightens.

"She's gone," he says softly.

"You don't know that," I snap.

"I do."

I give him a deep frown. "You don't know me. Stop pretending you do. You don't know what happened..."

He doesn't let go of me as I wrestle to break free. Then he says three words that make me freeze.

"I was there."

My blood turns to ice as my brain connects the dots. Is he really taking about...?

"The plane crash?"

He nods once.

I've replayed that crash a million times in my mind. It was always a dragon that pulled me out of the wreckage. Not a... not a...

My mouth drops open, and a fresh memory opens out like a flower blooming in my head. There *was* a dragon, flying in the sky above me, while I lay on the hot desert earth in the San Tan Mountains.

But something *else* dragged me from the wreckage. Something big, with a snout and paws.

Brown fur, gold eyes.

"*You* saved me." The words come out like a statement more than a question.

Ajax's jaw bulges, and he averts his gaze.

"I tried."

The fire flickers.

I can't breathe.

Then I look at the place where I saw Shelby running into the trees. "You saw her? My sister?"

He nods again. "I got her out, too. She was unconscious but... she never woke up."

I cover my mouth.

The sob escapes before I can stop it.

"I didn't know for sure. I mean, I remembered falling, and being alone outside the burning plane, but I always wondered—"

"She was already gone," Ajax says, firm. "Shelby didn't suffer."

My chest caves in. "You knew her name?"

"You cried out for her in your sleep."

"When?"

Ajax chews his lip. "I sat with you. At the hospital. For months."

I stare at him.

How the heck was a wolf shifter in my world? How did the hospital allow him to visit me?

How don't I remember any of this?

Ajax continues. "Before you ever saw me, I saw you. I've been watching over you since the crash."

My heart twists violently. "Why?"

He looks at me, eyes haunted. "I can't explain. Not fully. In short, I made a vow."

Tears spill down my cheeks. "I don't understand. None of this makes any sense."

"You don't need to understand. Not yet." His sights lower to my broken leg.

I want to argue. But I'm too tired. Too broken.

The pain, the memories, the truth—it's all too much, and I want to slip into sleep.

Ajax settles me back onto the blanket. His hand brushes my hair back.

"All right, Trouble, time to rest," he says, his voice sounding amused for once.

I let my eyes close, listening to the crackling fire and smelling his warm scent.

Sleep takes me.

And for the first time since I can remember, I don't dream.

Chapter 29
The Return and the Divide

I wake to voices.

Low. Urgent. Carried on the wind like whispers in the trees.

The tent flap shifts slightly, and with it, more sound filters in—frustration, argument, and... my name.

"She can't stay here. It's too risky."

"She's healed. We send her back to her school before they come looking."

A beat of silence.

Then Ajax's voice, firm and unshakable.

"No. She stays. She deserves the truth. She's already in this, whether she knows it or not."

Well, okay then.

I blink up at the ceiling of the tent, disoriented and slightly dizzy.

Ajax must have carried me inside.

The fire's long since died down to embers outside.

I move to sit up and half expect the pain to slice through my leg like a knife again. But it doesn't.

It aches, sure. But it's a dull throb. Manageable.

Cautiously, I swing my legs off the cot and lower my feet to the ground. I straighten up slowly, testing my weight.

Still no pain. Just pressure.

"Huh," I say aloud. "That was fast."

I shuffle toward the tent's entrance, poke my head out, and spot Ajax by the fire.

His arms are crossed, and he looks like he's two seconds from punching someone in the face.

He turns as I step fully into view.

I spread my arms, wobbly but upright. "Ta-da. Healed. Apparently."

He raises an eyebrow, then smirks, his expression brightening. "That's magic for you."

I grin despite myself. "Magic isn't so bad, right?"

Ajax's nose wrinkles, like I said a bad word. But he doesn't argue. He can't.

Without magic, I'd be hobbling around with a crutch, not much use in a war between dragon riders and wolves.

I notice the people from last night are around the fire, mid-discussion.

Their eyes snap to me. Not hostile, just wary. Like they were talking about me—which they definitely were.

Ajax gestures for me to join, but I don't sit.

"Listen, I appreciate the mystical healthcare plan,

but I need to get back. My friends have no idea where I am. They could be in danger."

"You're not going back," says a younger shifter with shaggy hair and too many piercings. "Not yet."

"Excuse me?"

Ajax steps forward, hands up in a peacekeeping gesture. "What Kai means is—stay. Just a little longer. Let us show you what's really happening, and you can make your own choice."

I cross my arms. "I've seen plenty. Dragons, curses, creepy tree monsters."

I'm more than ready to put as much space between me and the forest as possible.

Besides, after a good sleep, things seem clearer to me now.

Ajax is a stalker. The dragon saved me, not him. And now he and his pack are telling stories to lure me into their trap.

No. I won't fall for it. I'll go back to school, and with the help of Bo and Mari, I'll uncover the truth. The whole truth. And go from there.

Ajax shakes his head. "You've seen glimpses. Bits of broken mirrors. There's more—Siberious is hiding things. About Theridon. About the riders. About *you*."

"Me?"

Ajax walks up to me and towers. His shadow covers me, and I look up at him, with a nervous jitter in my stomach. "You might be trouble, but you're not powerless. The academy is lying to you."

I laugh, bitter. "Me? Powerful? Says who?"

Ajax crosses his arms. "Who told you that you had no magic?"

I hesitate. "Uh... Ms. Mauve."

The entire group tenses. But Ajax?

He goes completely still. His expression darkens like a storm rolling in over the hills. He balls his fists so tightly his knuckles go white.

"She's worse than Siberious," he growls.

A chill trickles down my spine. "You're joking, right?"

Mauve has a questionable approach to discipline and can come off as a bit harsh. But worse than Siberious?

No. I don't see it.

Ajax doesn't answer.

And I don't think I want to hear what he'd say if he did.

Images flash through my mind—Ms. Mauve gripping a student's arm in the hall that night. The way her eyes were cold, calculating. Char's body, lifeless, found shortly after, and Mauve nowhere to be seen the next morning.

I still don't know what it means. But the pieces are shifting.

Before I can dwell on it, a shadow falls across the clearing.

I glance up.

Dragons.

Three of them, massive and graceful, gliding through the clouds like silent sentinels. Their wings slice the air, their eyes gleam like stars.

Riders and Hunters

The wolves tense, muscles tight, breaths held.

All except Ajax. He watches them with something unreadable in his eyes.

"Do you think my dragon is up there?" I murmur.

"Yes," he says quietly. "But they're keeping their distance until...."

"Until what?" I demand, sensing Ajax's hesitation.

He gives me a strange look. "Until you make a choice."

The hair on my arms stands up. "A choice between what?"

"Truth and illusion."

I open my mouth to respond, but a howl rips through the trees.

It's close.

The camp scrambles.

Wolves leap to their feet, grabbing weapons, calling to each other in growled commands.

I stumble back, heart thundering. "What's happening?"

Ajax moves in front of me protectively.

But what bursts from the brush isn't a monster. Or an enemy.

It's Bo.

Sword drawn, hair windblown, eyes wild.

Mari is right behind him, her wand sparking with magic, mouth open in a battle cry.

"Back away from her!" Bo shouts.

Mari hurls a bolt of energy. It explodes against a tree, sending leaves raining down.

I throw my hands up. "Seriously?"

Bo skids to a halt, sword raised. His eyes lock on me.

I wave. "Hi. You can relax now. I'm not being murdered."

Mari nearly crashes into his back, panting. "What do you mean, not being murdered?"

"I'm fine," I say, arms still raised. "No murder here. Just... hospitality."

Ajax steps forward, hands on his hips. "Is this how you always show up to parties? Weapons blazing and zero intel?"

Bo glares. "Are you the guy who let her get dragged off into the woods?"

"Are you the friend who almost made her fall off a cliff?"

"Touché," Mari mutters.

Bo turns to me. "You've been with *him* all this time? Kayla. He's the enemy."

"He saved me. Twice."

Bo's jaw tightens. "We've been searching for you nonstop."

Ajax shrugs. "Could've tried harder."

Bo points his sword, the tip is a hair's width from his chin. "Say that again."

I sigh. "Cool it, you too. You both sound like characters in Mari's love story."

Mari snorts. She stuffs her wand in her holster, clearly sensing that there's no danger here. "So true."

Before the situation can escalate further, there is a loud rumble, and the earth shudders beneath us.

Then another tremor ripples through the ground.

And then—*crack*.

The world splits. The earth opens like it's being torn in half.

A magical pulse rips through the air, flinging us backward.

I hit the ground hard, the wind knocked out of me.

When I manage to sit up, the entire camp is chaos.

A wide chasm now splits the clearing in two.

The wolf shifters are on the far side, shouting and scrambling to regroup.

And on our side?

Bo. Mari. Ajax. And me.

The four of us alone.

"Well," I mutter, coughing. "That can't be good."

Ajax helps me to my feet. His face is pale, jaw clenched.

"We need to move," he says.

"Where?"

"Anywhere but here. The tremors, they're not natural. Someone's trying to separate us."

Mari spins, wand raised. "Is it the dragons?"

Bo swears under his breath. "This is a trap. It has to be."

Ajax's eyes narrow. "Not a trap. A test."

I glance at him. "How can you possibly know that?"

He doesn't answer, instead, he walks away with his hand resting on the hilt of his sword.

"Are you coming, or not?" he calls over his shoulder, his eyes darting in Bo and Mari's direction before landing on me.

I exchange a nervous look with Bo and Mari, then the ground trembles again.

With a shrug and a flurry of nervousness, we follow Ajax. Really hoping that we're not three little lambs being led to the slaughter.

Chapter 30
The Moon and the Nest

We walk in a tense silence for what feels like an age.

My leg is healed, but my muscles throb.

I'm so over walking and running.

Clouds roll over the stars in a sweeping hush, and an enormous orange moon rises, low and eerie. It casts strange shadows that stretch like ink bleeding across the ground.

And then those dang shadows start to move.

At least. That's what it looks like.

I stop and tilt my head, squinting at my shadow stretched out, long and distorted.

The shadow me waves even though my hands are still.

"That's not creepy at all," I mutter.

The group halts.

"No one moves," Ajax barks.

We freeze, with bated breath.

But our shadows make jerky movements, and the sight turns my stomach.

Mari hisses something under her breath as she takes out her wand. "Is anyone else seeing this?"

Bo swears. "This is not good."

I turn to him. "You've seen these things before?"

He nods grimly. "They're called the Hollowed. They're dark spirits trapped in the forest. They don't belong to a body, so they try to claim yours instead."

"Say what, now?" Mari squeaks, her face turning a sickly shade of white.

I swallow. "Oh, wonderful."

Ajax hacks through overgrown plants, revealing a hidden path.

"This way," he yells and steps through.

Before Bo can move, the shadow nearest to him detaches, pulling itself up like black sludge. It whips toward him, claws slashing.

My stomach twists at the ugly sound of ripping leather and flesh.

The scent of blood, hot and metallic, fills the air.

Bo cries out, staggering away.

But the shadow monster is not done with him. It lunges toward him.

Bo deflects it with his sword, the moonlight glances off the blade, and the creature screeches.

It shrinks out of the light and reforms in the darkness.

I suck in a breath. "Light is their weakness."

Another shadow detaches from mine.

It claws its way toward me like a nightmare coming alive.

I duck, roll, and kick it.

But then it grapples my ankles and slithers up my legs.

A burning pain sneaks up my thighs, every nerve is on fire as this disgusting thing is leaching me.

I try to wrestle free, but it's hopeless.

The beast is like smoke with claws, and it laughs. With *my* voice.

But it's twisted my voice to sound menacing. It strangles my throat and fills me with dread.

"Nope! Nope, nope, NOPE!" I wriggle away, my butt sliding mere inches despite my efforts.

Being attacked by my own freaking shadow that also laughs like me is more than enough to traumatize me for life.

Mari dashes over to me, she mutters a spell, and her wand glows like a flashlight.

My freaky shadow screeches like a wounded banshee and shrinks back, but hovers close by.

"Stop fighting and RUN!" Bo shouts, his arm hangs awkwardly as he limps to us. "You can't kill your own shadow."

"But your shadow can kill you," Mari adds, her eyes wide with terror at his arm.

Thick drops of blood trail his arm and fall to the ground like rain.

Her wand trembles. "Bo…"

He cradles his arm and shrugs away. "I'll be fine, just keep the light on and protect Kayla."

Ajax grunts, and the ground jolts as he's dragged to the ground, landing heavy and sudden.

Bo reaches out, spreading his fingers wide, and a golden tendril of light soars from him toward Ajax.

The shadow uncoils him and shrinks back.

I offer him my hand.

A flash of something crosses his brooding eyes. A mixture of distrust and surprise.

"Come on," I urge him through gritted teeth.

After a splinter of hesitation, Ajax grabs my forearm.

I hold him firm and yank on him.

He's back on his feet, and we're still holding each other, standing nose to nose.

He lets out a breath, it mists my cheeks, and a rush of tingles scatters over my body starting from my face, reaching all the way to the butterflies in my stomach.

Then, the contact is broken, and we rejoin Bo and Mari.

Ten or more Hollowed surround us, keeping just out of Mari's light.

With a final nod, we bolt.

Which is great. Because all I wanted to do after a day of walking is run at full pelt.

The trees blur in my peripheral vision. The world becomes branches and moonlight and screaming lungs.

But past the pain, something's different.

I'm fast.

Like, *really* fast.

My feet don't trip. My legs move like they were built for this.

Riders and Hunters

I leap over fallen logs like I've done it a thousand times. I don't even think, my body just knows what to do.

And then there's the senses.

I can smell the damp bark. The sickly-sweet ozone in the air. The fear-sweat clinging to Ajax's temples.

I can hear everything—the scrape of claws on bark behind us, the fluttering heartbeats of Mari and Bo beside me, the faint rustle of something stalking us from above.

None of it makes sense.

But I don't stop.

Is this what a major adrenaline surge feels like?

We break through the last line of trees.

"Whoa!"

The forest ends.

The ground beneath our feet drops away into a rocky basin—an enormous valley of steep crags and cliffs.

We skid to a halt, winded and wide-eyed.

Mari peers down. "That's... not an ideal place to fall."

Ajax frowns. "We've gone too far."

A tremor has us scrambling, and the ground crumbles beneath us.

I cry out and stagger backward, but the four of us stumble forward and tumble all the way down the slope.

The ground is hard. It beats me. Hard.

Elbow. Knee. Shoulder. Repeat.

We tumble, down, down...until we land at the bottom in a pile.

Groaning, we get to our feet and look around.

Bo cries out. But it sounds more angry than hurt.

He's holding his arm, biting his bottom lip with a grimace.

Ajax marches to him. "Your shoulder is dislocated."

Bo backs away and holds a glowing palm out to him. His pointed ears flash red.

"Keep away from me, wolf," he spits.

Ajax inclines his head and registers him for a moment. But then he ignores Bo's protests and grabs his hand and shoulder. "Try to relax, or this will hurt a lot more than it needs to."

Bo opens his mouth to retort, his brows knitted together, but a stomach-turning crack echoes in the air, and Bo floods the heavens with curses.

"Keep your voice down, fae," Ajax mutters.

Bo's red face matches his ears, and his voice lowers to a grumble.

I breathe and share a nervous glance with Mari.

Then we look around.

"Can anyone see a way out?" Mari asks.

There's a huge wall of rock surrounding us, too high and awkward to climb without rope.

All around us lay massive circular nests made of sticks, bones, and gnarled roots.

I squint.

There's something peeping out the nests. Glowing faintly in shades of gold, blue, and red.

I gasp.

"Are those...?" Bo starts to say.

Ajax's curt nod fills me with dread.

"Oh no," I whisper.

"Dragon eggs," Mari whispers.

She pulls out her wand again.

The eggs look like giant molten stones. Glossy. Cracked with firelight glowing from the inside.

We've fallen into a dragon nursery.

And we are so not on the guest list.

"Well, it was nice knowing you all," I say, resigned. "Where there are dragon eggs, there are dragon babies. And that means the big angry dragon mommas are not far away."

Ajax crouches and speaks in a hushed voice. "Everyone, don't move. Not one step more."

"Why not?" I whisper back. "Our chances of survival just dropped to one percent. There's nothing to lose now. So, why not make a run for it? Maybe Mari can magic us a ladder...or levitate us to the top?"

I look to her, hopeful.

She gives me a hopeful nod and lifts her wand.

But Ajax looks at me with his eyes sharp and intense, and my stomach tightens.

His dark hair covers most of his brow but the sweat on his temples gleam in the moonlight.

"If those eggs hatch and a dragon sees you before its mother..."

Mari gasps. "They imprint?"

"No. They *attack*," Ajax says flatly. "Unless you're dragon-blooded, they see you as food."

He gives me a knowing look, and my breath gets stuck somewhere in my chest.

Char's soulless eyes flash before my mind's eye.

Bo mutters, "I don't like idea of sitting here and waiting for death. We need to get out. Now."

"I'm with Bo," I say. "Now, it's not the best idea, but how about we try making a human pyramid?"

The group stare at me with dead eyes. Even Mari doesn't crack a smile. But *come on*. That one was funny.

"Fine. But if you hear *any* movement from within those nests, hide," Ajax says through gritted teeth.

We tip toe in a tight line following Ajax, who takes us to the edge again.

A breath floods the basin, and the chill in the air evaporates.

I glance at Mari.

She gives me a worried look and holds out her wand.

Bo mutters a stream of curse words.

"Do you hear that? Wings."

Bursts of wind flood the space as we hear flapping.

Something big is on the approach and...

The air is growing hotter by the second.

Mari nods to me.

I try to scale the side and sense an invisible force holding me at the hips. But when the wall steepens, something snaps, and I tumble back to the group.

"What happened?" I turn to Mari.

Her curls are frizzing at the ends, and she gives me a teary look. "I'm so sorry. Magic is energy... and I guess with all of the running, I'm too tired to carry you."

I swallow.

Ajax scrambles up the side but loses his footing and slides all the way down again.

Bo makes a valiant attempt, using his light lasso as a rope, with the end anchored into the side of the wall.

But the ground shakes again, and the wall crumbles away, leaving him to fall back again.

We look to one another, lost for words at this point.

And then my palm burns. Agonizing, blazing heat.

I hiss and clamp my teeth.

It's like the moment that dang necklace burned me.

Only ten thousand times hotter.

I yank off my glove and fall to my knees.

"Kayla," Mari whispers. "Your hand..."

The spiral symbol on my skin—the one that flared to life during orientation when the sky zapped me? Yeah. It's glowing again. Bright. Fierce. Like someone lit a flare beneath my skin.

I bite on my lip until it bleeds to stop a scream.

Ajax takes a worried step closer to me but pauses under Bo's glare.

Then Bo crouches next to me, face full of concern.

"I don't know what this means." Like he's

surprised that for once, there's nothing in his mental archives to explain this.

Ajax eyes it like he's seen a ghost. "I do."

"Cool," I say tightly.

Tears well in my eyes as the burning reaches unbearable levels. But I refuse to cry. "Then would someone please explain?"

Before he can, a roar splits the sky with a flash of lightning. Rain pours down. Freezing. Gloriously so.

Within seconds, we're drenched.

But the burning in my hand dulls enough to let me hold it up to the sky and get back on my feet.

The ground shakes. More rocks tumble from above.

I throw my arms over my head.

A cloud of dust covers my vision, and for a second, I think we're being buried alive.

But three massive shapes cut through the dust cloud from above, surrounded by rain.

My mouth drops open, as I take it all in.

Wings like sails.

Scales glinting like armor in the moonlight.

Droplets glisten like diamonds.

"Dragons," Ajax says, voice low.

His hand hovers over the hilt of the knife at his waist.

Bo and Mari exchange nervous looks.

"There are three... maybe they're ours," Mari whispers, sounding hopeful.

Bo nods, silent, but his eyes flash with something uncertain.

"What happens to us if these are not our dragons?"

I've never asked the question before. I never thought to.

Ajax sneers at the approaching beasts. "You better pray they are yours. Or they will feed us to their young."

My stomach twists.

We stand shoulder to shoulder, soaked and shivering. But no one backs down.

It's clear that whatever happens next, we won't go down without a fight.

But the closest dragon hovers right above me, gusts of wind press us so hard, we fall to our knees.

I drop my knife.

I don't feel like fighting.

The tattoo on my collarbone pulses, and the mark on my palm glows.

For the first time in my life, I'm not afraid.

I feel... drawn. Calm.

The red dragon at the front lands surprisingly soft and controlled, its claws dig into the stone with a crunch. Its wings furl in a graceful arc as it approaches—slow, careful.

And then it locks eyes with me.

A pulse of heat rushes down my arms and everything tingles. No. Not tingle, vibrates. *Everything*.

Like every single atom in my body is shaking at a speed so fast, so intense, I'll explode.

My breath catches.

Is this what it feels like when a dragon consumes a soul? Is this what Char felt?

The vibration subsides, but only a little.

I'm left feeling stronger, recharged. I stand, face to face with the beast.

My body moves on autopilot. I am no longer in control.

The dragon is impossibly big. With an infinity of dangerously sharp and beautiful scales. Scales of red and black and gold along the underbelly.

Yet, this formidable creature has an unmistakable presence and despite everything, I'm completely unafraid.

A memory flashes before my mind. The shadow outside the plane as it descended. The intrinsically detailed outline of it, as it circled the sky above me.

"I've seen you before," I whisper.

The dragon's eyes glimmer with a deep, old fire.

I step closer, and the huge eyeball swallows up my vision. I'm met with a picture of swirling stars. It's like the dragon holds an entire galaxy in its eye.

I take another step forward.

None of our classes prepared us for this.

We've studied theory. History. Magic. We've trained with wooden sticks and riddles and obstacle courses. The dummy dragons are an insult to the real ones.

But no one ever said what happens when your dragon finds you.

The dragon lifts its head and stares—stares—at Ajax.

Then my heart races.

Ajax is the enemy. A dragon hunter.

There is no telling what a dragon would do.

I remember what the teachers have told me at Theridon. Magic is about intention.

Maybe I can't turn water into ice. Or make a magic potion.

Maybe I can't even win in hand-to-hand combat.

I know I definitely couldn't win a fight with a dragon.

But maybe, just maybe...

I can use magic to communicate with a dragon.

My palm burns again.

My dragon.

I take a deep breath and focus all of my energy on the dragon's beautiful eyeball.

Then I speak. In my head.

Did you choose me?

I let the question hang and wait.

The dragon does not stir but keeps its gaze on Ajax.

Then, a female voice—not my own—fills my soul.

It's just one word, but the strength of it is like the sound of a waterfall, and it floods me with a sense of power and knowing.

Yes.

Chapter 31
Chosen

Emotion bubbles to my chest, and my nostrils flare as I bite back tears. But there's no time to dwell on it.

I focus my thoughts on the dragon again.

These are friends, not foes. Do you understand?

The dragon and Ajax hold each other's gaze.

The moment stretches taut like a bowstring.

I can't decide if the dragon is thinking about bonding with Ajax too or incinerating him on the spot.

Ajax gives a single, curt nod, as though they were having their own private conversation.

I blink.

Can he talk to her too?

A flicker of jealousy rises up, but I shove it down with a hard swallow.

Then the dragon turns back to me.

Get on my back. All of you.

"She wants us to get on." I glance over my shoulder.

Mari's wand droops slightly. "What about...?"

Her gaze shifts toward the other two dragons, nestled protectively in their nests. Their eyes glow dimly, but they are still and frozen, like statues.

My heart aches at the devastation on Bo's face.

He stares at the dragons like they've betrayed him.

I turn back to mine.

My dragon.

Even thinking it sends a thrill down my spine.

Are they not bonded to my friends? I ask.

A low, distant roar rumbles behind us.

No, she replies. *But they listen to me. I cannot say the same for the others.*

Another flash of lightning.

We turn.

A hoard of dragons crests the edge of the clouds, their massive wings slicing through the storm.

At least eight. Maybe more. All of them midnight-scaled and broad-shouldered, their claws flexing as they descend. There's nothing warm in their approach. They don't glide. They *prowl* through the air.

These are not welcome-party dragons, that's for sure.

They are hunters. And... we're the prey.

Smoke curls from the red dragon's nostrils.

Get on. Or stay here and burn.

"She really doesn't do small talk," I murmur. "She wants us to climb on."

"Well, she's got her priorities right," Mari mutters, already halfway up the dragon's leg like she's been climbing dragons her whole life.

Bo follows, though he slips near the shoulder.

"Graceful," Mari says dryly, as he joins her.

"Didn't realize my first time climbing a real dragon would be in the rain," he huffs.

I scurry up behind them.

My hands press into the warm, glassy scales. They almost hum beneath my palms, like her heartbeat syncs with mine.

Bo has a point.

My boots are slick with rain and mud, and I should slide right back down. But there's a magnetic energy that keeps me connected.

I climb to the top, swing my leg over, settling between two ridges that cradle me perfectly. Like they were made for me.

Mari grips my waist. "No sudden movements, right?"

"Well, don't fall. The way you have me in a death grip, if you go, I will too," I quip.

Ajax stays planted on the ground, arms folded like a statue carved out of butt-headedness.

I glare down at him. "Ajax. Get up here."

He doesn't budge. "I'd rather not put my life in the claws of a creature that could roast me alive."

The red dragon snorts.

You're testing my patience, Little Wolf.

He tilts his head slightly, as if he *heard* her, then shifts his glare to me.

"Did she just call me—?"

I bite back a laugh. "Yes."

"You sure she wasn't just talking to you?" he quips.

I frown at him, blinking rain out of my eyes. "Get. On. The dragon."

Behind him, the first of the dark dragons screeches, a bone-splitting, hollow cry that echoes down the cliffs like death's whistle.

The heat rolls over us in a wave.

Bo looks back. "Uh, Kayla? It would be really helpful if you could get your dragon to…you know…fly."

"On it," I call back.

"Ajax!" I shout. "Get your stubborn butt *up here* before your smolder becomes literal!"

He exhales. A sigh of pure exasperation. Like he's already regretting every decision that led him here.

But to my relief, he jogs forward, slipping once, catching a scale, then pulls himself up behind us.

"Finally," Mari grumbles.

"No one can know about this," he says, his eyes flashing dangerously at me.

I nod.

The wolf pack would probably brand him a traitor.

But there's no time to worry about that. This is life or death.

The red dragon lifts her wings slowly, like sails catching wind, and the air around us thickens with power.

Then we lift.

The storm drops beneath us.

The wind howls in my ears.

And the other dragons scream as they dive.

Riders and Hunters

But we're already flying.

Chapter 32
Sanctuary

The wind stings my cheeks as we fly.

Impossibly fast. Eerily silent.

But strangely—safe. And freeing.

My heart is galloping in my chest, but my soul feels still. Like something that was off-kilter has finally realigned.

It should be terrifying, soaring miles above forests and mountains on the back of a creature that could drop us or crisp us like bacon. But it's not terrifying.

It's *right*.

Below us, the trees blur into ribbons of silver and green, the moonlight painting the world in frost and shadow.

Mari clutches my waist like she's trying not to fall off a rollercoaster.

Bo's muttering what might be a prayer or a string of profanities.

Ajax, of course, is silent.

And then she speaks in my mind again.

Oh. Before I forget, you can call me Zephyros.

The voice isn't booming or guttural. It's calm. Measured. A little wry, like a teacher who's grading your paper while sipping tea.

I'm too busy holding on for dear life to channel a reply. So, Zephyros continues.

Or you can call me Zeph. Or Zephy. I used to be Lady Scales-a-Lot. It was a phase. We don't talk about it.

I smile.

You can call me Kayla.

Zephy's reply sounds firm, determined. *No. I shall call you Little Flame, the girl with a teeny-tiny mane of fire.*

Her words press a chuff of laughter out of me before I can hold it in.

"What?" Mari says, still holding me in a grip that will probably leave bruises.

"She's cracking jokes," I mutter.

"Jokes?" Mari parrots in surprise.

Zephyros–Zephy hums a low laugh in her throat, her wings dipping playfully.

I can also recite every line of a battle hymn and burn down a fortress with one breath, if you'd prefer that vibe. But I've found a little levity keeps me young.

I stare. *You're not what I expected.*

Zephy sighs in my mind.

I understand. No one ever expects a dragon with a sense of humor. We are a dying breed. It's incredibly difficult to find a mate. Most dragons value wisdom, or strength. Not sarcasm and sass.

My heart jolts, and everything falls into place.

If I hadn't known that this was my dragon, now I do. A well of emotion rises in my chest, and my eyes prickle.

We land on a high plateau in the mountains.

The air here is sharp and old, steeped in magic and silence. Mist drapes the cliffs like veils, and waterfalls gleam like silver threads in the moonlight.

Below us, nestled in a lush basin between three peaks, sits a hidden sanctuary. Circular pools shimmer in moonlight. Glowing runes pulse faintly from the stones. The whole place feels alive. Sacred.

"Whoa," Mari breathes. "This is..."

"Incredible," I whisper.

Bo mutters, "I'm not sold."

Still in a mood from not bonding with his dragon, I guess.

A twinge of guilt nips at me.

Zephy lowers her neck so we can slide off.

I hop off first. When my boots hit the ground, I feel energized and ready to face another adventure.

The mark on my palm only stings a little now.

Mari drops behind me and kisses the ground.

Bo flops dramatically onto a mossy rock, his chest heaving.

Ajax dismounts with ease, like Zephy is just a giant horse to him. He stands apart from the group, arms folded, eyes scanning every shadow.

"I have so many questions," I say, locking eyes with Zephy.

Then come, Little Flame, she replies in my mind. Her voice is warm and amused, but there's steel beneath it. *I have a lot to tell you, but let's begin with who you are.*

She slinks away from the clearing, the flicker of her tail guiding the path.

We follow until she brings us to a ring of ancient stones, overgrown with moss and vines. In the center, a fire burns low and steady, like it's been waiting for centuries.

Waiting for what? Who knows.

But it's giving me Indiana Jones vibes. I don't imagine a lot of humans or non-dragons get to see this place.

Mari squeals looking around. "Oh my gosh! This cave is so...magical. I can feel it in my bones!"

Bo snorts. "Magical? More like haunted." He folds his arms, his ears still red. "It gives me the creeps."

Zephy exhales softly, and I hear her sigh in my head. *They talk too much.*

I sense she's not going to give me any information with their bantering.

"Can you guys maybe grab some firewood or water? Give me a second."

Mari lifts an eyebrow. "You sure? I mean... are you safe to be left alone?"

Little Wolf stays.

I lift my brows at Zephy's response and meet

Ajax's frown with a smirk. "I guess we know who she was talking about earlier."

I turn to Mari. "I won't be alone. Ajax will be here."

Her gaze flickers to Ajax, and my brows lift in surprise at the way her eyes narrow on him with suspicion.

Once upon a time, Mari would have passed out with happiness at the idea of me spending some time alone with my dragon and a wolf shifter.

Now, she seems suspicious. More cautious.

Part of me pangs. I miss the innocent, hopeful Mari.

"I'm sure," I say with fervor.

"Fine, but if Kayla so much as twists an ankle, I'm hexing you," she says to Ajax, pulling Bo by the sleeve as he protests under his breath.

Once they disappear, Zephy coils around the fire, her scales glinting like burning coal.

Ajax lingers near the stones, arms folded, silent but ever present.

First things first, she says. *You already know you're not ordinary.*

"I mean, yeah," I say aloud. "Most people don't get zapped by sky lightning, start glowing, and have weird tattoos show up out of nowhere."

Zephy chuckles. *That mark is your bond. When you entered this realm, you awakened.*

"Awakened?" I parrot.

Your wolf magic was always there, dormant. But this land... the magic of dragons... it pulled it to the surface. You're not just human, Kayla. You never were.

I glance at Ajax. His expression is tight, jaw clenched.

My ears ring.

Wolf. Magic.

I look at him for answers.

Maybe I heard wrong. Maybe I'm imagining all of this.

Zephy's eyes gleam. *You were not supposed to survive that crash. But I opened a new path for you.*

I frown, not understanding.

Then Ajax steps in. "When your plane crashed, it opened a portal to this realm. That's how I was able to find you."

We both did. Zephy adds, sounding a little annoyed.

Ajax nods once. "I didn't know what you were then. But I knew you were... mine. I made a vow to protect you."

I try not to think about the word. *Mine*. It carries way too much weight.

"You imprinted," I murmur.

Mari will have a field day when she finds out that all this time she was right.

Ajax doesn't deny it. He just watches me like I'm still unraveling in front of him.

Zephy's voice coils around us again. *I watched you, Little Flame. Covering your grief with jokes. Drawing pictures of me in your notebook. I'll ignore the fact that most of those drawings gave me a disproportionately large belly.*

I can't figure out how a dragon can watch over me in my old world. Earth.

I never saw a shadow. Not since the day of the crash.

I run a hand over the glowing mark on my palm. The words bounce in my mind too fast to hold onto. "So, I'm bonded to both of you."

Yes.

"Dragon and wolf," I say, unable to grasp the weight of the fact.

Yes.

I look at Ajax, stunned.

He scratches the back of his neck. "This has never happened before. Wolves don't bond with dragons, and no one bonds to both."

I already figured that. But hearing it aloud hits harder. Like a weight settling onto my shoulders and refusing to leave.

I drag my hands on my face, my mouth is dry. I think I might pass out or throw up. Not sure which. Maybe both.

As if knowing exactly what I'm feeling, Ajax thrusts his water flask in my hands.

"Drink," he orders.

I take several greedy gulps, ignoring the musty taste and just focusing on the moment.

This is... too much.

If this is true, does Siberious know?

"No," Ajax replies for me. "If Siberious knew you're a wolf, you would be dead."

I shudder. "So, you can hear my thoughts, too?" I ask aloud.

Great. Just great. Nothing is sacred anymore.

Zephy keeps the focus on what is important.

You are the bridge between bloodlines that have spent centuries at war. The crack in the dam. You will bring both war and peace.

"I hate that that sounds poetic," I mutter.

Sorry, Zephy says dryly. *Would you rather I say; you're a target from both sides, many will fear you, most will want you dead, but if you come into your power, you can lead everyone to a world where dragons and wolves live in harmony?*

I squint at Zephy's starry eyes. Somehow, that's worse.

Footsteps crunch nearby.

Mari and Bo return with armfuls of wood and a canteen of water.

Bo eyes us warily.

Ajax and I watch them in awkward silence.

Don't tell them about this. Ajax's stern voice enters my mind.

I resist the urge to jump.

We can trust them. They're my only friends here.

Ajax's frown deepens.

Are you sure you trust him? He is Siberious's son. And she's a witch.

"So, what did your dragon tell you?" Bo asks, giving us a shrewd look.

Zephy snorts.

I smirk, then translate. "She says you're nosy."

Bo narrows his eyes.

Mari, glances between us. "So? What did she say?

Did she say where our dragons are? Why aren't they here?"

I look back at Zephy, who just blinks back. She doesn't even give me a single word.

"No," I say. "But she did tell me something...big." I glance at Ajax's severe expression and give him a shrug.

If you didn't want me to tell my friends, you shouldn't have told me. I glare at him.

"What? What is it?" Bo asks, looking from me to Ajax and scowling.

It's like he knows we're communicating in our minds, and he hates it.

I look at them, heart pounding.

"I'm...bonded to a dragon...and a wolf."

Mari's mouth opens. Closes. Opens again. Her cheeks flush, and her eyes sparkle. "I told you! Didn't I tell you? Oh, my freaking gosh! What if my story isn't fiction? What if..."

She clutches her cheeks in awe, with a faraway look on her face. "It's a *prophecy*."

Bo pinches the bridge of his nose while he rests his other hand on his hip. "I'm sorry, this is a lot to take in. You're bonded to this dragon and..."

"He's her mate. He imprinted on her," Mari says, nudging Bo with a tone as if to say, *Keep up, will you?*

I swallow. "Zephy—that's her name—she says I'm going to be a bridge between two enemies and, uh... bring peace to the realm."

Mari stares at me with wide, awe-filled eyes, speechless.

Bo is less enthused by the revelation. He turns to Ajax. "And you've just been, what? All this time you've been lurking in the shadows like her stalker?"

Ajax doesn't rise to it. "*Protecting* her."

"Sure," Bo mutters. "That's comforting."

Mari cuts in. "Okay. Tempers down. This is all such amazing news. There's no need to fight about it."

Bo throws up his hands. "Fine. Great. She's a bridge. Between enemies. Nothing could possibly go wrong. You know when Siberious finds out..."

Within a split second, Ajax is squaring up to him, his chest millimeters from Bo's. He fists his collar and growls. "But Siberious will not find out, will he? You will keep your mouth shut about this, or I'll silence you myself."

Bo wrestles free and staggers back. His eyes find mine for a moment, and my heart sinks. Behind defiance and anger, there's something so much worse.

Hurt.

"Is this what you want?" he asks me.

I stand frozen, my hands hanging helpless at my sides.

What I want? Do I even have a choice?

"Right. Okay, fine." Bo marches away, shoulders hunched.

Mari watches him go, her chest heaving. "I should check he's okay."

She looks to me, expectant. "What do you want to do? Come with us, or...?"

Her eyes flicker from Ajax to Zephy, unsure.

I look at Zephy. My dragon. At Ajax. My wolf.

At the fire. The future.

"I'll catch up with you," I mutter.

Mari nods, eyes soft.

I turn back to Zephy, but she nudges her nose against my chest. *Go with them. I want to talk to Little Wolf.*

Don't call me that. Ajax glowers.

Would you prefer Mr. Grumpy Pup? Zephy huffs smoke and tilts her head from side to side in a playful manner.

I resist a smile. "Zephy is a dragon. She can call you whatever she wants."

Ajax doesn't argue but still has a sour expression on his face.

Zephy is right, he is grumpy.

With a resigned wave, I leave the cave in search of Mari and Bo, trying not to think about what Ajax and Zephy could be talking about.

Bo's crouched near the edge of the fire, elbows on his knees, staring into the flames like they might tell him a better story than the one he's stuck in.

He doesn't look up when we arrive.

"Hey," I say gently, settling nearby. "That was... intense."

Mari kneels beside him, rummaging through her satchel. "You're bleeding."

"It's fine."

"You always say that," she mutters, already dabbing at his shoulder.

Blood stains the fabric of his shirt, a deep rust color now.

He winces. "It's not that bad."

"Then you won't mind taking off your shirt so I can clean it properly," she says, not looking up.

Bo grumbles something under his breath but pulls off his leather vest and yanks his shirt over his head.

I try to keep my expression neutral, but my eyes catch on the jagged wound slicing across his bicep. The blood is mostly dried, congealed in dark patches, but it still looks raw and painful.

Mari works in silence, pressing a damp cloth to the wound.

Bo hisses. "Could you try *not* to scrub the skin off?"

"If you wanted a gentle touch, you should've gotten yourself less mangled."

Then he shifts, turning his back slightly.

I freeze.

Two pale scars arc across his shoulder blades. Clean. Curved. Like they'd been made with precision. Not the kind of scars you earn in battle.

Mari gasps softly. "Bo...your wings."

He doesn't turn.

I swallow. "That's why you don't fly."

For a moment, all I hear is the fire, and Zephy's breathing behind us.

Then Bo says, voice flat, "Siberious clipped them. I was six."

Mari covers her mouth.

I stare. "Clipped them?"

He nods once. "He said wings made us weak. Made us long for freedom. He took them before we could even understand what we were losing."

A lump rises in my throat. "He did that to all of you?"

Bo's jaw clenches. "My brothers. My sister. None of us was spared."

Mari's hand stills on his shoulder.

"Why would you stay loyal to someone like that?" I ask before I can stop myself.

He finally turns his head, just enough to meet my gaze.

There's no fire in his eyes now. Only ashes.

"Pain teaches loyalty. One by one, my siblings rebelled against him. My father is an unforgiving fae. A ruthless king, even to his own flesh and blood. And... he's the only family I've got left."

Silence falls. Even the fire seems to quieten.

I hug myself, unable to comprehend his words.

Bo never once gave me the impression he had such a tortured past. One even darker than my own.

There are no words that can make it better, and even my snarky wit can't help.

So, I sit in silence.

After a while, Mari finishes tending the wound and helps him pull on a clean shirt.

Bo doesn't thank her. He just goes back to staring into the flames, eyes distant.

And somehow, I think that's the first honest thing I've ever heard him say.

I curl beside Zephy that night, her wing warm against my back like armor and shelter all at once.

Ajax keeps watch on the edge of the firelight. He

acts more like a bodyguard than a mate. Which is perfectly fine with me. Romance is the last thing on my mind tonight.

Are you okay, Little Flame? Zephy asks.

My brain is bursting with heavy information, and a whole book of new questions are on my mind. But it's too much to pick apart. Fatigue spreads through my body, making even a simple idea too overwhelming to think about.

"No," I whisper. "But I think I will be. What did you and Ajax talk about?"

Strategy. There is a war, and if we are to win and bring peace, we need you to be the strongest warrior there is.

I shut my eyes. *Sorry to disappoint, but I'm the worst person in the world to be a warrior. Uncoordinated, untalented...*

I pause as a hot mist of air rushes over me. One of Zephy's eyes hovers close.

Be kind to yourself, Little Flame. Words are held in the body. Those words will weaken you.

I fold my arms.

Maybe that's why I'm...

Another puff of hot air stops me in my tracks.

Careful, Zephy warns.

I swallow as I take in the weight of Zephy's advice.

Then I grit my teeth. *Fine. I will be a bridge between two enemies. A strong one. And no one will call me weak and untalented ever again.*

Good. Zephy nestles her face on the ground near me. *We train at dawn. I'll bring the fire. You bring the*

Little Wolf.

I crack a faint smile. "Do you ever stop being weird?"

Zephy lets out a low hum that rumbles the ground beneath me.

Never.

Chapter 33
Training and Totally Not Falling Gracefully

I never thought I'd be the kind of girl who trains with a sword while flying on the back of a dragon.

And I was right.

Because I suck at it.

"Hold it higher, Kayla!" Bo yells from the ground, shielding his eyes from the sun.

"I'm trying!" I shriek, clinging to Zephy's ridge with one arm while flailing my sword like I'm swatting at invisible flies. "Have you ever balanced on a moving furnace with wings while holding a glorified kitchen knife?"

I am majestic, thank you very much, Zephy chimes in. *And that's not a glorified kitchen knife. That's Starsteel. It once belonged to the Bladekeeper of Nethyx, I'd have you know.*

"Well, the Bladekeeper had better core strength than me!" I scream just before I slip off her back.

"KAYLA!" Mari's voice rises as her hands shoot out.

A cushion of magic catches me mid-air, slowing my descent like I'm being gently laid down by a particularly affectionate cloud.

I land with a soft oomph on the grass. My pride lands somewhere much harder.

"Third time today," Mari says, hands on hips. "I'm starting to think you're doing this just to make me feel useful."

"I like to keep morale high," I grumble, rolling onto my back.

Bo walks over, offering a hand. "Again?"

"Do I have a choice?"

You always have a choice, Zephy calls from above. *Just not a good one. If you don't learn to fight in the air, you're going to be plucked from my back and gobbled up in the next sky battle. There's only so much I can do to protect you, Little Flame.*

"I liked you better when you were quiet and mysterious," I grumble, wincing at the imagery.

Bo and I move to a flatter section of the field, swords in hand.

The red moon is high, the sky so blue it hurts, and I'm sweating through my training gear.

Bo, of course, looks like he just stepped out of a shampoo commercial. His freshly washed locks shimmering like actual gold. He rolls his shoulders and swings his sword like he never had any injuries at all. Much less a dislocated shoulder.

"Let's work on your grip." He steps closer. His fingers wrap around mine, adjusting the position of my hand. "And keep your stance wider. You'll have more balance that way."

His voice is low, focused. Kind.

It catches me off guard.

"You're surprisingly good at this."

He smirks. "Swordplay is my thing."

"Is that your only thing?"

His smile widens, cocky now. "Wouldn't you like to know."

I roll my eyes and swing at him.

He deflects, easily.

"Kayla," he says, parrying. "Do you trust me?"

I hesitate. My blade lowers an inch. "That's a weird question."

"Humor me."

"I—" My gaze flicks to where Ajax leans against a tree, arms crossed, watching. "I don't know."

Bo narrows his eyes. "What happened? With him?"

My head snaps back in his direction, and I lower my sword.

"You're awfully interested."

"Because I care," he blurts, then flushes red. "I mean—I care about the team. You're a liability if you're distracted."

"Oh, sure." I step forward, sword raised again. "Very convincing."

We spar again, blades clashing.

He's testing me.

I test him right back.

He shifts tactics. "Do you believe what the dragon said? About you. About Ajax being your... mate?"

"Her name is Zephyros," I correct. "Or Zephy."

I swing harder and shove him with my shoulder.

He blocks, but his stance falters.

Panting, I use the back of my hand to swipe the sweat from my brow. "I don't know what I believe."

"Strange," he says, backing up. "You usually have strong opinions about everything."

It's true, I guess. Usually, I do know my own mind. But here I am, caught in the middle of something that feels so much bigger than me. Than school. Bigger than dragons, too.

"Well, I'm sorry to disappoint you." I lunge.

Bo side-steps, and I cut the air with frustration.

"I'm just as lost as you are. But why do you want to know?"

Bo laughs, light and cool again. He blocks my attacks with ease. The clash of steel grates on my ears.

"I told you the day we met. I know things. Knowledge is power. And I'd say the answers to my questions might be the most powerful knowledge there is."

I glare. "Then you're going to be very disappointed."

He catches my blade and twists it from my grip. "Already am."

I grunt, annoyed, and reach down to pick it up.

"You know," I say, glancing at Ajax. "For someone who hates drama, you sure like to stir it up."

Bo's tone drops. "I just don't like him."

I set my jaw and hold his accusatory look. "Because he's a wolf?"

Bo's jaw bulges as he gives Ajax a suspicious side-glance.

"Because he watches you like you're his prey."

My eyes flick back to Ajax.

He's still in the shadows, leaning against the trunk like a statue. His muscles are taut under his training leathers, arms folded, ankles crossed. His black hair falls over his forehead, messy and wind-swept. He hasn't moved in twenty minutes, but I know he's watching.

His eyes glint amber in the light, like molten gold trapped in glass.

They're strange. Striking.

And dangerous.

I shiver.

And trip up on my own feet.

Focus, Zephy's voice cuts through my mind like a spoon through pudding. *Yes, your mate looks delicious to eat. But please, Little Flame. There are bigger problems here. Like your sword technique. And also, the incoming doom.*

I laugh under my breath. *Your pep talk needs a little work.*

"What's so funny?" Bo steps closer.

"Nothing. My dragon is just telling me how much she would like to eat Ajax."

Bo blinks. "I would pay good money to see that."

Zephy suddenly swoops down low, wings rustling the trees. She lands beside us with a thunderous thud, her starry eyes locked onto mine.

That was better, she says. *But you still fight like a sleep-deprived chicken.*

I blink. *Thanks for your uplifting words.*

Zephy shakes like a wet dog. She lets out a growl of annoyance.

Don't thank me until you've survived a sky duel. One wrong angle, and you're making a crater with your face.

She cranes her neck toward Bo. *He's got the rhythm of a rock. But listen to him.*

I pass on the message, and Bo raises a brow.

"You still want me to keep teaching her?" he asks Zephy.

I try to ignore the hint of hopelessness in his voice.

Zephy lets out of a puff of smoke.

Of course. The Little Fairy has good instincts. Shame about the intense jealousy of Little Wolf, though. It's quite unbecoming.

I snort. "I'm not going to repeat what she said."

Bo reads my expression, then his pointed ears turn red.

Zephy turns her huge head toward Ajax, who hasn't moved a muscle the whole time. *And you. Brood less. She needs encouragement, not a death stare.*

Ajax's jaw tightens, but he says nothing. His arms unfold slowly. He walks forward.

"I can teach her," Ajax says, voice low.

"No," Bo snaps, his forearm muscles flexing as he tightens his grip on his sword. "Kayla doesn't need..."

"I'm right here, you know," I say, exasperated. "I don't need two guys arguing over how to make me less terrible with a sword. I just need one of you to stop being cryptic, and the other to stop waiting for me to die on the spot."

Bo frowns. "Which one am I?"

"You know which one."

Ajax tilts his head, amusement flickering in his eyes.

I groan and turn away from both of them just in time to meet Mari's amused expression. "Having fun?"

I tug on my collar and puff a few strands of hair out of my eyes.

"If by fun you mean battling for my life while emotionally whiplashed—*absolutely*."

Mari gives me an unreadable look, not quite a smile but not a frown either. She blinks and looks at the two guys still in a heated debate. Then she shrugs at me. "If you're not flying anymore, I'm going to hunt. You good?"

I nod.

"Don't go too far," I say.

* * *

We resume training, this time with Ajax and Bo switching off.

It's a strange compromise to their disagreement.

They don't speak. They don't need to. The tension is thicker than Zephy's tail.

Bo teaches technique—clean, elegant, controlled.

When I make a right step, he flashes me a proud grin. When I fail to block his attack, he taps me on the nose with the tip of his broad sword. "Boop, got you."

I give him a *really?* look and take a jab.

He knocks my blade aside like it's an inconveniently placed leaf in the forest. Then he taps my nose.

"Got you again! You're being too reactive. Stop waiting for me to make a move and pre-empt what I'm going to do."

I drop my sword and raise my palms with a huff. "How the heck am I supposed to know what you're going to do?"

"Instinct," Ajax butts in. He's cast his jacket aside and rolled up his sleeves. His tanned arms are covered with intrinsic tattoos.

He steps closer. "Tune in to his heartbeat. It'll quicken when he's about to advance."

He picks up my sword and faces Bo. He takes a slow side-step, while Bo dips his chin and gives Ajax a look I can't read. Though I have enough sense to guess that he's not thinking about giving Ajax a hug.

"The eyes are the biggest tell," Ajax says. "They shift when he's being defensive. But when they're locked in, you know..."

Ajax and Bo spar for several heated minutes.

The air fills with dust as they perform what can only be described as a war dance.

Crossing swords, grunting and shrugging. They pummel the ground with their dusty boots.

Zephy watches, her eyes are squinted. *They really stink when they're excited.*

I turn to her, in surprise. *Excited? They're trying to kill each other!*

Zephy's laugh enters my mind. *Exactly. And they're showing off for you. It reminds me of two cockatoos trying to impress a potential mate.*

I turn back to Ajax and Bo.

They're playing dirty now.

Bo's thigh is split open, blood weeps from his leathers, gleaming in the red moonlight.

Ajax has a shiny new bruise on his left cheek. He spits on the ground, leaving a patch of blood.

"Is this really going to help me?" I shout.

But the two guys are oblivious to me.

I'm pretty sure Zephy is wrong. This fight is not about me anymore. It's a battle as old as time.

It's about winning. About earning the title.

Alpha.

* * *

Cycles pass, and riding Zephy begins to feel more natural. I'm able to brandish my sword in the air and move it with a bit more grace.

Hand-to-hand combat is still a challenge. Ajax and Bo continue to train with me.

Ajax teaches force. Momentum. Precision that comes from instinct, not form.

Every time Ajax corrects my stance, he doesn't

touch me, just points with the tip of his blade and mutters a word.

"Balance."

"Breathe."

"Strike."

While Bo cracks jokes and teaches me sequences to memorize. Like I'm not fighting but instead, simply playing a game of chess.

I can't work out if it's to keep me calm so I can focus, or if he's flirting with me.

But one thing is totally clear.

With Bo, I laugh. With Ajax, I sweat.

And I hate that I need them both to get it right.

But I do get better.

By the fourth moon cycle, the sword stops slipping in my grip. My muscles adjust. My legs remember how to hold me steady.

When Zephy takes off again, and I leap onto her back, something just clicks.

My blade moves with me this time.

I raise it above my head one-handed and roar to the skies.

We're soaring, and I'm not scared about what all of this means. Not exactly. Not anymore.

"Try it again," Bo calls.

I raise my sword as Zephy banks hard left.

My body leans with her.

I slash downward toward a phantom enemy in the sky.

Wind whistles past my ears.

My thighs squeeze around Zephy, and I don't fall.

When we land, I'm breathless but upright.

Zephy grins. *You're getting it, Little Flame. I'm proud of you.*

I grin right back. Sweat clings to my upper lip and temples. Adrenaline rushes through me, and I stab the ground with my sword, happy to be done for a while.

Ajax steps forward, offering me a flask.

I lick my dry lips as I take it.

Our fingers brush, and a rush of heat rises to my face, stinging my cheeks.

I don't look up.

Bo notices. Of course, he does.

"You need food, Mari is making us rabbit stew," Ajax says.

He joins Mari by the campfire, leaving me with Bo and his angry eyes.

He speaks quietly, head bowed, not looking at me. "Just be careful."

I take several greedy gulps of water. It's surprisingly fresh. "I am."

"No, I mean—with *him*." His voice lowers even more, but my wolf-senses pick up his words perfectly.

I wonder if Bo knows that Ajax can probably hear this entire conversation, and even if he didn't, he will when I replay it in my mind later.

A shiver rushes through me at the thought.

Ajax imprinted on me and can hear my thoughts.

Even this one.

And this one.

Oh shoot. I need to stop thinking about him.

Bo, oblivious to my foolish inner monologue, finishes his own. "He's intense, Kayla. Too intense. I've been watching him and all of this time, it's like he's waiting for something to go wrong."

I glance at Ajax.

He's sat next to Mari, holding a hollowed coconut, a sharp smile is across his features. Mari pours stew into the makeshift bowl.

He catches me staring, his left brow twitches, and a smirk crosses his lips.

My breath stutters, frozen under his sights. His eyes are lit gold in the light, and they burn right through me. Like always.

Bo follows my gaze. "See, he watches you like prey."

I shake my head. "No. Like something else."

Bo doesn't press. But his jaw is tight.

"I don't know what any of this means," I murmur. "The prophecy. The bond. The training. I feel like I'm standing on the edge of something huge, and no one's telling me what's waiting on the other side."

Bo studies me but gives a resigned sigh and takes my hand. "Then let's find out."

I look up at him.

I want to believe he's not working for his father. That everything he's told me is true. Because Bo brings a warmth and light into my life that makes me feel safe.

If I lost him—if he betrayed me—I would be broken.

"Together?" I ask.

His voice is a whisper, but it hits me like a thunderclap. "Always."

He releases me, and I hand over the flask.

He drinks while I head for the campfire, very aware of Ajax's burning stare.

Bo makes me feel warm and safe, yes.

But I feel something else entirely with Ajax.

Something that shakes the earth beneath me.

Something I can't name.

And that terrifies me more.

Chapter 34
Fractured

The next moon cycle brings more training. Just as I think I'm starting to get a grip and swing the sword, Zephy flies harder. Banking suddenly to the left, then the right. She jerks side to side, dodging imaginary adversaries. Now I've mastered the basics, she jumps up the difficulty several notches.

I slide down the glassy dragon scales and fall.

My inner thighs are raw, and every muscle in my body throbs and aches.

But the thing that gnaws at me most is the odd silent treatment I'm getting from Mari.

When I ask her what she's thinking or try to start up a light conversation, I'm met with one-word answers and narrowed eyes.

She uses her magic to rescue me, over and over. But instead of giving me pep talks or encouragement, she is quiet. Too quiet.

I think Mari is tired. We need to stop, I say to Zephy, eyeing Mari with caution.

We break for food, she sits beside me like a statue, only looking at her bowl but with a faraway look on her face. Her mood plant is slumped over her shoulder, wilting.

My stomach knots.

Something is wrong. I know it is. But I don't know what.

Hollie was like this shortly after the plane crash. At the time, I was too grief-stricken to notice...or care. And after several months, we drifted apart and went from besties to strangers.

My heart thumps uncomfortably.

I'm not letting that happen with Mari.

I decide to be direct.

"You're being weird." I spoon cold stew into my mouth without looking at her.

Mari doesn't laugh like she usually would. Her arms are crossed tightly, her jaw set in that way she gets when she's holding back a storm.

"I'm not being weird," she says, voice clipped. "I'm just being ignored."

I pause mid-chew and blink at her. "Okay... what?"

She shifts on the rock next to me, mood plant drooping even more like it's caught the vibes. "You and Bo. You're like this little dream team now. Sword training, riding lessons, exchanging long, meaningful glances..."

I nearly snort stew. "Meaningful glances? Please. I'm too busy trying not to die while hanging upside down from a dragon."

Mari shrugs. "Still feels like I've been replaced."

Riders and Hunters

That catches me off guard. "Mari..."

"You were my friend first, you know?" Her voice cracks a little, and it stings more than I expect. "I took you to the market. Encouraged you when everyone kept saying you were a freak. I wanted to bring Bo in, but not to take my spot. And now I'm, what-- the backup witch? A literal magical safety net."

"That's not fair," I say quietly.

Her eyes blaze. "Isn't it?"

I turn to face her fully. "Okay, yes, Bo and I have trained together, but that doesn't mean you're being replaced. You're still the coolest person I know. You're just... frustrated."

She looks down at her hands. "Yeah, well. Maybe I am. You've met your dragon, bonded with her, apparently you're some chosen wolf-dragon hybrid girl of prophecy, and I'm still sitting here with a plant that won't stop drooling and a dragon that won't even visit me in my dreams."

I soften, my shoulders lowering with my defenses.

This isn't about me. Or Bo.

"Mari..."

"No, don't pity me." Her voice gets sharper, eyes glistening now. "You've got two magical bonds now. You don't even know what you are, and still, everyone looks at you like you're the future. And me? I was supposed to be special. I was told I'd be special. Now I feel like one of those old coven guides—just here to teach a few beginner spells before fading into the background while the chosen one takes the spotlight."

"You're definitely not an old coven guide! You've not got a single wrinkle," I say gently, trying on a smile.

It fades under her scowl. "Don't mock me."

I raise my palms. "I'm not. I just—" I exhale. "I didn't realize you felt like this."

"Well, now you do." She brushes her rusty-colored hair back angrily. "And the worst part is you know I liked Bo. But you made fun of me for it. He waltzed in between us with his sword and his cheekbones and now—now you're looking at him like he's the answer to all your questions. Which is pretty insulting to Ajax, your *mate*."

I blink, stunned. "Wait. Is this really about Bo?"

She drags her hands through her hair. "It's about everything, Kayla! The war, the dragons, the secrets, you. You're changing. And I don't know where I fit in anymore."

I stand suddenly, the air too tight around me. "I'm changing because I have to. Because I've almost died like... four times this week. I didn't ask for any of this. You think I want to be some weirdo in a war who is supposed to bring two enemies together and lead everyone to peace? I wanted a simple life. A normal life. And now, now I'm going to a place that I cannot even imagine, facing dangers that aren't supposed to even exist."

Mari stands too. "And I didn't ask to be left behind."

We stare at each other. Neither of us backing down.

Several moments pass before I break. "I need space, before we say something we can't take back."

The words sound strange, like they're not my own.

I turn before Mari can say anything else and stomp off into the trees, steam practically rising from my ears.

My boots crunch over fallen pine needles and twigs, and I don't care where I'm going. I just need space. Air. Something that doesn't feel like it's slowly turning me into an emotional burrito of confusion and betrayal.

My breath puffs out in visible clouds as I shove past low-hanging branches, the night cooler now that I've put several campfires' worth of distance between us. Above, a moon glows full and bright, a perfect silver coin tossed into the velvet dark, as if the gods were playing "let's ruin Kayla's night" and this was their shiny contribution.

The trees hush behind me like they're gossiping.

I'd say something snarky, but I'm too tired to fight with foliage.

Eventually, I stumble upon the lake. The water is glassy and still, mirroring the moon in its depths. I crouch by the edge, unstoppering my flask and letting the silence wash over me like a temporary balm.

Then, there's a splash.

I glance up... and immediately regret all of my life choices.

Ajax is in the lake.

Bathing.

My brain halts like someone pulled the emergency brake.

I blink once. Twice. Hoping it's a trick of the light. But nope. It's full-on Ajax, half-submerged in silver-lit water, all lean muscle and jagged scars.

Moonlight drips down his shoulders like the universe is trying to seduce me.

Somewhere far away, there are gods snickering at me.

"Abort," I whisper to myself, backing away. "Abort the mission. Eyes front."

You know, Zephy's voice pops into my head, drowsy and unhelpful. *There are worse things to walk in on. At least now we know he's symmetrical.*

Heat rises to my face. *Not helping!*

Zephy sounds amused now, like she's enjoying every moment of this not-so-private conversation.

I grab my face in horror, knowing that our thoughts are not hidden from Ajax. For all I know, he's listening to every word.

Oh, I wasn't trying to. I'm just appreciating the aesthetics. Little Wolf is surprisingly big and broody, giving a tragic-past energy.

I clamp my eyes shut, cursing my dragon.

Stop talking. Stop it right now. He can hear you.

Every. Word.

My eyes flutter open again against my will.

I should look away.

I really should.

But my eyes seem to have entered some kind of

magical rebellion and are now locked on his back—a map of battles won and wounds survived.

He moves like someone who knows the forest will never defeat him. Fluid. Unbothered.

He turns.

Our eyes meet.

Panic detonates in my chest, and I drop into a crouch behind the nearest bush so fast I nearly face plant into a patch of suspicious-looking mushrooms.

A deep chuckle rolls out from the lake, smooth and infuriating. "Look who's spying now."

I clamber to my feet with all the grace of a startled squirrel.

"I wasn't spying. I'm...foraging for mushrooms." I grab a bunch and lift them in the air. "See?"

Don't eat those unless you want to die a slow death, Ajax's thought enters my mind.

The words scratch my brain in a way that makes me shiver. In a good way.

I drop the mushroom and brush my hands on my leathers. "Actually, I came down here to...to..."

I look around, searching for another excuse.

Ajax raises a hand, pushing dark hair off his forehead. The movement makes his abs ripple in a way that makes my mouth dry.

"Have you come to bathe too?"

You should, Zephy's voice enters my mind. *You stink, Little Flame.*

My mouth opens. No words come out. Because what even is this conversation?

"I'll wait until you're done," I shout to Ajax with a wave, cheeks blazing.

I pray to the gods that he didn't just hear Zephy. But his grin makes me want to curse the traitorous deities.

He wades out of the water like it's an epic movie scene—water streaming down his chest, every scar catching the moonlight like it's part of some poetic story no one has the full ending to. He's taut in all the right places, and his movements are so controlled, so confident. I get the vibe that he's enjoying every moment of this.

"Go right ahead." He grabs his shirt from a nearby rock.

He doesn't rush to get dressed. No shame. No pretense.

Just a wink tossed over his shoulder as he walks by me.

I turn so fast I nearly pull a neck muscle.

I keep my eyes glued to the dirt.

But... my brain wants to peek and find out what Zephy means about him being symmetrical.

Just once.

For *science*.

* * *

Later, I find Ajax again at the campfire, crouched with quiet precision, skinning a rabbit. The stars above us are needles of light in the black sky. The air is cool and still.

Riders and Hunters

Mari and Bo went hunting ages ago, and haven't returned yet.

Zephy is curled around the camp, asleep. Every so often, she lets out a strange snore that sounds suspiciously like the word "pineapple."

I settle down across from Ajax, pulling my coat tighter.

He doesn't look up, but his posture shifts slightly, like he's always aware, always calculating.

"I'm sorry," I say softly, breaking the silence.

"For what?" His voice is even.

"For earlier. The lake thing."

He shrugs, slicing cleanly down the rabbit's belly. "I wasn't exactly complaining. Besides, it was bound to happen eventually."

The fire pops between us, throwing flickers of light over his sharp jawline and the dark fringe of his hair.

My gaze drifts to the angry scar trailing across his shoulder. "Where did you get those?"

He doesn't flinch. "War. Training. Living. Being a wolf in a world that thinks we're monsters."

I hug my knees to my chest. "Do you ever wish you weren't one?"

"Sometimes." He wipes the blade clean with a cloth. "But then I remember it's saved me. The instincts. The rage. The refusal to go quietly."

His eyes flick to mine. "It's saved you too."

I arch a brow. "Debatable."

He doesn't smile. Just studies me with a gaze that burns too deep. "Is it?"

I glance down at my boots. "I don't know what to believe anymore."

"Good." He throws a rabbit bone into the fire. "That means you're paying attention."

I frown. "That's bleak."

"It's realistic. Everything you've been told, every story, every enemy—it's all someone's version of the truth. Even mine." He pauses. "But there are some things I know."

"Like what?"

He jabs his thumb in the direction of my dragon. "Zephyros is strange. Loud. A little obnoxious. Probably addicted to those fried circle things you made her try."

"They were onion rings," I correct him with an eye roll.

"Whatever. But she's not a killer."

I nod slowly. "She's weird. But not evil."

"But it's important to remember that she's still a dragon," he adds, his voice distant.

"Yeah. And dragons have teeth." I give him a pointed look. "So do you."

His lips twitch. "Only metaphorical ones, I'm sure."

I grin. "Weird. That's what I was gonna say."

Our hands rest near each other, palms open to the fire's warmth.

His pinky shifts. A breath of movement. Then it brushes mine.

Just a light touch.

Soft. Warm. Tentative.

The hair on his hand tickles my skin.

I freeze.

So does he.

I tilt my head toward him, heartbeat climbing into my throat.

He's a giant flame, and I'm a moth, helplessly drawn in.

A rush of heat floods me, and it's nothing to do with the campfire. There's something more, but I don't know what it could be.

His golden eyes flick down to my lips.

I lean forward a little. So does he.

The fire crackles like it knows something's about to combust. That whatever happens next, nothing will be the same.

I can feel his breath on my lips now. I hold still, waiting for him to close the space.

His velvet lips brush mine, and I swear, if he says something snarky in this exact second, I'll—

"Hey!"

Bo's voice slices through the night like a dagger.

I flinch so hard I almost roll into the fire.

Ajax exhales slowly, jaw locking.

Mari appears behind Bo, rubbing her arms. Her eyes avoid mine.

"We've been talking," she says.

Bo steps forward. "We're going back to Theridon."

My stomach drops. "Now?"

"Immediately," Mari says.

I look between them, the fire still warm at my side, the space between me and Ajax humming with unfinished things.

"Are you serious?"

Bo nods. "We need to go back and warn the students. Tell them the truth about Siberious. Most of them probably won't listen, but we have to try."

Ajax rises slowly. His shadow looms across the fire. "You won't be welcomed back. Everyone thinks you died in the trail."

Bo glares at him. "We'll come up with a story. Kayla..."

His eyes land on me, and something inside me stutters.

"Are you coming with us?"

The question hangs like a noose and tightens round my neck.

I look at Ajax, filled with confusion.

I don't want to be split up. I want things to stay exactly how they are.

"I'm not ready..." I begin. "I need more time to... to..."

I lock eyes with Ajax.

To plan what happens next. To learn to fight and win. To awaken my wolf. To find out how I feel about Ajax.

Bo's eyes dull, and he exchanges a knowing look with Mari.

"Fine. We'll tell them you died during the challenge. It won't be too hard for anyone to believe," Mari says.

The words cut deep. But I blink fast to stop the tears from welling in my eyes.

"Great," I say through gritted teeth.

And like that, they're gone.

Ajax sighs. "You should get some sleep. We've got a lot of work to do."

I hug my knees and stare into the fire. "In a minute."

The wind shifts, scattering sparks into the dark.

Behind me, Zephy sighs in her sleep.

And just like that, the moment—whatever it could've been—is gone.

But the heat in my chest?

That stays.

Chapter 35
The Cost of Magic

It starts with a sound.

Not a roar. Not a screech. Something deeper. Raw. Guttural.

A dragon's cry. But not one I've heard before.

Zephy lifts her head from the ground so fast, the wind kicks up embers from the fire and sends them whirling around us like startled fireflies.

Her huge eyes are wide, frantic, reflecting something I can't see yet.

"Mari and Bo just left," I say, voice barely above a whisper. "It's okay. It's probably just—"

It's not them. Zephy's voice slices into my mind like a blade. *I am sick. The air feels... Something is terribly wrong.*

She lurches to her four feet. Her wings unfurl with a violent snap.

I jump up next to a startled Ajax.

Zephy's tail lashes, tearing through the soil and sending sparks flying. Her scales glow red, then gold, then red again like she can't decide whether to rage or run.

"Zephy!" I shout, stepping forward. "What's going on? Talk to me!"

I can't—I need—I have to— Her words stumble through my head like a broken song. *They've done something. Or...doing something now. I feel it. A thread is snapping and—*

"Wait. What thread?" Ajax braces with his hand on his sword.

The hairs on his arms are on end, and the flash behind his eyes makes me wonder if he's trying to decide whether to shift or not.

Zephy's eyes find mine, and for the first time since we met, I see something that doesn't belong in a formidable creature like her.

Terror.

The alpha calls me, I have to go.

She beats her wings, the wind knocking me off my feet, and launches into the sky with a scream that splits the night.

I stare after her, mouth open, heart racing.

"ZEPHYROS! Take me with you!"

She doesn't look back.

Silence crashes around us.

The fire crackles like it's trying to fill in the blanks.

Ajax steps up beside me, his jaw tight. "That's not good."

"You think?" I snap, dragging my fingers through my hair.

He doesn't respond. Just watches the sky, muscles

coiled like a loaded crossbow. Then, without a word, he steps back and shrugs off his coat.

"Uh," I blink. "Now is really not the time to get shirtless again."

But it's not that kind of moment.

Because his whole body shifts—bones stretching, skin rippling, hair bursting over his form in a violent cascade. In seconds, the man is gone, and the massive brown-haired wolf with golden eyes is standing in his place.

He glows with magic this time, he stands in a blue aura, and the energy pulses, taking my breath away.

"Oh." I breathe.

The wolf nods its head toward the ledge, then crouches low.

"You want me to get on you?" I ask, feeling foolish for talking to a wolf.

Though I don't know why. I've been exchanging sarcastic remarks with a dragon all this time. Surely, a wolf is no different.

I expect Ajax's voice to enter my mind, like always. But there's only silence.

The wolf nudges my waist with urgency.

I swallow.

"I just—okay. No saddle. Got it. Very rustic."

I climb on, and the moment I bury my fingers into his thick fur, it feels...intimate.

Too intimate.

I try not to overthink it, but it's hard when I'm straddling a guy who just turned into a massive apex predator and is now sprinting full speed down a craggy mountain with my thighs clamped around his ribcage.

We move like smoke, cutting through trees and leaping over rocks.

Zephy was right. The air...feels different.

It's heavy, still...almost like a storm is on the way.

My senses go wild.

I can hear everything—the rustle of birds in the trees, the flap of distant wings, even the soft pants of Ajax's breath as he runs.

I can *smell* everything—the sharp scent of pine, the rich musk of damp soil, the wild, overwhelming smell of him.

Sweat. Magic. Wolf.

And something else.

My nose wrinkles, and my stomach twists.

Blood.

A thick, coppery scent that curls into my lungs like smoke from a burning building.

"Ajax..." I whisper, pulling gently on his fur.

He stops with his ears pricked. His body stiffens beneath me.

Then he howls.

A long, mournful, guttural sound that rips through the trees like a curse. It ends in a whimper.

I slide off his back, nearly falling, and stagger beside him.

"What is it? What happened?"

But I already know.

I feel it.

Riders and Hunters

There's a pressure in my chest. Something ancient. Something cold.

Then—noise. Celebration.

Voices. Laughter. Howling.

It's so jarringly out of place I almost scream at the wrongness of it.

Ajax shifts back, breathing hard. He yanks on his clothes and boots. His eyes are troubled.

My ears prick up at the sound of celebration, and I'm drawn to it.

I walk away, deeper into the trees.

"Kayla..." Ajax says, his voice low. "Brace yourself."

We walk forward.

The trees part, and the world tilts as my eyes land on a terrible scene.

There's a clearing.

At least twenty people in hunting gear stand in a semi-circle, each one holding a weapon of sorts.

Bows, arrows. Knives and swords.

In front of them, a pack of wolves, at least a dozen of them, their mouths stained red.

Fangs bared. Tongues lolling.

And in the center—

No.

No, no, no.

A small dragon. Gold. Wings crumpled. Tail limp. Blood slicking the ground in a pool around her still form.

Her chest rises—once. Then exhales a final breath.

The air shifts.

I don't mean metaphorically. I mean the realm itself reacts.

Something deep in the earth cracks.

Like a piece of the magical fabric holding everything together just got torn loose.

I stumble back, one hand on my chest.

Ajax catches me, takes my arm, and makes us crouch in the bushes, hidden from view.

I turn to Ajax.

His face is grim. Furious.

"That dragon..." I whisper. "She wasn't even full grown."

"A fledgling," he says. "Barely past hatching."

The wolves don't stop celebrating.

One of them wrestles with the dragon's body, then stands on hind legs and raises a bloodied bone like a trophy.

My stomach turns.

Then, one by one, they start to shift—back into people.

Young men and women with wild eyes and stained teeth.

And they're smiling.

Smiling!

To my deep relief, Ajax's face darkens, and he does not join in the celebration.

An elderly woman approaches, dragging a sack with two wrinkled hands.

"Take the scales, boys. Every last one of them. They fetch a pretty penny at the market."

My heart shatters, and I look away as a group with knives swarms the baby dragon.

Ajax grabs me by the arms and drags me away.

We stumble deeper into the forest, and my brain spins.

"That dragon," I say again, voice hollow. "Could she have bonded with a rider?"

Ajax doesn't answer.

But he doesn't need to.

I feel it.

Like a string has snapped deep inside me.

If hatchlings can bond, that would explain why some riders don't meet their dragons right away. Maybe they have to wait until they grow.

My throat constricts.

Another student is dead.

Just like Char.

My legs threaten to give out, but I lock my knees because if I fall, I might not get back up.

That dragon was just a baby.

A helpless fledgling.

And now she's... gone.

Ajax places a steady hand on my back. His warmth anchors me for a second. Just long enough to hold my insides together.

"They don't know," he says quietly. "Bo. Mari. The others."

My eyes snap to his. "What if it's Mari? She was so upset about not meeting her dragon. What if this is why?"

My voice is a croak, barely audible over the pulse pounding in my ears.

Ajax blinks, caught off guard. He covers his mouth as he takes it in.

"She's always smiling," I whisper. "Even when everything's awful. Always looking for the good in people. That dragon—she was gold, bright, warm... that was *so* Mari."

At least... until Mari got weird and depressed.

I shake my head.

My thoughts are spiraling, and I can't seem to stop them. "No. No, maybe it was Bo. The color, those scales, they matched his light magic. His hair. The whole glowy golden warrior thing he's got going on."

I suck in a sharp breath. "What if—what if we just stood here, watching a piece of them die? And we did nothing about it!"

The words fall out of my mouth, too fast, too raw, and I can't pull them back. The truth of it hits me like a punch to the chest.

I start to tremble.

Ajax doesn't hesitate. He wraps his arms around me and pulls me into his chest, solid and warm and real.

I resist for half a heartbeat, and then I collapse against him, fisting his shirt in my hands like it's the only thing holding me together.

"They're okay," he murmurs into my hair. "You're okay. Just breathe."

I breathe.

One.

Two.

Three shaky breaths that don't feel like enough but have to be.

The moons shift when the wolves are done and leave the clearing.

Ajax and I walk in and kneel by the mutilated body. They did not even leave one scale on its delicate frame.

Tears prickle my eyes and fall hot and wet on my cheeks.

I turn to Ajax. "This is what you did?"

Ajax frowns. "No. This is another pack. More ruthless and brutal. Mine would never hunt a juvenile."

I wipe my cheeks with my sleeve and sniff. "But you'd do this to a fully grown dragon, huh? I feel so much better knowing that."

Ajax raises his palms. "Listen, Trouble, you know I wouldn't…"

"Don't call me that," I spit. "How can you be part of this? How is this okay? It's barbaric."

Ajax's eyes turn downcast. "I don't need to explain myself to you. I worked with the information I had at the time."

"Wow. Okay, so it's like that?" I cross my arms. "Not even an apology."

Ajax scowls and is about to retort, but his gaze flickers to the deceased baby dragon, and he pauses.

The silence that follows is deafening.

Chapter 36

The Cracked Path Back

I don't know how long we stand there.

The air's too thick to see the moons. The silence, too loud.

The blood on the ground is starting to dry in rusty streaks, and the scent of magic—dark magic—still clings to my skin like smoke after a fire.

I want to scream. I want to tear down the trees and rip open the sky and demand answers from someone. Anyone.

But instead, I breathe.

Ajax shifts into a wolf and pounds the ground with his paws, clawing the dirt. When he's done, he shifts back and marches into the forest.

I'm left with what looks like an open grave, and the weight of the situation threatening to push me inside.

When Ajax returns, his arms are laden with branches and vines.

"What are you doing?"

He doesn't reply. Instead, he sets to work. Grunting and focused.

I hug myself, looking up at the covered skies and hoping for any sign of Zephy. Her lack of presence has ripped a giant hole in me already.

I can't imagine how I survived my whole life without her.

Maybe it's the bonding process, but when she's away, it's like a part of me is missing.

More grunting. Then a thump.

I tear my focus away from the clouds just as Ajax is covering the hole with dirt.

The body is gone, all that is left is a large patch of dried blood.

I drop my hands. "You buried it?"

Ajax pushes in a makeshift cross and pats his legs. Finally, he gives me a look.

It's intense, the kind of look that says a thousand words.

My stomach knots.

"They don't know," he mutters. "Bo and Mari. They don't know this is happening."

My heart lurches. "Then we have to tell them."

He nods once, sharp and sure, then glances to the edge of the clearing. "This isn't over. We need to move. Fast."

"Should we fly?"

He hesitates, and I look up again with a frown.

Right. No dragon.

Mine's currently MIA, likely on a vengeance quest. Maybe shopping for revenge accessories.

I wouldn't blame her.

So, no Zephyros.

Just Ajax.

He doesn't speak, just shifts. That same ripple of muscle and magic rolls through him, the bones snapping, reforming, hair bursting like a storm cloud until the man is gone and the wolf stands in his place.

Without ceremony, he crouches.

I sigh. "I really need to stop riding you like an Uber."

He huffs. Possibly a confused wolf snort.

I climb on.

His fur is warm beneath me, thick and strong.

I wrap my hands tight in the scruff at his neck, and he launches forward without warning.

This time, it's different.

This time, I notice everything.

The speed. The way the trees blur past us like brushstrokes. The sharp cold on my cheeks. The scent of his fur—woodsmoke, pine, something deeper.

My senses have never felt this alive. Every time my senses are awakened, it's more profound. Sharper.

Every bird call is louder. Every root and rock registers in my brain before we pass it.

And the smell. Oh gosh.

My nose wrinkles.

Blood.

Again.

Not the old kind. Fresh.

A new pulse of dread coils in my stomach.

The forest isn't just dying—it's bleeding.

I lean closer into Ajax's fur. "I don't like this."

He doesn't respond. But I can feel it—his muscles tensing, his ears twitching. He doesn't like it either.

We break through a grove of ash trees, their leaves silver under moonlight. Everything here feels... off. The colors wrong. The energy twisted.

And then we see it.

A unicorn.

Dead.

Lying in a shallow stream, its horn snapped clean off. Blood leeches into the water like ink in paper. A crow perches on its flank, pecking.

I gag and cover my mouth.

Ajax stops, panting.

"What is happening to this place?" I whisper, sliding off his back.

He shifts back slowly, skin pale, jaw clenched. "No one hunts Unicorns. They're sacred. But now... it's like there are no rules. Anything is free game."

I swallow. "You think wolves did this?"

Ajax's jaw bulges. "Probably the same ones we saw earlier. The horn is missing."

"Let me guess... It'll fetch a pretty penny on the market?"

Ajax shakes his head. "Underground market, maybe. But if they tried to sell it to any ordinary folk, they'd end up hanged."

I step closer to the unicorn, ignoring the bile in my throat. Other than the missing horn, there's not a single scratch on its perfectly white body.

Its eyes are open.

Wide. Empty. Hollow.

"I saw Char like this," I murmur. "Nothing inside. Just... gone."

Ajax says nothing.

But I see the rage simmering just below the surface.

We walk after that. Quiet. The tension between us is a thin wire strung too tight. Neither of us wants to say what we're both thinking:

That we might already be too late.

It takes another moon cycle to reach the outer wall of Theridon.

The sky is orange, and it looks like dawn.

Only it doesn't feel like dawn on Theridon.

Clouds hang low like smoke. Fog creeps along the ground. The castle looms in the distance, shrouded in silence.

"I don't remember it being this..." I search for the word.

"Haunted?" Ajax supplies.

"Yeah." I squint at the skies for a second, then it hits me. "There's no protective rain, either."

We move carefully. The guards at the front gate are gone. The towers unmanned.

Red flag number one.

We slip through the servants' garden entrance and enter the east wing.

I expect to be swarmed by students or at least hear the familiar drone of spellcasting.

But the halls are dead quiet.

Too quiet.

I'm starting to get that "bad horror movie" feeling. Any minute now a cursed suit of armor is going to decapitate me.

We creep through the lower levels. Everything's dim, even the enchanted torches that usually blaze with overcompensating gusto.

I reach the Dining Hall doors and peer through the crack.

There's a meeting underway.

Whispers.

A bunch of teachers and some officials I don't recognize are deep in conversation. Their voices are low and urgent. At the head of the table: King Siberious.

My breath catches.

He looks... older.

Paler.

His skin is stretched too thin across his gaunt cheekbones. And the sparkle in his eyes is gone.

He's not the polished, smug monarch I'm used to.

His hands tremble as he speaks, but I can't hear the words.

"I need to get closer, I can't hear much from here," I whisper.

Ajax frowns. "The room is probably enchanted. We should wait and spy from a better vantage."

"You say spy. I say dramatic entrance." I wink at him.

"Okay, Trouble. But don't cry to me when they catch you."

I meet his disapproving look with a wink.

"I'll be careful."

I slip through the side corridor and duck under the curtain alcove that runs at the back of the hall. There's a decorative tapestry and—bonus—a hole in the wall. Perfect.

I press my eye to it.

Now I wish I could read lips. Because their voices are muted and muffled.

Ajax is right, the hall is enchanted.

I squint, using the best of my lip-reading skills and muffled hearing to make sense of the conversation.

"...one rider lost," Mauve says. "No external injuries. Just like the others."

"Then it's true," Madame Hexley adds. "The bond. The death link. If the dragon dies..."

"...so does the rider," King Siberious finishes.

My heart drops into my stomach.

The teachers fall silent.

One of them, a woman with sunken eyes, asks, "Should we tell them? The students?"

"No," Siberious says immediately. "Panic will destroy what order we have left."

Mauve leans forward. "Perhaps they deserve to know the risk—"

"They knew the risk the moment they chose to become riders," Siberious snaps.

A heavy silence follows.

And then someone whispers something I can't quite hear. I can only see the back of their head.

I lean closer, straining my ears to catch the words

"heart of the mountain."

The words pummel me in the chest, though I have no idea why.

I lurch back and almost land on my butt, but Ajax is right there to catch me. As always.

He yanks the curtain back in place and motions for me to retreat. This time, I don't argue.

We move quickly, heart pounding, ducking back into the hallway.

I lean against the stone wall, trying to process.

"What did you hear?" Ajax asks.

I tell him.

His jaw tightens. "So, it's true."

"They're dying, Ajax. Dragons. Students. And they're covering it up."

His gaze is stormy. "Then we do what dragons do best."

"Which is...?"

He smirks. "Burn everything down."

"But first, we find Bo and Mari."

Ajax nods, but his tense jaw tells me something else. That's when I hear his thoughts.

I'm not sure they're here.

The thought sickens me. But I press on, refusing to let my mind go to dark places. Not yet.

We reach the dorm tower just after sunrise. There are still no students. Just silence.

Until—

Click.

A low buzzing behind the training wing.

Ajax and I spin toward it, hearts beating fast, chests heaving.

My eyes fly to the weapon rack. Glowing with an ancient power.

And right there... Bo's sword.

It's humming with golden light, pulsing, vibrating, as if reacting to something.

Or maybe just missing someone.

Ajax notices too.

"It doesn't mean anything," he tries to comfort me.

But my stomach twists.

Bo would not give up that sword easily.

Then, from somewhere above us, a door creaks.

Footsteps.

And a hushed voice.

It's soft.

Familiar.

"Kayla?"

Mari steps out from the shadows. Alive.

But pale.

And alone.

Chapter 37
The Secrets We Bury

"Mari?"

My voice cracks on her name, like it's too fragile to say out loud.

She freezes at the top of the stairs, half-shadowed in the morning light. Her curls are frizzed beyond belief, and her usually bright eyes look hollow. Like someone turned the light off inside her.

"Kayla?" she says again, in a breathy whisper.

And then she's running.

I don't have time to react before she slams into me with all one-hundred-and-I'm-not-gonna-ask pounds of her. Her arms lock around my shoulders like a vise.

"I thought you were dead," she chokes. "Or— worse. That you'd become one of them."

I glance at Ajax, who raises a cool eyebrow but wisely says nothing. Meanwhile, Mari talks at a hundred miles an hour.

"So much has happened. All I've been thinking

about is the last thing I said to you. I'm so sorry. So, so, sorry."

"I missed you too." I pat her back awkwardly. "No offense, but you look like you lost a fight with a banshee."

She snorts into my shoulder, when she pulls away, she leaves a patch of snot and tears on my shirt.

I don't care.

"You should see Bo," she mutters.

My breath hitches with hope. "Is he okay?"

She looks at Ajax, wary, then nods slowly. "Yeah. He's... alive. Moody as heck. But alive."

I let out a breath with sweet relief.

We step into the empty dorm wing, Ajax trailing behind us like a silent shadow.

Mari gives him a wary side-eye but doesn't comment. Yet.

"Where is everyone?" I ask.

"Most of them are gone," she says softly. "After the memorial. A bunch of students left. Some of them... They didn't make it through the challenge."

I stop. "Wait. What?"

"The one we were all supposed to complete." She swallows. "More people died, Kayla. And the teachers aren't talking. They just keep saying it's an unfortunate loss. That not everyone is suited for the rider path."

My stomach lurches.

"How long have I been gone?" I ask, suddenly dizzy.

"Five moon cycles."

Five.

How is that even possible? It felt like two.

Ajax meets my eyes. "Time behaves differently in this realm. Even more so, when you're around dragons."

Of course, it does.

Mari guides us to one of the abandoned dorms, now turned into a temporary hideout. Bo's sitting cross-legged on the floor, shirt off, bandage running across his arm like a sash of bad life choices.

He looks up, and the tension in the room spikes like someone lit a fuse.

"You're alive," he says flatly.

"Last I checked."

He doesn't smile. Just stands slowly, eyes flicking between me and Ajax.

I swear, I can feel the testosterone standoff in the air.

Bo's eyes narrow. "I see your guard dog's still following you."

Ajax folds his arms, unfazed. "Woof."

I slide between them before someone decides to whip out a weapon. Or worse, a monologue.

"Stop. Everyone's cranky and traumatized as it is."

Bo doesn't laugh.

Mari sits beside him and clears her throat. "We've been talking. We were going to come find you. But something happened."

She looks at Bo, like she's not sure how much to say.

Bo sighs and speaks first. "A dragon bonded to me."

My breath catches. "Wait—what?"

"Three nights ago," he says. "Golden. Huge. Kinda judgy."

"Did he have a name?"

"Yeah. Arion."

Mari cuts in. "But then... he disappeared."

"What do you mean disappeared?"

Bo's jaw tenses. "I mean, one second he was there, and the next he was gone. Like something pulled him away. Last I heard his voice in my mind, it was emotional. Like... he was trying to say goodbye."

That sinking feeling in my stomach turns into a full-body chill.

"What if he died?" I whisper.

Bo looks away. "I don't know. But I felt something. A tearing. And since then, my magic's been—"

He holds up his palm.

Where there would usually be swirls of yellow light, there's...

Nothing.

Mari bites her lip. "My wand has been acting strange too. Like the magical connection is there, but distant. And I had a vision of a dragon, Kayla. A green one. But she never came to me."

I shiver. And the sense of foreboding is worse as Mari and Bo give me the same worried look.

The kind of look that says, "Where's your dragon?"

"Zephy left me. She said something about going to the alpha. Maybe that's where all the dragons are."

Riders and Hunters

We sit in silence, the weight of what we've all experienced weighing on us like the ceiling's about to fall in.

Ajax finally speaks. "The Heart of the Mountain. It's dying. That must be it."

Bo rolls his eyes. "We're really desperate now, clinging to bedtime stories."

Ajax ignores him. "It's a real place. The source of dragon magic. Killing dragons is weakening the connection."

"So, what? We're supposed to believe you're one of us now?" Bo asks Ajax, dryly.

Ajax squares up to him. "There is no us and them. Don't you get it? Kayla is the one to bridge both sides."

My heart leaps at the sound of my name coming from Ajax's lips.

"Zephy's warning…" I whisper. My heart begins to bleed. Just thinking about my dragon hurts.

Mari's eyes widen. "Is she okay?"

"I don't know," I admit. "She panicked and left. I haven't felt her since."

Mari's hands fly to her open mouth.

But I'm not done. My voice sounds strange as I tell them about the baby dragon's death. How poachers took every last scale.

Tears leak out of Mari's eyes.

Bo stands abruptly. "We need to go. Find this heart. Maybe that's where we will find our dragons. And then maybe our powers will return."

Mari nods. "The council wants to go there. I'm

sure it's not for anything good. If we get there first, then maybe we can do something to fix this mess."

I glance at Bo, who looks resolved. To Ajax, who has his sights on the stone floor.

He doesn't blink. "I know where it is. But it's a long walk. We will need to move quickly to get a head start on the council."

We nod as a group.

We gather supplies that night. Whatever we can find that hasn't been confiscated or corrupted.

The plan is simple: We leave before the next moon cycle. Head toward the mountains. Find the Heart. Find out what we can and hopefully, reconnect with our dragons.

Try not to die or get caught by the enemy in the meantime.

No pressure.

As we sit around a flickering lamp, I watch the three of them.

Bo—gritting his jaw, wound tight, like he's trying not to feel anything at all.

Mari—quiet, watching him. Watching me. Her fingers twitching like she wants to cast a spell and vanish.

Ajax—leaning against the wall, arms crossed, gaze locked on me like I'm the only thing in the room.

We're together again.

But everything's changed.

I stare at the glow of my dragon mark, pulsing faintly on my skin.

The world is dying. Magic is bleeding. And I'm still trying to figure out who I am in the middle of it.

Rider?

Wolf?

Traitor?

Leader?

Tomorrow, we find the heart of magic.

And I pray it hasn't already stopped beating.

Ajax clears his throat, prompting everyone to look at him.

"There is something I need to do first."

"What?" Mari and I say in unison.

The lamplight flickers across his darkened features. "I need to talk to my pack. Tonight."

Chapter 38
The Ones Who Will Not Listen

The air in the wolf camp is tense enough to strum. A dozen warriors stand in a loose circle around a fire pit that's more smoke than flame, growling and muttering among themselves like the pack is one spark away from tearing itself apart.

Ajax stands in the middle of them, tall and defiant, his eyes wild with urgency. While I stand flanked by Bo and Mari.

We try to stand with presence, but Bo and Mari's diminished powers have hit their confidence. Their shoulders slump, and the desperation is written all over their faces.

"You have to listen to me," Ajax growls. "Killing the dragons will not cure us. It won't lift the curse. The opposite is true. It will end us."

"This is useless," Bo mutters in my ear. "Who does he think he is, trying to end centuries of prejudice with a speech?"

"It's worth a try," I whisper back. "All he needs to

do is put doubt into one wolf, and the rest of the pack will follow."

A ripple of snarls passes through the group, and the pack looks at Ajax with matching expressions of suspicion.

"You sound like them now," one of the older wolves barks from the back. His wild mane of hair sticks in all directions, and his face is covered in jagged scars. "You've gone soft and brainwashed."

"You must listen to me, magic is breaking and with it, the people are descending into chaos." Ajax takes a step forward. "When a dragon dies, the rider—"

"We are not riders," another cuts in. A woman this time, lean and sharp as a blade. "We were born wolves. Not bonded. Not chosen. Cursed. Killing magic will unleash us from our eternal damnation. If a few kids have to die, then so be it."

A chorus of agreement surges around her, low and guttural.

Mari and I exchange worried looks.

But Ajax holds his ground, jaw clenched. "We are not cursed. We are alive. Strong. We've survived everything this world has thrown at us because of the wolf. Not in spite of it."

"We survive because we fight," someone spits. "Because we kill the beasts that took our lives from us. Don't be fooled, Ajax. Dragons suck souls and looks like they've already started on yours, too."

My hands ball into fists at my sides. Beside me, Bo shifts his weight, looking ready to jump in with something sarcastic and sharp. Mari's jaw twitches, but she keeps her mouth shut. Smart move.

Ajax breathes hard. I can see the struggle in his eyes—the old loyalty, the love for these people, crushed beneath the weight of everything he now knows.

Ajax presses on, raising his voice over the growing growls of the crowd. "We're wrong about dragons. They don't devour souls. They don't even want to kill us. And the packs? They've taken this war too far. I saw them with my own eyes, mutilating a youngling for a few coin. And don't forget, when dragons die, magic dies. If magic dies—"

"Then we're free," Branor snaps, his broad arms folded across his chest.

There's a hardness in his expression telling me it would take something bigger than a calm discussion to crack his resolve.

"No," Ajax roars. "Then *we* die. We DIE. Including you, Branor. Even our younglings."

That lands.

Silence.

The fire crackles, and a rush of whispers wash over the group. Wind rushes through the trees like it's trying to hide from what's coming.

And for a second, I think maybe it's worked.

Maybe he's gotten through to them.

Then a boy bursts into the camp, panting and wide-eyed.

"I found a dragon," the scout says, breathless. "In the eastern glen. With a witch. They're alone."

A collective hush falls over the wolves.

And then everything moves at once.

Branor leaps into the air and lands in wolf form. A tall woman shifts into a black one, her fur matching the braid that rested over her right shoulder. Half the group starts running toward the trees. The air fills with excited howls.

"No—wait!" Ajax shouts, running after them. But he stops after a few steps and lets his arms hang useless by his sides.

He's too late.

The hunt has begun. And we're out of time.

* * *

My senses are on fire as we follow. We don't stop running.

Bo curses under his breath. "Your pack are a bunch of psychopaths."

Ajax doesn't answer. His face is stone.

I can tell he's blaming himself, and I want to say something comforting, but now is not the time for therapy. We're trying to beat a pack of wolf shifters to a dragon who might already be dead.

The forest thickens around us as we race deeper into the glen. The air is electric, charged with magic and tension.

My senses sharpen like razors.

I can smell sap, blood, wet bark, and—

"Smoke, turn left," I say.

Ajax's wolf ears flicker, but he darts in to the left

path. Bo and Mari fall behind, unable to keep up with us.

We press forward.

When we slow to a nervous walk, Mari catches up, her wand flickering with light, casting a weak glow on the dirt path.

Bo draws his sword and twirls it once. Then twice. Show-off.

"I swear," Bo mutters. "If we get there and that dragon's already dead, I'm going to lose it."

"You've already lost it," Mari says, half-breathless. "That's your default state now."

Bo's ears redden. "I mean it. This whole thing sickens me."

Ajax, back in human form, breaks through a patch of bramble with a grunt. "Keep your energy. You'll need it."

The red moon's barely rising now, casting orange-gold light across the canopy.

The glen opens ahead.

And what I see punches the air out of my lungs.

A small dragon—silver-blue, scales shimmering like frost—is curled around a broken stump. Her wings are torn. She's breathing shallow. Shivering.

Alive.

But not for long.

Wolves are closing in.

I count five. Branor's in front, axe raised. Two others are flanking the sides, weapons drawn. The others circle in wolf form, herding her in like prey.

"She's barely breathing," Mari whispers, horrified.

"Not for long," Bo mutters, eyes narrowing.

Ajax doesn't wait.

He steps forward and shifts, body bursting into fur and fury. He charges the wolves with a howl that splits the sky and shakes the ground.

The wolves pause, startled, unsure.

I don't hesitate either.

I sprint after him.

Bo follows, sword raised.

Mari flings a stun spell at the nearest wolf, knocking him backward.

We dive into chaos.

Ajax slams into Branor, knocking him flat.

They roll across the ground in a flurry of claws and growls.

I throw myself in front of the dragon, arms out.

"Stop!" I shout. "She's not your enemy!"

A wolf lunges at me.

Bo slices him mid-air, slamming him into a tree. When he withdraws it, the blade gleams with blood.

Mari casts a protective force around the dragon. It flares golden, just in time to block a thrown spear, but it shatters.

Mari curses and mutters the spell again.

The wolves regroup. Their eyes are wild. Snarling.

"You protect it? You traitor," Branor growls.

"I protect life! All life is precious!" I shout, thinking of Mr. Pinewood and our first Mystic Botany class.

Whether it is a blade of grass, a wolf, or a dragon. All life is precious. I *will* protect it.

Riders and Hunters

The baby dragon whimpers behind me.

Ajax, blood on his snout, faces down his own people. His voice thunders in my mind as he speaks to the pack.

Look around you, he growls. *She's not fighting. She's scared. If you kill her, another bond will break. Another rider will fall. Do you want that blood on your hands?*

Silence.

Heavy. Uncertain.

The youngest of the wolves steps back.

Then another.

Branor glares, breathing hard, nose bleeding. "You've changed, Ajax."

Ajax nods. "I've *evolved*."

Branor spits on the ground. "Then you're no longer one of us."

He turns and runs into the woods.

The rest follow.

We all stand still for a long second, just breathing.

The dragon curls tighter.

Bo drops to one knee beside her. "Hey. It's okay now. You're safe."

She blinks at him. Big silver eyes with a scatter of twinkling stars shimmer like pools.

Mari kneels too, reaching out a careful hand.

Bo closes his eyes and holds out his palms. A beam of light pours from him to the dragon, and glows on its wings.

Mari lifts her wand and mutters under her breath.

My eyes widen as I watch with bated breath.

An invisible force heals the torn wings before us. And the dragon lets out a surprised cry, before purring.

"I think she's going to live," Mari whispers. "And being near her makes me feel stronger."

Bo nods. "My powers are back."

I can't help myself. "Well done, Captain Obvious."

I share an amused look with Ajax, who is back in human form and getting dressed.

Bo stands. "We can't stay here." He looks to Ajax. "You've had your chance to convince the wolves. Now we do this my way. We go to the Heart of the Mountain."

Ajax grits his teeth but gives him a curt nod. "Agreed. If we can't convince the wolves to stand down, we need to get a message to all of the dragons to stay away from the forest."

"The problem is that only fully grown dragons can let us in to the Heart of the Mountain," Bo adds.

"But our dragons are gone..." I begin, but my voce falters under Mari's pointed stare.

"Not all of them."

She points above my head.

I swivel and crane my neck.

My chest explodes with joy, and my face breaks into a huge goofy grin.

Then a beautiful voice enters my mind.

Hello again, Little Flame. Did you miss me?

Chapter 39
The Mountain Speaks

The air is thin and sharp as we climb toward the mountain. Each breath scrapes at the back of my throat like sandpaper, and my legs are already threatening mutiny.

I'm pretty sure my thighs are going to sue me for magical negligence.

Zephy circles overhead, her enormous shadow sweeping across the jagged cliffside. Every time I glance up, I catch the glint of her red scales against the sky, like a comet made of fire and sarcasm.

You're getting weak, Little Flame. You really should've packed snacks, she says directly into my head, her mental voice as breezy as a spring morning. *An apple, maybe. Possibly a small goat. Unless you're watching your waistline, of course.*

I grunt and hoist myself over another rock. *You weigh half a mountain, and you're judging me?*

Zephyros snorts. Literally. A puff of fire bursts

from her nostrils above. *What can I say? I get my entertainment from roasting people. Figuratively.*

Behind me, Mari groans. "If I ever make it off this trail alive, I'm charming a ladder to follow me everywhere."

"Why stop there?" Bo says, clearly winded but trying not to show it. "Just enchant the mountain to carry you like a chaise lounge."

Ajax is silent, as usual, though I notice he's positioned behind all of us. Watching our backs. Or maybe just watching me.

I don't know how to feel about that anymore.

The ground is so steep, we're practically crawling our way. The heat of the earth burns hot, the higher we climb, and everything in me tingles.

"I swear this path wasn't here before," I mutter, frowning at the strange new ground. In place of normal moss and mud, there's a sleek brick road.

"We're getting close," Ajax finally says, and he's the only one of us who doesn't sound out of breath. "The Heart of the Mountain only appears to those called by it."

Of course, it does. Because nothing in this world can ever be labeled and clearly signposted like a normal magical death trap.

After what feels like a century of climbing and Mari threatening to marry a rock if it meant we could rest, we reach a ridge that overlooks the valley below.

And there it is.

Nestled in the cradle of two cliffs, half-shrouded in

mist and glowing faintly like the ember of a dying star —the Heart of the Mountain.

It's not a temple. Or a fortress. It's a cave, pulsing with golden light, veins of glowing crystal spiderwebbing across its entrance.

Zephyros lands beside us, her talons crunching into stone. She doesn't speak for once. Just stares at the cave, her eyes burning with something I've never seen in her before.

Fear.

"What is this place?" Mari asks, her voice low.

Zephy doesn't look at her.

The first dragons were born here, she says quietly. *And the first magic with them.*

I translate for Bo and Mari.

The ground beneath us hums with power. Not the sharp kind of spell work or the warmth of bonding. This is deeper. Older. Like the heartbeat of the world itself.

I'm reminded of Madam Hexley's class. When she talked about the different kinds of magic.

This is definitely not ordinary. My body shivers, takes it all in.

"I've got a bad feeling about all this," Mari whispers.

"Join the club," I mutter.

Ajax moves to the front, his steps slow but purposeful. "We need to go inside."

"Do we?" I peer into the pulsing cave. "Because it's giving off strong 'final boss' energy. And I'm not sure I'm ready."

He doesn't answer.

Instead, he marches forward.

Inside, the air is thick and buzzing, like walking through static. The walls pulse with dim golden light.

I can feel Zephy in my mind, her thoughts suddenly... muted.

I cannot follow you, she says.

"What? Why?" I stare at her, incredulous.

This is rider ground. What lies ahead is not for dragons. Not even for me.

I frown. "But I thought only a dragon can take you to the Heart of the Mountain. It can't be for riders only."

Zephy shakes her head. *Oh, Little Flame. There is still so much for you to learn. Let me tell you this, a dragon will take you to the Heart of the Mountain. But only a dragon rider can go inside.*

I don't like that answer, but I nod.

Mari, Bo, and I press forward. Ajax stays near the entrance, eyes wary.

"I'll keep watch," he says.

"Try not to brood yourself into a coma," I say, more affection in my voice than I intended.

A twinge of worry hits me somewhere in my midriff. Being apart from Ajax, especially now, feels... unnerving.

He smirks. "No promises."

The cave narrows until we're walking single file.

Bo's light magic glows faintly from his palm, illuminating runes etched into the stone.

"The air is thick with magic," he murmurs, a smile crossing his face. "Can you feel it?"

I shiver again and give him a nod. Then I look around in awe at the markings in the walls.

"They're in dragon script," Mari says.

"You can read it?"

"A bit," she says. "I took a language elective."

Of course, she did.

We reach a chamber with a circular floor and jagged walls that form a dome of crystal and rock. The air hums louder here, vibrating with unseen energy.

I feel it deep in my bones—like my blood is singing.

And then the walls shimmer.

Images flash across them, glowing gold and white:

A woman with fiery hair riding a dragon into battle.

A man kneeling in front of a beast with obsidian scales.

A child, no older than ten, shifting into a wolf under a silver moon.

Mari gasps.

"They're... memories," Bo says. "Or prophecies."

"Maybe both," I whisper.

My mark burns on my collarbone.

Then I see her.

A little girl with red hair, laughing as she dances barefoot through a field of golden grass. My breath catches.

Shelby.

The image lingers for just a second, then vanishes into light.

I stagger back. "That was—"

"I saw it too." Mari grabs my arm. "You saw a girl, right? Was she you when you were little?"

I shake my head, and my hands begin to tremble.

"I don't know what's real anymore," I whisper.

How do I explain to Mari that I've been having visions of my dead little sister?

The cave shifts again. The light dims. A voice echoes—genderless, ancient.

"You have come seeking truth. But truth demands a price."

"What price do you seek?" Bo calls out, his voice low and soft.

"The same it always has. Loyalty. Sacrifice. And blood."

Great.

Classic creepy cryptic wisdom.

A pedestal rises from the center of the room. It holds a blade, silver and gleaming, shaped like a dragon's wing.

"We can summon all of the dragons from here." Bo lifts the knife. "We just need to—"

A shout interrupts the moment.

It's from outside.

Ajax.

I don't even think. I bolt.

I burst from the cave, heart pounding, and nearly run straight into Ajax's chest. He's breathing hard, one hand bleeding, the other gripping his side.

"What happened?" I demand.

"Siberious and Mauve," he says, his voice tight. "They were already here, they summoned the dragons already and instructed them to go to the forest looking for Kayla."

Then he points—past the cliff. Toward the trees.

Smoke rises in thick black coils.

Mari and Bo rush out behind me. Zephy lands hard on the ridge.

It's burning, she says. *The whole forest is on fire.*

Ajax's face is pale. "The wolves. They set it ablaze. Hunting for another baby dragon."

I stare at the smoke. *Another* one?

I look at Zephy. "The nest? Have the eggs been hatching?"

She blinks, and a sense of knowing fills me to the brim until tears well in my eyes. All of these fresh, innocent juvenile dragons are in danger.

"Why do I get the feeling that all of this is part of Siberious's twisted plan?" I ask, thinking aloud.

"We need to stop this, what should we do?" Mari asks, catching on.

I wipe my eyes and sniff, then give Zephy a hard look. "Can you fly us back to the forest?"

She hesitates. *I can take you. But the air is thick. Visibility will be bad.*

"Bad air I can handle," I say. "Losing another dragon? I can't."

We mount.

And the sky turns red as we fly.

Chapter 40
The Ashes of Truth

The clouds are screaming, bursting my eardrums.

Or maybe it's the echo of my own.

Zephy cuts through the smoke-choked sky, her wings beating like war drums against the blaze.

Beneath us, fire devours the trees, licking hungrily at the branches, sending up plumes of orange and black.

Somewhere below, something roars. Not a grown dragon. Something smaller.

Its wounded cries claw at my insides until my organs bleed.

I clamp my eyes shut and pray.

Not again. Not now. Please.

Bo and Mari are behind me on Zephy's back, crouched low against her scales. I can feel the tension rolling off both of them.

Bo's jaw is set like stone, and Mari has her hand clenched around her wand, lips moving silently as she preps spells.

Ajax gallops below us in his wolf form, weaving between burning trees with terrifying speed. He's a blur of smoke and ash-covered fur, a ghost in the flames.

My chest tightens every time I lose sight of him.

The fire's spreading too fast, Zephy warns. *We won't reach the young one in time.*

There's pain in her voice that shakes me to the bone.

"Yes, we will," I say, more command than hope. "We have to."

She doesn't argue back, much to my relief. I don't have the energy to argue with a negative dragon.

She dives.

The heat blasts into us like a furnace as we drop. Branches crackle. Smoke clogs my throat, and ash stings my eyes.

"There!" Bo shouts, pointing to a glade where the smoke thins.

It's another baby dragon. This one is burnt orange. Its wings folded tight over its body. Trapped beneath a fallen tree. Flames curl toward it, and it doesn't move.

"No!" Mari gasps.

Zephy lands hard, talons scraping against rock.

I leap off her back before she even settles and run at full pelt.

Ajax is right next to me in wolf form.

A burst of flames blocks out path, but I'm too full of adrenaline to stop, so Ajax and I run right through it.

"KAYLA!" Bo shouts after me.

Too late.

The heat singes my eyebrows. My leathers scorch at the edges.

I duck and roll on the other side of the fire wall. I skid on my knees across the rocky ground under the smoke and reach the fallen tree, heart pounding like a war drum.

The orange dragon twitches.

"Hey," I whisper, crawling the last few paces to it. "I've got you. Hold on."

Its eyes flutter open. Blue. So very, very blue. Like little whirlpools of stars.

Ajax uses his huge body to raise the tree just enough to free the dragon from its prison.

"Bo, help me!"

He's beside me in a second.

Together, we heave.

Mari chants behind us, sending a gust of water to douse the nearby flames. They hiss angrily but die back in wisps of smoke.

The tree groans. Lifts higher.

The wolf pants, misting the air with hot breath.

Bo and I try to pick up the dragon, but even though it's small, no bigger than a Great Dane, it's heavy.

Too heavy.

We yank on its front legs instead.

"Come on. Get up. Get up quick!" I mutter to it.

The little dragon wiggles out, stumbling to its feet. It looks up at me, dazed, and then stretches its wings.

Zephy lands beside us. Her gaze is unreadable.

She is unharmed. You did well, Little Flame. she says.

I nod, breathless, heart still thundering. *I had a lot of help, but thanks.*

Zephy nudges the youngling with her huge shout. *Fly back to the nest, Andora, your mother is looking for you.*

We stand in a circle as a group and watch the dragon take to the skies with shaky wings. After it disappears in a cloud, I look down to meet Ajax's golden eyes.

He's human again, shrugging on his hunting jacket.

Then I look to Mari, who is taming her wild curls into a ponytail. Then Bo, who stands expectant and broody with his hands placed on his hips.

Everyone takes a collective breath.

"That was too close," Ajax mutters.

No one argues.

But I nod to the sound of crackling fire, of the burning forest down the path. "And it's not over. You did good, Mari, to put out these fires, but there's still so much to do."

Then the air changes.

A coldness ripples through the smoke, and my instincts make me shudder.

The fire dies. Not naturally. It just—disappears.

All signs of smoke and chaos erased with it.

An unnatural mist covers the clearing and before

anyone can ask what the heck just happened, two figures emerge through the haze.

One in crimson.

One in gray.

King Siberious.

Ms. Mauve.

My stomach sinks so fast I swear I hear it hit the ground.

Siberious looks calm. Regal. Like a man who owns the sun.

Ms. Mauve, on the other hand, looks like she's been crying for a hundred years and turned her cheeks gaunt and hollow.

Bo steps in front of me instinctively.

Mari grabs my wrist.

Ajax is somewhere by my side. His breathing comes out in short, angry bursts.

Siberious lifts a single hand.

"There is no need for any of that, we're not here to harm you," he says, the calm tone in his voice reminds me of a hunter talking to prey in his clutches, just before he's going to slit their throat.

No one moves. No one backs down.

He takes a step closer. Zephy rears on her hind legs and bears down, teeth on show.

Shall I bite his head off? I might break a tooth on his thick skull, but it would be worth it.

I give Zephy a look. *Not yet.*

"I commend you," he says, his voice like velvet over steel. "That was a daring rescue. Brave. Foolish, but brave nonetheless."

My mouth is dry. "You knew there was a dragon here?"

Siberious blinks too slow, like a parent preparing to explain quantum physics to their curious toddler.

"Of course."

Mari gasped. "And you would let it burn to death?"

Siberious's gaze slides to Bo for a moment. Then he meets my horrified gaze.

"I let nature take its course."

Ajax snarls. "You lit the match."

Mauve steps in, her wings shimmer as she speaks. "You don't understand what's at stake here. None of you do. This is all a lot to take in. To digest."

"Then explain it simply," I snap. "Or my dragon will digest *you*."

She looks at me, and for a second, just a flicker, she looks sorry.

"The dragons are too powerful," she says. "If left unchecked, they will destroy us all. They are not your friends. They are not pets. They are not gods. They are the embodiment of chaos."

Zephy growls from behind me.

She's lucky I don't eat fairies. Their guts stick to the roof of my mouth. But if she keeps talking, I may have to make an exception. She smells like dragon.

My mouth falls open.

"You're feeding off them," I say, the pieces clicking together. "You're stealing their magic."

Siberious smiles. "I prefer to call it borrowing. Channeling. Containing."

He inclines his head at me. "You've tasted it too, Kayla. Do you remember? In my office."

My throat constricts.

The drink he gave me that heightened my senses and made me feel...everything, all at once. "That elixir was... dragon blood?"

Mauve sighs. "You've never been the brightest student. But really? Do we have to explain everything?"

Mari coughs and mumbles to me. "Magic, not blood. The elixir was their magic."

Siberious smiles at Mari. "Yes, Marigold. Magic."

Bo's face pales. "You're bottling their magic. You said dragons are to be protected. It was our sacred vow... Was all of that just—"

"Would you rather the world burn?" Siberious's eyes are dull when they land on Bo. "Would you rather wild magic consume your cities, your loved ones? And destroy everything we've worked so hard to build?"

Bo just shakes his head. Either too sickened to speak, or unable to dishonor his father.

Fury bubbles in my chest.

"I'd rather you not lie to teenagers and throw them into your twisted little Hunger Games," I snap. "All this time you've been using us as bait, killing us when we're an inconvenience... just so you can keep your power."

He sighs. "Oh, the dramatics of youth. Spare us the guilt trip, Kayla. I had enough of that from Charlotte."

My mind freezes. "You killed her. She found out the truth, and you killed her."

Mauve blinks. "Her dragon died tragically in a thunderstorm. That is all."

Zephy steps forward with a roar. *Lies! I was there. They hunted Cornelius. Not wolves. Not hunters. Them. I can smell his blood on that woman's breath!*

My stomach lurches at the words, then I scowl at Siberious and Mauve, as rage burns through me, threatening to burst me into flames.

Zephyros. I've heard enough. Kill them both.

Zephy roars, letting out a jet of fire.

But Siberious and Mauve stand cool and collected.

Mauve waves her hand in a flourish, and the fire bursts into millions of sparkling glitter. Floating in the air.

Siberious lifts his hand as Zephy charges forward.

She freezes mid-step.

Siberious snaps his fingers.

Her body goes rigid, her wings stuck, pinned to her back.

I scream. "Let her go!"

"She belongs to us," Mauve says. "As do you."

Bo charges. His light magic flares like a whip.

Ajax follows, shifting mid-sprint into his massive wolf form.

Mari conjures fire balls and tosses them, screaming like she's possessed.

Chaos erupts.

I duck under a blast of magic but get knocked by an invisible punch and tumble away from the group. I spit blood and jump to my feet, ready to go again.

But then I meet Siberious.

He stands unmoving, like a storm around the eye. He watches me. Just me.

"So, you've heard the prophecy. But I don't see it." His judgmental gaze washes over me as I stagger forward, brandishing my sword.

With a wave of the hand, my sword flies out of my clutches and buries itself in a nearby tree.

My hands ball into fists.

But Siberious's lips curve upward. "They're wrong. You're not a wolf. You're not magical. And there's nothing special about you, Kayla Whitman. You were just a sad girl who never recovered from a plane crash. Trapped."

I shake my head, panting. "How do you know about…?"

Siberious laughs, soft and dangerous. "I know all about you. I know you have had nightmares ever since that day. I know you distanced yourself from anyone who loved you. And you destroy anything you touch."

His gaze flickers to the group up the hill, deep in a battle with Mauve, who takes them on single-handedly.

"They will die because of you, Kayla," Siberious says, too simply. His discerning stare hits me square between the eyes.

"They will die," he repeats. Slow and deliberate. "Because they die for a cause. For a lie. About you."

The weight of his words crushes me until I fall to my knees.

He towers, a twisted smile etched on his wrinkled face.

"The dragons call you the bridge," he says softly. "And bridges? They are made to be broken."

He raises his palm again. And this time, I *feel* it.

A pulse. Deep in my chest. In my mark.

Pain.

Zephy cries out, locked in place.

I scream.

The world tilts...

Everything goes dark.

* * *

I wake to snow.

It's not real. But it *feels* real. My skin tingles with the cold. The wind howls.

I whip around, searching, searching for my friends. But I'm surrounded by white barren wasteland.

I scan the skies, looking for Zephy, but I'm all alone.

Then, there's a voice.

Feminine. Familiar.

"Kayla."

With a sharp inhale, I turn around and meet the person who called me.

My sister.

But she's older. Taller. Glowing with golden light.

"Shelby?"

Hot tears well in my eyes, and I stumble to her.

She's solid and warm when I throw my arms around her narrow frame. The familiar scent of coconut shampoo washes over my senses as I bury my face in her hair.

Maybe this is real after all. It's too grounding.

Maybe Shelby made it to this realm too? Or maybe we all died in that crash, and I've just finally crossed over to whatever this wasteland is.

Limbo?

Heaven?

Something else?

When we break apart, she smiles. Tender and sad.

"You have to wake up."

I frown. "I am awake."

Shelby's smile vanishes, and her eyes harden. She dips her chin.

"No, you're not. He's trying to take you. You have to fight back."

Her words hit me like a million tiny knives. But my brain is unable to understand them.

"Who?"

But she's gone.

A roar shatters the scene.

Zephyros charges through snow. And rams into a wall of gold light.

Siberious stands beyond it. His robes bleeding, red and dangerous.

But nothing is as unsettling as his smile, which doesn't quite reach his eyes.

"You belong to me now."

I wake for real, this time.

Coughing. Crying. Alive.

Bo's face hovers above mine, blood on his cheek.

Mari sobs somewhere nearby.

Ajax leans over me, his hand on my heart. "You're okay. You're okay."

Zephyros is beside us, weak but alive.

"Siberious..."

"They're gone." Bo's face is unusually pale. "I was so close to breaking Mauve's neck with my light whip, but she suddenly vanished. Like a wisp."

Mari hugs her knees sobbing.

Ajax turns to her. "It's alright. She's alive. She's okay."

I guess he's talking about me.

Mari finally takes a look at me, praises the heavens, and throws her arms around me.

"You were jerking and twitching. The screams will haunt me for the rest of my life," she mumbles into my neck. "I thought Siberious was going to kill you right there and then."

I take a shaky breath as I stand.

"Maybe...maybe he did," I wonder aloud.

I look at Zephy. *I saw my sister. She was real and solid.*

Zephy nods. *I saw her too.*

My heart skips a beat.

If my dragon saw her, then maybe it wasn't a strange afterlife. Maybe...

But before I can speculate on it all, Bo gives me a look.

"He knows who you are. He knows about the prophecy."

"I know." I rub the dragon tattoo on my collarbone. It pulses.

The pain is dull, but it's still there.

Mari sniffs and whispers, "He wants to use you."

"No. He wants to break me."

Ajax meets me with a searching look, then he casts his sights around the group with a grim expression.

"Then we will break him first."

Chapter 41
When the Sky Breaks

Siberious and Mauve left behind a savage path of destruction. Now that they are gone, the illusion that everything was fine in the forest is gone too.

The ground is silver and crunches beneath my boots. Ash falls like snow, coating everything in a blanket of silence. Every step forward feels like walking through a graveyard of what we've lost and what we could still lose.

We move as one, quieter now. The adrenaline has worn off, leaving behind fatigue and the kind of dread that sinks into your bones and builds a nest there.

I steal glances at my friends.

Mari's brows are tight with worry, her lips pressed in a hard line.

Bo's movements are sharp, clipped, and erratic, like he's burning inside and has no way to cool down.

Zephy flies above, casting long shadows over the scorched earth. She hasn't said a word since we started walking, but I can feel her still in the back of my mind. Her emotions swirl like a hurricane—rage, confusion, and something quieter: grief.

Ajax walks beside me in his human form, silent as ever, but his hands clench and unclench at his sides.

I've grown used to his quiet brooding, but now it feels heavier. Like even he doesn't know what comes next.

"We need to regroup," Mari says at last. Her voice is hoarse, and she doesn't meet my gaze.

"We need to hide," Bo says. "Siberious won't just let us go. Not now."

"Let him come," Ajax growls. "I'm tired of running."

Usually, I would agree. It feels like running is all I've done since I stepped foot in this realm. But the alternative twists my stomach into a knot.

I'm not ready to face him again.

Not smart enough. Not strong enough.

Watch your words. Zephy's voice enters my mind.

I bite my lip at the reminder, then give the sky a nod.

Bo spins on Ajax. "And what, you want to take him head-on? That man just froze a dragon with a hand wave."

Ajax shrugs. "I'm not afraid of him."

"Well, maybe you should be!" Bo shouted. "You don't know him like I do. What he's capable of."

"Enough!" I snap. "We're wasting time."

The silence that follows is thick.

I walk a few paces ahead, needing distance from

the tension snapping in the air like live wires. I try to think—about what we saw, about what it means.

Siberious said I'm the bridge. And bridges are meant to be broken.

The mark on my collarbone burns again, and I wince, pressing my hand over it.

Bo notices. "Are you okay?"

I nod. "Fine."

He doesn't believe me. I can see it in his eyes.

When the moons shift and night falls, we set up a small camp in the ruins of an old tower. Its stones are blackened with age, and the top has long since crumbled, leaving open sky overhead. Zephy curls protectively around us, her body forming a crescent that blocks the wind.

Ajax and Mari sit afar off, looking at the stars. I can just make out their faint voices, sharing stories of the constellations.

Bo sits beside me, passing me a canteen.

"You're quiet," he says.

I shrug. "What's there to say? Everything I knew was a lie. My school trains teenagers to be sacrifices, my mentor's a soul-sucking psychopath, and apparently, I'm the bridge between warring magical species. Oh, and I nearly died today. Again."

He huffs a breath—almost a laugh, but not quite. "That about covers it, I guess."

The fire crackles between us.

Bo leans back on his elbows, staring at the stars. "Do you think we'll ever go back to normal?"

"What's normal?" Mari asks, glum. She settles next to me with a sigh.

Her mood plant is a sad tinge of gray, slumped over her shoulder, looking more like a dying weed than a plant.

Bo looks up at the sky. "I don't know. Class. Training. Complaining about breakfast options."

I smile faintly. "If I ever see another bowl of plain oatmeal, I might cry with happiness."

A long silence passes. The kind that feels more like a conversation than the ones filled with words.

Ajax approaches the fire and stares at it with a deep frown. "It's getting cold. I'm going to get some firewood."

Mari picks up her wand. "I'll go with you. Maybe on the way, we can find something to eat that hasn't been scorched."

I watch Mari and Ajax disappear into the tree line with a heavy heart.

"I'm sorry," Bo says suddenly.

I jerk my head in his direction. Surprised. "For what?"

"For being…difficult. For not trusting Ajax. I shouldn't have left."

"You had every reason not to trust him." I nudge him. "He's a wolf shifter. You've grown up believing them to be the enemy."

"But I should've trusted you."

I look at him. "Bo…"

He sits up. There's something raw in his expression now, like a storm cracking just under the surface.

"I care about you, Kayla. I don't know how to say that without sounding like an idiot. But I do. And if something happens to you, if Siberious gets to you, I swear—"

"Stop," I whisper, reaching for his hand. "Don't say it. We're going to make it. All of us."

He closes his fingers around mine. "I hope so."

Just then, a sound cuts through the night.

Wings. Heavy. Many.

Zephy lifts her head with a sharp hiss. *We have company.*

I hitch a breath as Bo and I break apart.

"I can hear them, to the east." I curl my fingers around the hilt of my sword.

Man, can a girl not catch a break?

Dragons. Five. No—six. Their shapes blot out the moon.

In their shadows, a pack of wolves.

Mari and Ajax tumble into the campsite.

"They're hunting again." Ajax drops an armful of logs onto the ground. "Get out of the path, they're heading right for us."

We grab weapons.

Zephy launches into the air, bellowing fire across the sky. *The alpha forbade us from flying over the forest. I shall remind the dragons to follow command.*

Before we can scramble away, the wolves reach us. Snarling and thrashing the air like wild beasts.

The clash is instant. Bo and I fight back-to-back, Mari casting shields and flame.

Ajax leaps into wolf form.

It's calamity—claws, fire, spells bursting like flares.

My ears throb at it all, and my heart pumps fresh adrenaline through me.

Then, a cry.

Bo.

I turn.

A wolf has its giant jaws clamped over his side.

A gut-wrenching crunch breaks my heart and when the wolf lets go, Bo falls heavy and awkward.

The impact thrusts a cloud of dust in the sky, and the wolf leaps away.

Time slows.

"NO!" I run toward Bo.

He's on the ground, lips pale, breath ragged.

"It's that bad?" he gasps.

Blood leaks from his mouth, and he pants.

I press hard on his side, but he cries out.

"Bo, no. Stay with me, okay? We're not done here!"

I scream for Mari. But she's too busy deflecting the wolves. A flickering protection spell covers us.

Wolves hit the barrier and yelp, like they've struck an electric fence.

I turn back to Bo, tears misting my vision.

"Bo, you're going to be fine." I try to sound calm.

But Siberious's words echo in my brain like a war drum.

They will die, because of you.

Bo touches my face. His calloused fingertips graze my cheek, and I wet them with my tears.

"Bo, hold on. Just wait a little longer. The wolves

will move on, and then Mari will fix you right up," I say more to myself than him.

Bo's ears turn ashen gray, and his eyes turn distant.

A soft smile breaks through.

He whispers, "See you in another life, Kayla."

And then, he's still.

Mari shrieks, and the protective field shatters. She looks at Bo, clutching her face.

Before I can speak—before I can scream again—a guttural, wounded shriek cuts through the sky.

A dragon.

Not Zephy.

Golden wings beat downward with panicked force as what I can only assume is Bo's bonded dragon, blazing with light magic, crashes through the trees.

The dragon lands in a burst of radiant fire, its eyes wild and glowing. It screeches as it lowers its neck, nudging Bo's body with frantic care.

"Wait—" I choke out, reaching toward them.

But it's too late.

The dragon scoops Bo's limp form into its claws, and with a furious, heartbroken roar, takes to the sky. It vanishes into the clouds, trailing fire and light in its wake.

"BO!" Mari screams.

Ajax drags me back, even as I thrash against him.

"He's gone, Kayla. We have to move!"

But my heart is broken open.

And the war has only just begun.

Chapter 42
The Weight of What's Gone

The world is quieter now, but not in a peaceful way. It's the kind of quiet that comes after an explosion. The kind where your ears ring and your heart doesn't know how to beat properly anymore.

The kind where someone is gone.

We make camp deep in the forest, away from the smoke and ash, away from the blood.

It doesn't matter how far we go. The ghost of Bo's last words follows me like a shadow I can't shake.

See you in another life.

Zephy coils herself around the perimeter of our camp as usual. Her body, normally warm and humming with life, is still. Her scales have lost some of their luster, dulled by grief. Every now and then, I feel her pulse in my mind, a quiet ripple of sorrow, like waves lapping against a shore at midnight.

Mari hasn't spoken since Bo was taken. She hasn't cried either, which somehow feels worse. Her right palm is blistered from holding her wand too tight, for too long. Her cheeks are pale. Her eyes—blank. The mood plant is black and motionless on her shoulder.

Ajax paces. He's been pacing for over an hour, jaw clenched, hands twitching at his sides like he doesn't know whether to punch something or turn into a wolf and tear through the forest.

I sit in silence, hugging my knees, staring into the flickering campfire.

The heat should be comforting, but it doesn't touch me.

I'm cold again.

"He's not dead." I startle both of them.

Mari doesn't move.

Ajax stops pacing. "Kayla—"

"No," I say, louder now. "He can't be. He said—he said—"

My voice catches.

I bite the inside of my cheek until I taste blood.

"Zephy," I whisper, turning to my dragon. "Can you sense him? Can you reach his dragon?"

A long pause. Then, her voice, quiet and tired in my head. *There's a tether... faint... but not completely severed. Siberious has him.*

I close my eyes, releasing a shaky breath. "He is alive. Zephy says he's back at the school."

Ajax crouches beside me. "That doesn't mean he's safe, and he's mortally wounded."

I glare at him. "I don't care. If there's even a chance—"

"I know," he says gently. "We'll find him. But we

have to be smart about this. If we charge back to Theridon now, we'll get killed."

Mari speaks at last, her voice flat. "Siberious let us go. Why?"

I look at her. "What?"

"He let us go," she repeats, her fingers curling in the dirt. "He had us. All of us. He and Mauve could've ended it. But they didn't. Instead, they just left us. I think he wanted Bo to be taken. He wanted us to run."

The fire crackles between us.

"I think," Mari continues, "he's clearing the board. Letting the game reset. Putting the pieces where he wants them."

That idea sends a chill down my spine. "And what piece are we?"

I let the silence settle over us again. Then I push to my feet.

"We can't just sit here."

Ajax tilts his head. "What do you suggest?"

"We find the wolves," I say. "Your tribe. They need to hear what happened. They need to know the truth."

Ajax's expression tightens. "What's the point? They won't listen. They didn't before. What will change now?"

"They will this time." I look at him, firm. "Because this time, *I'll* make them."

He studies me for a moment, then nods. "Fine. But we go at dawn. You need sleep first."

Sleep? The word tastes foreign. Like a language I forgot how to speak.

Besides, there's an old saying that goes *'there is*

no rest for the wicked'. Judging on my life, I must be really evil.

Still, I lie down near Zephy's side. Her scales warm beneath my cheek.

Mari curls up beside me without a word.

I stare up at the sky, cursing all the stars that watched everything happen. And did nothing.

Now, they dare to twinkle, as if this is just like any other night.

I wonder if Bo's looking up at them too.

Siberious will heal him, I decide with my teeth gritted. *He's going to be fine*.

He has to be.

Dawn breaks sluggishly. The forest is still cloaked in mist when we set off, following the path back to the ridge where Ajax believes his people may have returned.

The walk is mostly silent, broken only by the occasional bird call or the crunch of boots on leaves.

Zephy flies above us, weaving between the clouds.

Mari lags behind, lost in thought.

Ajax keeps pace beside me.

"You okay?" he asks.

I glance at him. "Do I look okay?"

He shrugs. "No. But I figured I'd ask anyway."

There's something steadying about him today. Less snark. More... weight. Like he knows we're crossing into territory we can't come back from.

When we reach the ridge, smoke curls faintly into the sky. Campfires.

Ajax and I stop and exchange a knowing look.

The tribe.

With a nod, Ajax shifts into his wolf form and howls—a low, eerie sound that echoes through the trees.

A moment later, a chorus answers.

By the time we reach the clearing, we're surrounded.

Wolves circle us, tense and on edge. A few shift back into their human forms, eyeing me with suspicion.

"It's her," one mutters. "The dragon girl."

Ajax shifts back, standing protectively between me and the others.

"I need to speak to your leader." I force my voice to stay calm.

"Why would we listen to you?" one of the older wolves snaps, stepping forward. "She is a rider, not a wolf."

"She's both," Ajax growls. "And if you'd shut up and listen for once, you'd realize that might be what saves us."

An older man steps forward. His silver-streaked beard and lined face mark him as one of the elders. His eyes, sharp and calculating, land on me.

"Speak, girl."

I take a breath.

"You've been fed lies to hunt dragons," I say. "But it's not for the reason you think. You're working for King Siberious. He's using dragons to feed off their magic. But listen, when dragons die, so does magic. And when magic dies..."

Murmurs ripple through the crowd. "What foolish nonsense."

"Lies," someone hisses.

I press on. "A dragon was killed last night. A young one. And when it died, a student at Theridon died too. No wounds. Just... gone. Hollowed out."

The elder narrows his eyes. "How do you know this?"

"I saw it. I felt it."

"You bonded to a dragon. Your magic is tainted."

"No. My magic is *connected*. That's the difference. And if you keep hunting them, you'll destroy the balance holding this world together."

A long silence follows.

The quiet gives me courage. After a reassuring nod from Ajax, I continue.

"Siberious wants you to hunt dragons. They are not the enemy. He is."

A sea of suspicious eyes beam on me, and I swallow hard. But I stand my ground, staring everyone down and waiting for their judgment.

Then, a sharp howl cuts through the tension.

Another wolf, breathless, bursts into the clearing. "We found another. A big dragon, it's trapped. In the western pass."

The wolves begin to stir. Excited. Hungry.

"No." I step forward. "Don't do this, it's a trap."

They ignore me.

Ajax's face hardens. "If you touch that dragon, you will doom us all."

The elder lifts his chin. "We made a vow to hunt dragons. And hunt dragons we shall. Every. Last. One."

And with that, the pack takes off, shifting mid-sprint into wolves and disappearing into the trees.

Ajax looks at me. "We have to stop them."

I nod.

Zephyros dives overhead, roaring.

The chase is on.

Chapter 43
The Dragon Hunt

The forest blurs as we run. Twigs snap. Leaves scatter.

Zephy circles above us like a blood-red omen, her screech echoing through the trees.

My boots slam against the ground, lungs burning.

Ajax runs ahead in his wolf form, swift and silent as a shadow.

Mari struggles to keep up, panting and muttering spells under her breath to lighten her steps.

Every part of me screams. Not from exhaustion—but urgency.

The wolves are ahead. And they're going to kill a dragon.

Another one. And another rider will fall.

What if this one is Mari's?

The trees thin.

We crest a ridge, and I catch my first glimpse.

A clearing. Flattened brush. Scorched earth.

In the center, a small dragon, its scales a pale, icy

blue, it's not as big as Zephy. Like the size of an elephant.

And circling it—wolves.

Not in playful arcs.

In hunting formation.

"NO!" I leap down the ridge.

One wolf lunges.

But Ajax hits him mid-air, snarling, teeth flashing.

They roll, crashing into a tree.

Mari lands beside me, wand in hand. "We can't kill them, they're not evil. They just don't understand what they're doing!"

"I know!" I shout. "But we have to stop them!"

She throws up a barrier, a crackling dome of green light.

The wolves hiss and reel back, unable to pass through.

The dragon makes a wounded cry and flattens its body to the ground.

Zephy dives overhead and lets out a roar that shakes the sky. She lands behind us, wings spread wide, her shadow engulfing the entire clearing.

The wolves hesitate.

Until a voice cuts through the tension like poisoned silk.

"Well, well. Playing guardian now, are we?"

Mauve steps out of the trees, her silver hair pinned into a perfect bun. Her eyes gleam like glass. Too cold. Too knowing.

"Mauve," I hiss. "You followed us."

"Don't flatter yourself, girl. You're a walking disruption. Rather easy to find."

Ajax growls low beside me, blood on his muzzle. He shifts, half-wolf now, fangs still showing.

Mauve eyes me with something resembling pity. "I warned you. I told Siberious this would happen. One girl. One broken plane. And now you've cracked the whole world in half."

"You're the one killing students," I snap. "You and Siberious. The dragons aren't the enemy. You are."

Her smile turns cruel. "Sweetheart. You bonded to a dragon and a wolf. And yet, you aren't one of them. How useful do you think you are with that pitiful sword on your hip? You're no one's hero. You're an abomination. A stain to be erased."

Zephy roars, but Mauve only lifts her hand. She slashes the air with a flick of her fingers.

A wave of dark magic hits Zephy.

She stumbles, one wing collapsing with a crunch. Her head swings dangerously low.

"ZEPHYROS!" I scream, running to her side.

Pain surges through my shoulder. Hot. Wild.

Zephy and I are bonded. That means she feels my pain, and I feel hers.

I crouch to her. *Be brave. Stay with me.*

She's too powerful. There's too much dragon magic in her veins. Zephy's voice is faint.

Her galaxy eyes begin to fade, like someone is blotting out the stars.

No.

Something inside me snaps.

Something ancient.

Something not human.

I open my mouth and expect a scream to fly out of it, but no. It's something deeper, harsher.

A growl.

The atoms in my body tremble at lightning speed. Faster than ever before as pure rage floods every part of my soul.

I keep a steely look on Mauve's satisfied smirk.

She's raising her hand again, ready to make the final blow on my dragon.

But she pauses, and her gaze lands on me again. Mouth open to form the perfect O.

My bones crack. Limbs stretch. My spine arches. My fingers become claws.

I launch into the air with another growl.

I collapse, gasping, snarling. And I'm not Kayla anymore.

I'm a wolf.

Sleek, golden fur, my vision is crisp.

The world sharpens.

I can smell Mauve's perfume, bitter and oily. I can hear the heartbeat of every wolf in the clearing.

And I run.

Straight at her.

Ajax blocks me. "Not now!" he growls. "She's not alone."

I spin, snarling, confused.

And then, behind her, something moves.

Siberious.

Astride a massive, onyx-black scaled dragon.

He's here.

He raises a hand.

The wolves go still.

The air ripples with raw power.

It crawls over my fur, down to my bones.

The harshness in his countenance makes my stomach turn. Surely, there is only one reason a father would turn this cold. This far gone from any sense of humanity.

Bo is gone.

"You've made your choice, Kayla Whitman." His voice is calm. Too calm. "There will be no forgiveness now."

Zephy lifts her head, struggling to rise to her feet.

The young blue dragon stumbles to her, hiding under her massive, wounded wing.

Siberious snaps his fingers, and the sky ignites.

Fire. Not from a dragon. From magic. A wall of it.

"Mari!" I howl—my voice warped, still wolf.

She casts a dome around us, shielding us all from the blaze.

Ajax grabs me by the scruff and pulls me back.

RUN! His voice shouts in my head.

I nudge Mari's back with urgency, and she takes the hint, climbing onto my back.

We flee. Back into the forest.

Zephy takes to the skies, her wing is at an awkward angle, and she's bleeding. But the younger dragon flies beneath it, propping it up.

The fire chases us. So do the shadows.

Branches whip past my face.

My paws bleed.

Mari gasps.

Mauve's cackle fades behind us.

The forest is burning.

And we barely escape.

We collapse in a ravine just as the red moon dips low in the sky and the silver one begins to rise.

Zephy lands hard beside us, too weak to hold herself up.

Mari drops to her knees. "I—I don't know if she'll make it."

I shift back, collapsing into a heap.

Sweat. Blood. Ash. Naked.

My head spins.

Mari tosses me her satchel, and I shakily pull on a cotton dress.

Then Ajax pulls me close, brushing soot and sweat from my forehead.

I tremble uncontrollably in his arms.

"You shifted." He gives me a proud look.

I nod weakly. "I didn't mean to. It just... I was so angry. So primal..."

He nods. "It was time."

The baby dragon cuddles against Zephy, tiny and shaking next to her.

Mari wastes no time, muttering spells over her wing.

I sense the magic pouring into Zephy, it floods me with a soothing sensation.

When she's done, Zephy drops into a deep sleep, too exhausted to stay awake a moment longer.

I lay on Ajax's chest, his heartbeat thumps against my ear. "At least, we were able to outrun them. We saved the dragon and got away."

Mari hums deep. "No, Mauve was just startled that you turned into a wolf. I don't think she expected that to happen."

I cradle my head, trying to ignore the pulsing pain in my temples. "They let us go again."

Mari weeps, not for the dragon. Not for Bo.

But for everything.

And the heartbreak that is yet to come.

Chapter 44
The Edge of Everything

"I can't sit here and do nothing. I'll go and find us some water," Mari mutters after trying and failing to sit in stunned silence.

Zephy and her little dragon snooze, ignorant to the storm of emotions in my chest.

Then my gaze flickers back to Ajax, who can't stop grinning.

"Will you stop that? We're in the middle of a war, and you're looking at me like you've already won."

Ajax's forehead reddens. "I'm sorry," he says, but he doesn't look it. "I'm just replaying it in my head."

I try to scowl at him, but it's impossible under his triumphant smile. "Stop it. Things are bad. Really bad. You can't be happy."

"Yes, I can." Ajax takes my hands and grazes them with his thumbs. "You were amazing back there."

Butterflies.

"But I couldn't control it, who knows what I'll do next time."

Ajax's hand moves to my jaw, tentative. "You don't have to be afraid of what you are."

"I'm afraid of how out of control I feel," I whisper. "I'm afraid of what I might do next."

Ajax's eyes glow like stars in the darkness as he studies me. "You saved our lives."

I grit my teeth. "I couldn't save Bo."

There it is. The truth, raw and sharp.

Maybe if I had learned to shift earlier, maybe if I was stronger, I could have saved him. He'd still be here.

His expression falters. "Kayla..."

"I saw Siberious, he was grieving," I say. "I *smelled* it on him."

My voice breaks, and so do I.

I fold in on myself, but Ajax catches me. His arms wrap around me like a shield.

I don't fight it. I'm too tired. Too broken.

Too guilty.

He holds me close, hand cradling the back of my head like he's afraid I'll unravel. "Bo wouldn't blame you, and neither do I," he murmurs into my hair. "He knew the risks."

I don't answer. Only giant, wracked sobs tumble out of me.

I haven't cried for a long time. After the plane crash, I cried myself to sleep. That is...until everything went numb, and the tears refused to come.

Since then, I've had control. I could shut off my emotions and keep them at bay while I faced whatever crazy challenge hit me.

But now... now I'm soaking Ajax's shirt with tears and snot and making a total fool of myself. But I can't stop. I won't stop.

It's all too much.

"Bo wouldn't want you to fall apart," Ajax murmurs into my hair.

"I'm *already* falling apart," I whisper, clutching his soggy shirt. "I don't know who I am anymore. I'm not just some girl who survived a plane crash. I'm not even human. I'm a monster with fur and teeth and—"

Ajax's mouth is hot and wet and... stuck to mine.

The kiss is sudden. Desperate. Not polished or poetic, just raw emotion colliding with emotion.

For a heartbeat, I kiss him back.

I give in. Letting him carry my weight as he peppers my lips with kisses.

Soft. Lingering. Tender.

It's not fireworks.

It's a lifeline. Like he's trying to kiss me better.

Trying to heal me.

But Bo's ashen gray face enters my mind, and guilt burns away at my insides until I press my palms on Ajax's chest and push him away.

I tear my lips away and bite back tears.

"I—no. I can't. I'm sorry."

Ajax's eyes widen. "Kayla, I didn't mean—"

"It's not you," I say quickly, hating the hurt written all over his handsome face. "It's me. It's Bo. It's everything. I don't know what this is. I don't know *what I am*."

I drag my hands over my face and sniff, trying to center myself.

I can't go kissing boys when the world is on fire and I'm a hair's width away from death at any given time.

Ajax takes in my thoughts with several nods, and he gives my hand a squeeze. "It's fine. I get it."

An ache gnaws into my chest as I chew my lip, torn.

Part of me does want to forget everything and enjoy smooching the hot brooding wolf shifter. But it feels wrong.

Not now. Not when so much is at stake, and I still don't know how to be a bridge that doesn't crumble.

"I just need time," I whisper.

Ajax caresses my cheek, his warmth sends a rush of tingles from my head right down to my toes.

"I'll wait as long as it takes."

My heart squeezes as I nod back.

That's the thing about Ajax. He means it.

* * *

We wake to the smell of ash and the sound of wind whispering through the charred remains of the forest. Trees that once stood proud now curl like skeletal fingers toward the smoky sky.

Zephy sleeps nearby, her wounds bandaged with strips of Mari's cloak and healing moss.

Mari is still asleep. Her head rests against a tree stump, her cheek smudged with soot. She clutches her wand even in dreams. She hasn't let go of it since the fire. Since losing Bo.

Ajax is already up. Shirtless again—seriously, what is it with this guy and shirts?

His chest is streaked with soot and scars, his dark hair wild, but his movements are precise as he sharpens a blade near the edge of the ravine.

I stretch, wincing as every muscle screams in protest. "Do you sleep at all?"

He glances at me, one eyebrow raised. "Do you?"

Fair.

I spent the night thrashing around, trying to get comfortable, but my brain wouldn't let me relax. I replayed our kiss a million times, until it was burned into my memory.

Sleep only came when I literally passed out from exhaustion. But thankfully, I didn't dream.

I never do when I'm with him.

I stand, brushing ash off my pants. My body is still sore from the transformation. From running. From the near-death everything. "So, we should make a plan, right?"

Ajax stabs the blade into the dirt. "We don't have time to run. Or hide. The dragons are rallying. Mauve and Siberious will come for us. We either wait to die or fight."

I sit beside him, eyeing the scorched horizon. "Do we even have a chance?"

His jaw clenches. "With you? Maybe."

I snort. "Because I turned into a furry rage monster one time?"

He chuckles, low and soft. "Because you care. You throw yourself into danger for strangers. That's not something Siberious will ever understand. He leads with fear. You lead with fire."

He reaches over, brushing a lock of hair from my cheek.

My breath catches.

"And because you're stubborn," he adds, his voice quieter now. "Ridiculously stubborn. You won't let them win."

We sit in silence for a moment, the tension of upcoming danger coiling in my body like fog.

Then I ask the question I've been avoiding. "What happens if we lose?"

He looks away for a moment, looking at the rising red moon.

"Then we lose together," he mutters. "Nothing else matters."

My stomach flutters in a way that has nothing to do with impending doom.

He leans closer.

The firelight reflects in his amber eyes. There's something unspoken in the air between us, charged and crackling.

His hand brushes mine.

And I don't pull away.

"Kayla," he murmurs, voice rough, "I've been thinking about what you said last night, and I don't know what this thing is between us either. But I've never—"

"GUYS!" Mari shrieks.

Riders and Hunters

We both jump apart like guilty teenagers.

She's pointing toward the sky.

Dragons.

Hundreds.

Not the cute, gold, red, and blue colored dragons. The jet black gnarly ones with jagged outlines, shadows of death in the sky.

All flying toward Theridon.

Zephy's tired voice enters my mind. *The alpha has commanded all dragons to join the king and prepare for battle.*

Nausea ripples up my throat. "Battle...with who?"

Ajax answers. "Who else? The wolves kill younglings. Pretty sure that makes Siberious and Mauve look like they're the good side."

Mari's breath hitches, and she pulls her curls back into a ponytail. "Siberious uses the wolves to keep the dragon population down. He won't support an attack."

I give her a surprised look. "Maybe he doesn't have a choice. A hoard of assassin dragons is on the way to Theridon Academy."

Giant, ear-splitting roars flood the air and streaks of red and orange snake across the sky.

"Well," I mutter, heart hammering. "That escalated quickly."

I turn to Zephy. "Are you good to fly?"

She gets on her legs and shakes like a giant, awkward dog. The makeshift bandages and bits of moss go flying.

You have heart, Little Flame. But do you really want to go flying into the fire?

I get up and start to pace. "If dragons start killing wolves on Siberious's command, it will only drive a deeper forge between both sides."

Ajax sheathes his sword with a nod. "Even the moderate-minded packs like mine will not rest until every last dragon is dead."

Mari shrugs her jacket tighter with a shiver. "What is Siberious plotting? He needs dragons, for the power. He doesn't want wolves to become unhinged."

Ajax hums, then his intense gaze shifts to me. "I think he's willing to risk everything to prove a point."

I narrow my eyes on him as a memory crosses my mind. "The prophecy. He'll do anything to stop it from happening."

We all look to the skies.

"Even if it means burning the whole world down."

Mari's words send my blood cold.

We gather supplies and climb Zephy.

The moment I'm on her back, the world shifts.

She speaks in my head, her thoughts a storm of panic and sass.

Oh great, the final battle. Let's just hope my scales hold up better than your sarcasm, Kayla.

"You love my sarcasm," I mutter.

Like I love chewing on a cyclops's eyeball. Hold on tight, Little Flame. Things are about to heat up.

Ajax rides behind me. His arms around my waist are strong and warm.

I hate how safe I feel. Like this moment, despite everything, is where I'm supposed to be.

Mari is behind Ajax. "I'm not ready for this."

"Neither am I," I shout back.

Zephy growls. *Speak for yourselves. I'm ready to bite someone's face off. Maybe two someones.*

As Theridon comes into view, my stomach flips.

Smoke curls from the towers. The banners have changed. No longer gold and red. Now they're black.

The skies are barren of rainclouds, offering no protection.

The gates are wide open.

Waiting.

My breath stops.

It's a trap.

We land on the edge of the courtyard, cobblestones still slick with old blood.

What's left of the students and teachers gather at the far end, all wearing blank expressions.

Are they enchanted? Fearful?

It's impossible to tell.

Siberious stands at the top of the stairs, draped in shadows. Mauve beside him, her silver hair gleaming like ice.

He spreads his arms in a false act of hospitality.

A chill snakes up my spine.

"Welcome back to Theridon, Kayla. I had a feeling you'd return. You have too much left to learn."

Ajax growls low behind me.

I step forward. "I'm not here for pleasantries."

"No," Siberious says softly. "You're here to die."

He raises his hand.

The courtyard erupts into chaos.

Spells fly.

Fire rains from the sky.

Zephy dives, scattering soldiers.

Mari lets out a battle cry and launches a ball of flame into a stack of guards, sending them fleeing.

Mari stands tall, smiling, her wand glowing.

A fiery inferno jets over a group of students, who cower, cradling their heads.

Just before they are incinerated, Mari casts a protective bubble over them.

"Get inside the school," she orders them.

They do as they're told.

I fight with both hands carrying my sword. Awkward, but I make it work.

I duck, swing, parry, and pray.

Ajax transforms mid-sprint, his massive wolf form crashing into the guards like a wrecking ball.

He howls.

I flinch. Wishing I could transform at will. But nothing happens.

The battle swirls around me like a storm of color and pain. Fire spells lighting up the courtyard, steel on steel, the crackle of wards, and the shriek of commands.

But my eyes are locked on the sky.

Black dragons circle above, like sentinels, their wings slicing through the clouds like scythes. Ominous. Waiting.

I turn toward the stairs, toward the monster in human skin I used to call Headmaster.

"You need to stop them," I shout. "Call them off!"

Siberious watches me with an infuriating calm,

like I'm a particularly irritating gust of wind rather than a girl standing in the ashes of his broken legacy.

"I assume you've mistaken their target," I say. "You know, unless your new plan is to torch the rest of the forest and finish the job the wolves started."

Mauve laughs, a cold, elegant sound, like a sword being unsheathed. "You really are dim."

Great. That's two insults before breakfast.

"We're not going to *destroy* the wolf packs, darling," she purrs, drifting down the steps like this is some high-society garden party. "Not when they're doing such a marvelous job *harvesting*."

"What?" My voice scrapes raw. "Harvesting what?"

"Dragon younglings." Mauve smiles like she's sharing a good wine recommendation. "Eggs. Hatchlings. The usual. Siberious gives them permission, the packs stay loyal. Everyone wins."

Zephy's roar cuts through the sky like a war cry, and the moment I blink, she's gone from my side, nose-diving toward Mauve like a freaking divine missile.

"No, Zephy. WAIT—!"

Mauve doesn't flinch.

With a flick of her wrist, a pulse of silver magic slams into Zephy mid-air.

It's like watching someone hit a bird with a brick wall. She crashes into the courtyard fountain, the stone basin shattering into a thousand shards.

Water explodes upward and floods the cobblestones.

"Zephy!" I scream, sprinting to her.

My boots splash through the mess as I skid to her side.

She's curled awkwardly in the rubble, her wing pinned at an unnatural angle, her scales cracked.

She lifts her head with a pained groan. *Honestly,* she says, her voice rasping through our bond, *for a Little Witch Fairy, she's got a strong punch.*

"You're alive," I breathe, pressing my forehead to hers.

Of course. Also, you smell like wet wolf.

I turn to Siberious, heart in my throat, anger scorching my blood.

"Then what are they doing?" I point skyward. "Why are the black dragons circling? Why is the alpha commanding them to attack the wolves? On *your* orders?"

Siberious descends the stairs one step at a time, radiating magic like he's walking through a storm he controls.

"They're not going to attack the *wolves*." He stops right in front of me.

I have to tilt my head to meet his eyes.

They glow like hot coals.

"Just one," he says.

A hush falls around us, as if even the chaos knows something's shifted.

"What?"

"You, Kayla," he says softly, almost like it's a kindness. "You've brought chaos. Disorder. Weakness. Since your arrival, balance has unraveled. Wolves are questioning their bonds. Dragons are choosing to rebel. Even the humans are listening. The prophecy spoke of the end of our world. And you..."

He leans in, his breath ice. "You are that end."

I rise slowly, every muscle trembling but refusing to buckle. "So, what? You think killing me fixes everything?"

Siberious lifts his chin like a man preparing to deliver a final sermon. "I make this vow: When you die, I will make peace with the wolves. Theridon will return to order. And the realm will survive."

My heart hammers like a trapped bird, but I meet his gaze and refuse to blink.

"I've looked death in the face too many times to be scared of yours," I say, voice shaking but loud. "You want me? Fine."

Ajax shouts something behind me, but I don't turn around. I can't.

My feet move on their own, until I'm standing alone between Siberious and the flood-stained rubble.

I drop my sword. It lands with a hollow *clunk*.

Mari's gasp cuts through the air.

I kneel.

Because maybe this is how it ends. Or maybe... maybe this is how it begins. Maybe I become the bridge by letting myself break.

I close my eyes.

Suddenly, I'm home.

The smell of cinnamon rolls in the oven. Mom laughing in the kitchen, Dad doing that stupid dance with the spatula, and Shelby chasing me through the hallway with socks on her hands like puppets.

I could live in this memory forever.

Peace swells in my chest.

"Do it," I whisper, opening my eyes.

Siberious gives Mauve a nod.

She steps forward, her palm crackling with power.

But instead of aiming at me, she turns her hand toward Zephy.

"No!" I lunge, but I'm too late.

A beam of devastating force explodes from Mauve's palm.

Straight at my dragon.

Chapter 45
Ash and Embers

My body moves before my mind can catch up.

"No!" I scream, lungs splitting.

My vision blurs, heart rupturing, soul clawing its way out of my chest.

Mauve's palm pulses with raw, coiled power, aimed right at Zephy.

My dragon, crumpled and bleeding in the rubble, barely lifts her head. She doesn't even brace.

I lunge forward, useless and too slow.

A *shriek* cuts through the air like a blade.

A whip of *light* snaps around Mauve's wrist, wrenching her arm to the side.

Her magic arcs harmlessly into the sky, dissolving into smoke.

"What the—" she snarls, spinning with a snarl, yanking against the glowing tether.

Her movements are jerky, unbalanced.

I stumble to a halt, blinking through tears and ash.

The whip... It leads upward.

I follow the line with my eyes, and for a moment, *just a moment,* my heart stutters.

A figure stands tall on the stands above the courtyard, haloed in light and shadow.

Short, golden hair. Red pointed ears. Confident stance.

"Bo?" I choke out, hope slamming into my ribs like a wrecking ball.

But no.

It's not Bo.

It's *Eliyah*.

Wings unfurl behind him, massive, iridescent, and *real*. Not the illusion of a Fae teacher trying to blend in. No, this is full celestial mode. Feathers like blades, light pulsing at the edges.

And he's not alone.

Teachers descend behind him—Professor Rell, the grumpy elf with a terrifying aim; Madam Faiza with her storm-colored cloak swirling in magic; even old man Eltarion who's been asleep in the library since I arrived.

Eliyah lands in front of Siberious, the ground cracking beneath his boots. He lifts his chin and speaks in a voice that carries across the shattered courtyard like a thunderclap.

"King Siberious and Ms. Mauve, you are hereby under arrest for treason against the Realm and its Sacred Orders."

The world holds its breath.

Siberious glares, but Mauve steps back, warily eyeing the teachers surrounding them.

"On what authority?" For the first time, her voice is shaken.

Eliyah squares his shoulders and shakes his hair out of his eyes. "On the authority that I am chief law and order officer at Theridon. Authority you bestowed on me, big brother."

I follow his gaze on Siberious, and my jaw hangs open.

Brother?

Mari rushes to my side, her wand still crackling.

Ajax's hand curls protectively around my arm, his wolf form slowly shrinking until he's back in human skin, breath coming hard and fast.

We stare at Eliyah. Bo's uncle.

My brain scrambles to connect the pieces.

"What... how did he...?" Mari whispers, clearly struggling to process this too.

"Does it matter?" I murmur, blinking hard. "He just saved Zephy."

Eliyah's gaze finds mine. It softens for just a moment.

"Kayla. Go. Take your dragon to the Heart of the Mountain. She won't survive without the old magic."

My throat tightens. Words fail me.

I nod.

Just nod. And everything in me cracks.

Zephy groans beside me, lifting her battered head.

I'm not a fan of needing rescue, she mutters, even as her legs tremble trying to rise.

"Yeah, well..." I brush blood from her scales. "Try getting used to it. We're fragile disasters now."

Speak for yourself, she says. *I'm just temporarily inconvenienced.*

We take off into the air, slow and awkward.

Zephy doesn't fly so much as *drift*, carried by magic and sheer stubbornness. Her wings tremble, barely able to stretch fully.

I sit on her back like she's made of glass.

Below, the courtyard shrinks, and the wind whips around us like whispers of what we've escaped.

Chapter 46
The Heart of Danger

The journey to the Heart of the Mountain is quiet. Too quiet.

No one dares speak as Zephy flies low, drifting more than gliding, her wings sluggish and trembling beneath us. Every beat looks like it might be her last.

The black dragons let us go.

But I feel them watching. *Waiting.*

Zephy's voice nudges into my mind, faint and thin. *They're not finished with us. The Alpha is still hunting. For me. For you. We've broken something sacred, Little Flame... and they want it buried.*

We reach the base of the mountain by nightfall.

The air hums with energy, ancient, thick, and strange, like the mountain itself is dreaming.

A massive cave yawns before us, dark and pulsing faintly with soft golden light, but Zephy doesn't go inside.

She veers toward a shimmering lake just outside

the entrance and collapses into the shallows, letting the water lap over her scorched scales.

At first, I panic. "Zephy?"

But she exhales a long plume of steam and groans. *Warm. Feels... like magic. Like home.*

A soft glow spreads through the lake around her.

Her wounds begin to close.

Ajax crouches by the shore, his hand on her massive neck, whispering something I can't hear.

Mari tugs on my sleeve. "We should gather food. There's a grove of berry bushes back near the ridge. It's safe. I think."

I nod, and we slip away.

The mountain looms behind us, casting a shadow over everything. But the stars are bright, and the air is clear.

We pick in silence at first.

I watch her hands tremble as she fumbles with the berries. She's trying so hard to stay together.

Then she breaks.

"I can't stop seeing him," she whispers.

I look over.

Mari's face is streaked with tears, and her lip quivers like she's barely holding on. "Bo. His body. Mangled. Bleeding."

I set the berries down and walk to her. "I know."

She covers her face with both hands, sobbing now, chest heaving. "How do I keep going when it hurts like this? When it feels like my heart's been ripped out and stomped on, and I'm supposed to just... *keep breathing*?"

I swallow hard, my throat burning.

"I lost my family in the crash," I say softly. "My parents. My sister. Shelby... She was annoying and loud and always singing off-key. And I still hear her sometimes. I *see* her sometimes, in my dreams. I didn't know how to keep going either."

Mari lowers her hands, mascara smudged and eyes rimmed red.

"But she's not really gone," I continue. "None of them are. They're in every step I take. Every fight I choose. That pain—it means they mattered. It means we *matter*. And I hold onto that."

She looks at me like I just cracked the sky open.

"I loved him," she says. "I didn't realize it until he died. Until I saw them take him."

"I know," I say.

She presses her forehead against mine for a moment. Just breathing.

When we return to the lake, Zephy is stretched long in the water, steam rising in thick curls around her. She looks... better. Stronger.

Ajax glances up at us, one hand still on her neck. "She'll make it."

Zephy groans. *Barely. But I'll take it. Also, next time I charge into battle, maybe just tie me to a tree first.*

I sit beside her, nudging her snout gently. "You scared me."

I scare myself sometimes.

Mari drops the berries into a bowl made from a large leaf and hands them around.

No one really eats. We just *sit*.

Then Zephy's voice nudges into my mind again, clearer this time. *The Alpha never meant to have the dragons kill the wolves.*

I blink. "What?"

The message was muddled, she continues. *I would never have allowed them to attack my rider. One of the black dragons—Thalos—confessed as we passed. The true message was... cryptic. Only meant for those loyal enough to decode it.*

"What was it?"

'The Bridge Must Burn.'

I repeat the sentence in a whisper.

The words settle over us like a blanket of ash.

Ajax stands slowly, jaw clenched. "Someone carved that outside the cave."

"What?" I ask.

He gestures toward the mouth of the Heart. "Come see."

We approach the stone just outside the entrance. Ancient. Cracked.

Faint runes pulse along its face. And in blood-red script, fresh and jagged: THE BRIDGE MUST BURN.

My breath catches.

Mari's fingers close around mine.

Ajax's voice is low. "The bridge between wolves and dragons. Between old magic and the new world. You threaten them, Kayla."

Zephy's growl hums like thunder in the earth. *We threaten them.*

A twig snaps.

Ajax is instantly in motion, sword drawn, standing between me and the trees.

Mari rises beside him, wand glowing at the tip, her face pale but steady.

Zephy lets out a warning growl, her wings half-flared.

I hold my breath.

A shadow breaks from the tree line. Slow. Deliberate.

A cloaked figure steps into view, hood drawn low, face hidden.

We brace.

The air charges around us, thick with magic.

The water glows brighter.

Then, just as Ajax shifts his weight to attack, the figure lifts a hand.

"Not everyone wants you dead, Kayla."

THE STORY CONTINUES in Book 2 of The Magic of Dragons: Wolf Blood

Author Note

I've been writing stories since I was five years old. Fantasy has always been my greatest love, and when I was barely 14 years old, I wrote an epic fantasy story.

My parents encouraged me to contact agents and publishers, but I only got rejection letter back. However, my dad told me to keep them and treasure them.

"They are part of your story. And you should be proud of them."

When life happened, I grew too busy and distracted to write.

Instead, I married the love of my life and had our three sons, Ryan, Alexander and Nicholas.

My spare time was spent playing with make up and selling it over social media. Some called me "successful" but I was just having fun.

Then the very worst thing happened:

My dad unexpectedly passed away.

Author Note

He was my biggest fan. The person who would tell me I could do impossible things. And I believed him.

When he passed, my whole world split in two.

Now, my heart looks like a patchwork quilt. Sewn back together, but cracked and not the same.

I couldn't post online about make up anymore. So I lost my business, and my spark.

But one day, I was clearing out my father's possessions and found an envelope with my name on it.

Inside, was a hard copy of my book. Hope Island.

The story my dad so desperately wanted me to share with the world.

It has been two decades since I wrote that story. I've grown as a writer, and my passion for mythology has only magnified.

The Magic of Dragons includes many aspects of Hope Island.

From shadows that try to eat you...

And stories of betrayal and war in a world of monsters and magic.

This series is written for him.

For my sons.

For me.

For you.

For the readers who read Lord of the Rings under the covers, with a flashlight during the night.

For the readers who loved How to Train Your Dragon and Twilight. And want something more.

For the readers who have lost a loved one. Suffered a chronic illness.

Author Note

For the readers who live with daily pain.

For the readers who need to escape into a world without time, or technology, or politics, or calories.

This series is your escape. Your safe space.

A place where you can be powerful and broken at the same time.

Where you can make life long friends who will stand by you even when the skies are on fire.

Kayla's story is just beginning, and the next book will include more POVs.

I can't wait for you to join me on this adventure and if you loved this book, it would mean the world to me if you would leave a review.

And the most valuable form of advertising is word of mouth - so please tell your friends and family about The Magic of Dragons!

Until next time,

Keep reading!

Laura

Xoxo